THE FARM

THE FARM

Clarence L. Cooper, Jr.

First published in 1967 by
Crown Publishers Inc., New York.

First published in Great Britain 1996 by
Payback Press, an imprint of Canongate Books Ltd,
14 High Street, Edinburgh EH1 1TE

British Library Cataloguing-in-Publication Data
A catalogue record for this book is available upon request
from the British Library

ISBN 0 86241 600 0

Typeset in Minion and Serif Modular by
Palimpsest Book Production Limited,
Polmont, Stirlingshire
Printed and bound in Finland by WSOY

For My Jean: for always Us

About the Author

By all rights, Clarence Levi Cooper, Jr. should be mentioned alongside the names of the greatest American novelists of the last fifty years. And he probably would, if not for the misfortune of being a good three decades before his time, and having pre-occupied himself with writing quirky, in-your-face fiction about flawed, villainous men, whom readers – both black and white – found objectionable. Consequently, Cooper is not only not on the list, he's nowhere close; all of his audacious works are out of print and forgotten since their first publication.

Born in Detroit in 1934, Cooper got married, developed a monstrous drug addiction, did a two year stretch in the Iona Penitentiary, wrote for and edited the black daily newspaper the *Chicago Messenger*, and published two novels, all before his twenty-seventh birthday.

The first novel, *The Syndicate* (1960), was published by a sleaze-and-schlock house under the name, Robert Chestnut. It was quickly forgotten. *The Scene* (1960) was published in hardback by Crown, and proved to be a different story. Focusing on a world populated by dope-fiends, lesbians, whores and pretty boys, and written in a style that evokes an unholy mix of Jim Thompson and a prison library reading list, Cooper sprung onto the literary scene like a raging animal set free from his cage. And the critics noticed. The *New York Herald Tribune* remarked: 'Not even Nelson Algren's *The Man with the Golden Arm* burned with the ferocious intensity that you'll find here. He writes with a personal authority that can only be called shattering and the searing exactness of one who has lived through the horror.'

Unfortunately, Cooper was still living through the horror, and by the time *The Scene* hit the streets, he was serving another lengthy stretch. Over the course of the next two years,

Cooper turned out three more impressive manuscripts, and a slew of whacked third-person, autobiographical notes that prove far less truthful than his fiction in reporting the details of his life.

'How these books ended up in the slush pile at a low-end house like Regency is something of a mystery,' says famed novelist Harlan Ellison who, during the early 1960s, was doing it all for the Chicago-based publisher. Although the two men never met, through their correspondence Ellison formed the opinion that Cooper was a 'very literate, very troubled individual'.

Cooper's troubles only multiplied. Released from jail, and unable to write in a world of temptation, Cooper again fell into drug addiction and petty theft, and would spend much of the mid-sixties in lower Manhattan, haranguing former friends and associates for money, and looking for a place to hang his hat. John A. Williams, who knew him at the time, describes him as 'a disappointed man who was unable to override his frustrations at the reception of his books'.

'So much of what we know of ourselves is such a lousy God Damn Lie,' explains John, the hero of *The Farm*. Released in 1967, it was Cooper's last book, and his most personal. This enigmatic statement would foreshadow the final years of Cooper's life, the few details of which include a rumoured decline into homelessness, slow suicide through alcohol and drugs, and eventual death.

In the only known review of *The Farm*, the *Negro Digest* savaged the book for its 'flawed characters', 'over-writing' and 'gratuitous and affected prose construction', while admitting 'there is a small coterie of readers who swear by Clarence Cooper, Jr. . . . and is, they maintain, one of the most underrated writers in America, a Richard Wright of the revolutionary era.'

The One Part

At the crossroads of, and what might have served as the entrance to, the night-bleary little town, our headlights plucked out 3 signs that proclaimed, in the laughter of red-sparkling reflectors,

GOOD
EVIL
SAME

1

We saw a niggerwoman dead on the road.

Let me tell you how it was, for it was ghastly bloody abstraction. It horrified my bottom gut, gave a taste to the mouth like tangerines and beer, and while I sat there, back-seated, cuffhaltered, the reality of death, the sudden exhibition of it, caused me to itch deeply in a shameful sexual way.

In exactly this way we saw her, we3, 2marshals and me:

The sun had never shown its grimy winterface. The road, as far as here, was fast enough,

but somewhere in Ohio we'd met an evil swath of useless white dust that danced in billions on the windshield and blinded all for 20miles or more.

'Shit, it's cold. I wanned to be in Louie by tonight.'

The motor surged us ahead irritably.

'Warmup in a panna pussy,' and the other laughed, then thought quietly of what he'd said.

I was only half listening. I'd tried to cancel these government types out longago, in Toledo, when they found out I didn't talk, didn't even eat on the government expense reserved for these trips. It was as though I traveled in a dead state, because if I *hadn't* been dead, and said the things I felt and needed to scream, crushchew, slobberout, they would have shot me for mad, and they were too ignorant to fill out the forms, the quadquintsexsepticates, the government requires in such instances. All I wanted to do was to get the hell to where it was we were going and ease my raw, travelsplintered ass. The trip from Danbury Correctional Institution was the worst I'd ever experienced in a lifetime of riding in the backseats of copcars.

The roads in this southern part of the country are like depraved, usedup old faggots – they swish and flick their bony asses around obscenely, as though they'd really been good for anything except a sexcrime the day they'd been born, mockeries of everything 1 would naturally expect from them. That's why we didn't see directly, being involved in the perversity we traveled on, and my mind had gone out of me blankly and hadn't announced its return until the wind seemed to part the curtain before us, and it was as though we'd entered another dimension, and then I was all wary attention. The cars directly ahead of us, humpbacked with the greasy snow, were checkerboarded over the road. To my right, over the dead rigid manhigh shoulders chalked unevenly in white, I saw smoke, like something in a war movie, rising in a thin black rapid piss-stream toward the latrine of the sky; but this was at least several hundred yards ahead, around curves we had yet to manage.

'Must be a accident,' I mumbled.

'Yeah.'

And you could feel the anticipation building. And I could feel my wrists straining against the steel. And as we crept along with the other snowmonsters, a lousy bloodstink seemed to ooze out of us, because we instinctively knew something had been killed and we lusted to be part of the grotesque exhibition of death, to drink it in with our senses and feel relieved, for some basic reason none of us would ever admit to.

But we came instead on anticlimaxes of what we expected to be It: cars hugged against the shoulders inexplicably with staring-out white faces, at me, a black 1, as we slowly cruised past; these unexplainables looked themselves like horrible accidents in their whitecovered waiting, bumperbumpered at 90-degree angles. So that when we got there, suddenly, with the slickered statetrooper, hands stuck out in kuklux grimness, standing right yonder in the middle of the road, suddenly shot up out of the asshole of it like a big dirty white formless turd, we almost missed what had caused all this.

But no, we were meant to see, even though the trooper forced us to speed up, 'Speed up! By Gawd, move that Gawd Damn Thang!' piercing right through the windshield and our inside silence, like a bullet, his mawmouth all raw and red inside as his nose and the edges of his slippery eyes. But we were meant to see:

The smoke coming from the assend of some kind of car I couldn't tell the make of, since I'd been locked up so long and didn't giveashit what make was what, high over us as we passed, at an attitude and angle that was impossible for any other reason than it'd been struck and sliced away by the furious momentum of the other car just below that hung like a 7, bent by the ergs of irresistible force, hood dripping like the nose of a Harlem drunk slobbering 2quarters of the way onto the road. So we saw it.

It used to be a convertible, but now it was absurd, it was confusion, and I couldn't help wondering about the sexual way people *put* themselves into cars, and it seemed only right, just then, that things like death should happen in them, for if orgasm doesn't come of these things, then it's coitus interruptus and isn't right, but this was right, you could see, in every aspect – there was the jism of it all over the road. It was good; it was right and final.

But I had only an instant to cop all this, like a booster, because the trooper bounced his boot off the end of our car and marshal 1 looked at marshal 2 and stomped on the gas. We skittered and slid dangerously toward half a hundred, and we were gone.

But we had seen

in a flash of that instant the black woman crimped in the catastrophe of the smoky simmering wreck. She lay with her arms spread, like a female Christ or a woman who has just busted her nuts, eyes wide in the way of those dead in the last shutter of seeing before nonseeing. Somewhere, some instant in that moment of deathhappening, the bridge, or possibly Safety Glass of the windshield, had come inward like a butterknife to slice her head directly down the middle of the fore – even the nose, as though an expert scalpel had been at work – clear to the back of the head, so that her thick justdone hair sprayed like fine black blossoms in the wind and the snow clung to it, like the tiny hairheads of

Medusa, looking somehow majestic and imperially rude in this kind of being,

as a fireman with bent head and bucket hat swung a torch around the doorjamb that creased her into the hook of the 7.

And there was the opulence of blood all over the road. Her black head had been parted in such a way as to reveal the teeth completely and bring the smile to my lips as we passed. In that moment I felt kissed, tongued, and my mouth was full of her blood – it was I, it seemed, who'd just made her come to death. And Oh it was then I felt my own almost-arriving, to feel my face flushing, to smell what her dead cunt must be as I slightly touched her attitude of needing, and at that moment I heard 1 of Them say up front, involuntarily, mouth bitter with the shock of it,

'Gosh, Bob, did you see that niggerwoman?'

My lips were chapped and peeling, and I ate the skin of them, a sort of selfconsumption that gave my belly a gurgling kind of justification.

Over the last of the hills, our rolling snowclogged thing carried us, then down a long, betterbuilt road, where we followed a winterfilthy Esso truck to a scrubbrush junction. Then left, I think. Yes, left. Then to a 40-inch path, it seemed, a hogpath; then quickly to the right, as I said,

'Is this right?'

'I dunno.'

'Alwus git turned around comin out here.'

'I think you right. See that house? That's Capun Koyle's, I remember, from the last time we came. Now, you gotta take the tit yonder, to the left; that's the disposal plant there. I bet there's a lottashit goes on in that place.' Gigglegiggle.

Overhead, the sky had suddenly gone red, as though it had sucked up the blood of the black woman behind us, marred near the horizon with pusblacks and goregreens. It came into the car and stained the pale faces of the 2 and more clearly defined the sharp edges of their cheeks and mouths and made their shadowy throats look as though something had been chewing-chewing, almost through, then puked in disgust what it had tasted. My eyes had belched a crud of fatigue, and I watched its patterns in the dying sun: blue and green checkmarks and opal ditto signs with bright pink brilliances in the shapes of cunts. Through all this the Place rose suddenly when we came upon it, carved as it was on the sillyhilly landscape.

'There she is.'

'There she is,' the Other agreed.

'Never been here before, huhboy?' But I didn't answer. 'That's the Farm.'

She rose proudly. She had spires and Roman cornices and Greek ramparts and punk American Depression symbols of electricity that coursed about the pregnant dirtybrown marble belly, and She pronounced the smug disunity of her period with disordered extensions and low, latched-on excrescences, and windows, windows, thousandsandthousands of windows that hadn't been washed in decades, and stared like the cataract eyes of a square caterpillar onto the peacefully curving road that led into the black socket of her navel.

'Yep, that's her.'

'Yep,' said the Other, smiling in the pyrotechnics of the sun, eyes and mouth drooling filthy colors.

'Betya never been this far south before, huhboy? You being raised in the City? We get a lot of boys come down here outta New York, right, Bob?'

'Right.'

'You gonna like it down here. I bet you like it better than that other place. They even got women, and volunteers come in from the street all the time – they call um Winders.' He turned to face me directly, eyes leaving the road and what he was doing, determined to draw me out. 'They got things for you to do down here. What do you do?'

'Time.'

'Naw.' He laughed. 'I mean when you ain't doin that.'

'Time.'

I had despised the little nigger who ran Classification and Parole in the other fedjoint I'd been in Up Noff, a nappy-headed little Napoleon, who hadn't liked me much better till later, and then it was too late, for even now I hate him as he must remember me fondly, and those mornings, those Saturdaymornings, I used to come up to his office and rap to him about bullshitum absurdum and pretend to this Elder Brother-Father an inability to cope with the Nickel, the 5years I had to do, and how badly I needed his advice, 'Please advise me, Mr. Reb,' while I choked down the need to lace my black fingers around his throat and choke him once for each letter to my woman he'd sent back as 'unauthorized' because we were married only in commonlaw, and all the other countless petty cruel things that only 1 black man can do to another.

We came into something like a rear portico facing a parkinglot, but the lot was empty, and I didn't, couldn't, realize what day it was: and from where we came to stop there were faces, the faces of broads, staring out high windows at us, the manymany wide eyes of women twisted peering. I felt a certain pulling at my belly, being away from them for so long, with only my woman once at an earlier period before she died, in the visitingroom of the other joint, me sitting there touching her knees and snorting her gingery woman-musk, sitting on my swipe, which was long and hard and aching for her – so it took me a while to come around now. And it was bad. I was wrinkled and stinking from the long ride, and they probably thought I'd just come off the street, ugly and creasednasty from some Dante's CountyJail.

'Lookit the whores,' I said, raking up the parkingbrake.

We got out. We walked up the long path from the car, the broads still looking, and me walking with my hands in front of me, coat twisted round in a way you couldn't mistake DANGEROUS PRISONER, and up the tinyshort steps of the shiny-metal enclosed porch; before me the marshals carrying my penitentiary bags with a few assorted pictures and my toothbrush marked *made in lewisburg pennsylvania*, and 1 marshal's coat undraped in the snappy mountain wind to show his BuckJones scabbard with little wigwam traces and the dirtylittle heat, a .38, that appeared almost rusted and made the whole thing look like it was part of a cast.

My eyes smarted in the wind, started to dribble like rivers, made me look, I know, like I was crying my way into the joint. But we got inside finally, where the 2 guys rang the bell, and we stood there waiting for over 20minutes, waiting for a bitchvoice I could hear from the inside of the new face panelling with peekhole, who finally came, all pink and spotted about the nose and mouth, like a dead fish,

who said, unbelievably, 'Oh, YALL! Dew *look*it yall!' spread the door with a jangle of keys at the belt of her plump white waist, 'C'mon IN. Dew you boys cum *in*!' not fast enough, 'Now – c'm – there, now. Cold out there?' led us to a sittingroom, or something that looked almost civilized, with pictures by Rembrandt and Matisse – but no, I'm wrong in looking at the signatures: they're the work of dopefiends.

She glances at me friendly, rubber red ring of mouth, 'How dew you feel, boy?'

'All right.'

'Not sick?'

'No.'

1 hand on top of a solicitous other. 'From another federal institution?'

'Yes.'

'Which 1?'

'I have the papers right here,' 1 said, opening his folio.

'You have the papers?' she said.

'Yeah. Here.' He scrambled around. 'We picked him up from Danbury. Doin 5years for Sale of Narco.' He grinned at me. 'He ain't got too much time left, but he say he does time all the time.'

'Oh, then. Oh, yall just come with me.'

'Him too?'

'No, he'stahstay right here.'

'Well, what should I do withim? We got to sign in.'

'Just leave him here,' she said.
'With the handcuffs on?'
'You can take the handcuffs off. It'll be all right.'
'Okay. Here.'
'You got the key, Bob.'
'I thought *you* had it.' Searching in all pockets, shifting bags and folios around awkwardly. 'I didn't have it.'
'I don't . . .' fingers in breastpockets. 'Naw, I couldn't have it.'
'Maybe I've got it': They all turned to look at me, then decided I was joking, and they laughed quite sloppily about it.
'OH, *I* got it,' 1 of the fools said, and twisted my wrists about sharply, plunging the plug in the little socket, turning.
My hands were free and breathing. I felt my chest expand.

So they left.
I stood there, turning around slowly. Windows ahead of me, like observation portals; there are green and purple flowers on the papered walls; 2 broadbrimmed silverhatted lamps. On a coffeetable, several issues of the joint paper, with photos on the front page. It's called the *Times*, with a logoscroll blaring silly little maxims having to do with Honesty. The front page shows broads and guys, looking as though they were into something. Stageshows, broads dancing in tights, all close-cunted. PATIENT COUNCIL'S SHOW A SUCCESS.
I heard the laughter of a woman, the answering laughter of another,
and they were the laughs of blackwomen, curved and curlicued and very hip at the end of the tip of each phrase.
A man's brownface, fleck of gold in the front tooth, looked in on me. He had a graying moustache, and I recognized him immediately as Douglas Gaines, an old hustling partner of mine from Brooklyn. It shook me a bit. I'd heard that he was busted, about 6months after I fell, but I didn't know they'd sent him down here. I've known Doug for years, since the 1st time I met Joyce and we got hooked up together. He

was always crazy about our kid, Joye, and I heard when I 1st started this bit that he was dropping off a little bread every fewdays for her medical expenses.

He seemed to dig who I was, but left quickly down the hall. To my left, a shielded grill to hide his escape; to my right, nothing. Quiet. I hear somewhere a tiny sad bell.

I touch my face; it is cold and scintillating with the inside warmth.

Way off, a trumpet, cc, highhigh, with a little splah in it.

1 of the cops came to the window to look and make sure I was still there.

Then that horrible woman came to the door with both cops and, as they started out, leaving, grinning at me, and she unlocked the door with her keyset to let them out, moaning all the while, whirling round to me,

'YALL be all right now, and him? I'll take care of this boy all right, won't I, son? Okay, now. Happy trip, boys. And you, you know what *yew* must do? Yewmuss start callin' me here and now Miss Sweet Lorraine.'

She smiled.

13½

The smiling doctor stuck his finger up my ass and felt around my balls. He looked at me very nicely.

Then Miss Sweet Lorraine came and gave me a blue suit with a USNshield on the lefthand pocket that had drawstrings around the waist.

Then a little guy who looked like the Monster's Igor, with even a hump and the same nose and jawline. 'Heah, heah,' he waved in the same way Igor used to wave the Monster into some hole in the ground, 'this way, this way,'

'okay, sign right here.'

'Sign what?'

'This paper here.'

'For what?'

'Becuz it's part of the rules you got to sign.'

'I thought they dropped that rule.'

'Not'sfar as I know, which means you gotta sign.'

'I'm almost sure they dropped that rule.'

'I don't know nothin about it.'

'What does it say?'

'What? What?'

'What I'm going to sign.'

'It's a release.'

'To release my dead body? and my effects?'

'And other things. But you got to sign.'

'Where?'

For a moment he raised his eyes to look at me, and then something came between us when he said 'Here,' pointing, softly.

I didn't sign. I said there were enough things signed by me already, the OKAY to inspect my mail, and other papers no 1 let me read. I took them through a few changes, even Miss Sweet Lorraine. And then I signed just at the moment they were most convinced I wouldn't.

Then they took me up to Skidrow, where all the earlier admissions lived, on the second floor; there were guys only minimally sick, I could see, most of them, however, there was a New York crowd that was interesting, and I ran into a guy I knew once in my kidhood.

And the next day, even though I hadn't seen any stuff for over 2 years, a stupid nurse came on and gave me a goofball.

From my window, I stare up at the 6floor arches of another unit, and again I hear the voices and laughingsounds of women. There is a stain of time on that façade, just like the ones it leaves in the ground.

Below me is a courtyard with a surprising accumulation of garbage. The windows are painted, but each night a girl-figure perches, a shadow in her bedroom through the slant of her window all the way down. And we merely stare back and forth to each other for hours into the night.

There was TV. I watched it a lot. Same thing in the other joint: it got so all I looked forward to was TV in the evening, became something of another sort of dopefiend – so I got hung up in it again, especially on the ladies' programs, because there was a young blonde in 1 segment who turned me on, and this was 1 basic reason.

But there was a little slumkid, a Winder, who came to the dayroom at the same time, who at 1st addressed me as 'Oyea,' though I couldn't figure out why the hell why unless I looked like some black Spanish cat he knew. Anyway, he sat with me and rapped like a boil or cyst would rap if they could speak. Always asking snotsnoop questions about where yafum? you know Undertaker outta New York? 116th? You a prisoner? how much time you doin? is it hard doin' time for the feds?

He irritated me most by sayin over and over he could just eat the crotch out of the blonde's pants. It would've been tastier to eat the crotch out of the blonde.

Once a day a sappylooking little doc came around, zipping around saying goodbye, and 1 day somebody gave him a clue and he finally came lisping over to me, with much batting of eyes,

'I'm Dr. Uxeküll. It's not a difficult name when you say it with a hard v. And you're Mr.— yesyes. How do you feel?'

'Not very much.'

'You mean Not Very Well.'

'I mean not very much.'

He couldn't quite see, but his mouth twitched smilingly as though he did. 'You mean . . .'

'Not very much.'

He sighed in relief. 'Well, at least that's something on our side, eh? Have you ever been here before?'

'No.'

'Well. How did you get here? I mean you must have come here some sort of way.'

'Isn't it in the record?'

'Well, you can plainly see I don't have any records with me. I couldn't consult records I don't have, could I? Are you a prisoner?'

'Of course.'

'Then you're free of a physical addiction, though sometimes we get some directly in from the jails who're still in a sickstate. Then you haven't been, in 1 of those, I mean?'

'No.'

'How long have you been off narcotics?'

'It's hard to remember just now.'

'3years?' he prompted smilingly. '2? is it closer to 2½ than 3, or is it less than 3 and more than 2?'

'I think it's less than 3 and more than 2.'

'What was your drug?' he went on with great haste. 'I mean what were you on?'

'Hairron.'

'Do you remember how many bags a day, or how many you were using, that is?'

'Less than 3 and sometimes more than 2.'

'Well.' He brightened. 'How do you feel, fella?'
'Not very much.'

Today I went through the whole row; I'm struck by the freedom, the lack of restraint. I'm like a horse without a spur in its ass.

This place is fascinating, with its almost hotelrooms, and the huge barred grill at the end of the tier that stands as an oblique barrier to what I know is some part of a women's unit. I wondered if the girl in the window would be around there somewhere, and my mind began clicking hungrily over schemes and visions of fucking her, but there was no way.

Each day I came to the grill and listened, but only once did I hear words that amounted to sense, and that was when 1 bitch called another 1.

There is a little black Sister, an employee, who comes up with the lousylunch wagon, who is marvelously hooked up, with very hostile eyes, so much so they seem not to see you, but all the while she *is* seeing you, you know, and she responds by putting the thinnest portion possible on my plate. She has wild black hair growing far down on her forehead, and a thrilling Hottentot little ass under her white uniform. Her feet are big, like snowboots pointed with All-Brite White Polish for All Shoes. But her legs and the rest of her are terribly hooked up,

and the way she treated me is possibly because of the way I used to stand in 1 of the dayroom corners eating my spaghetti, staring at her while she served the rest of the 50more, and I knew she felt as though she was the thing I was eating so deliberately as I watched her.

2

Let me comb the nappy hair of my memory well,

because I wasn't at all as dead as I seemed or felt. My transition between the Skidrow and Shootinggallery took only a few days, 1 reason being that I had no Jones, no habit, on arrival, and therefore had no need for withdrawal. But still, I was coming awake, like the monster they thawed out of a block of ice in a movie I saw once.

Skidrow is the 1st floor a dopefiend hits; then the Shootinggallery is next. They're merely hospital tiers divided by the dirtywindowed dayroom.

I crept from 1 side to the other, looking at the preposterous junkiefaces, mottled and drab and touched under the skin by the dirty fingertips of stuff, sniffing snot back, largely trying to impress everyone they met that they were sick. 1 kid stops talking to me in the hall and runs into the shithouse adjoining his room: I hear him gargling bile, and he comes back in a while, a large patch of yellow spit on the lapel of his USNrobe, moaning,

'Ohman, ohshit, ohshit I'm sick and they won't give me nothin but goofballs.'

'That handles it.'

I'm suddenly not on his side. 'What?' he says. 'You muss be kiddin. I need some *stuff*, not fuckinggoofballs. They don't do nothin for me by tomorrow, I'm checkin outta here.'

'That'll fix um.'

'I'm serious,' he complains.

'So'm I. It muss be sweet to check in an out of the penitentiary whenever you get ready.'

But he doesn't cop my meaning, and at this time I'm the only con on the gallery among the 50some, and word gets around to the rest of the Winders that I've got some kind of fuckedup attitude.

At lunch, when I bring my tray back and empty it in the garbagebucket next to the steamwagon, I ask the little Sister when I'll be going into population.

'Why you ask me?' she says snottily. 'I don't know.'

'You sho don't.'

'What?'

'You sho won't, will you?'

'I sho won't what?'

'Play dominoes with me. I see you playin with the other guys. The white guys.'

She's embarrassed. 'Of course I'll play with you, Mr.—'

'Yesyes.'

'It's my job to play with the patients.'

'I play for keeps. Whatever I win off you, you won't get it back.'

'But we won't be playing for anything.'

'Ohbut we will. I always bet my life in any game I play.'

She looks at me oddly off the hump of her linenwhite shoulder, deepbrown eyes slowly coming to light with the realization that the greatest need in my life at that moment is to spread her soft black thighs and fuck the living breath out of her,

and I see her flush, the way blackpeople flush, with almost indecipherable tones of browns and blues about the eyes and very base of jawline, and shudder, a repulsed kind, and I know she'd felt some freakish sort of thrill, as I watch her tiny softhard ass retreating quickly with the steamwagon down the long sicklygray Shootinggallery row.

Some guy came in, a Brother, telling me how bad the stuff was in New York. He had beard like scrubcactus growing in the black eroded desert of his face, and his long hands were swollen from bad hits, where he'd ruptured the veins and they'd gotten infected, but they were now smooth and fleckless of life, like those of a badlyhandled corpse in a jackleg black funeral parlor.

'It's garbage,' he said about the New York stuff. 'I was usin Seconals.'

'You ever run excretals?'

He blinked at me. 'What?'

'Excretals, man. They're made by the Small Intestinal Combine. They really handle it.'

'Habitformin?'

'Just like stuff, only you don't have no bowel trouble.'

'Wow. Expensive?'

'Depends on your shot. A guy can make a pig outta himself off anything.'

'Where can I cop?'

'Your corner grocer. Try the meatcounter, the cangoods, the vegetablebin, the—'

Art Mondré, outta Montreal, was probably the only whiteman I've ever regarded with respect. In the summer, we used to sit on the stonebenches of the other joint, and I'd listen while he ran the lineage of Boobus Billicus Americanus to me, while the sun baked our brains and we stared unseeing across the nickelanddime yard with its 2tenniscourts and a couple of screws in the shade of the gymwall and education building,

or while we were on our job together in the laundry, running the 1,000sheets we had to do each week through the bastard GSA mangler that rarely worked properly, and he used to tell me

'Boobus has gotta be eliminated, ya know? I mean, ever since the Crusades he's been gettin bigger and bigger as a group. You can't even isolate him any longer – he's gettin into everything, even stuff.'

'And politics.'

'Oh,' Art'd laugh. 'He's been in that for a longtime now. Lookit the President today – you ever see such a perfect example of a turnipeater? Now it's worse – Boobus has gotten into the blackrace. It's the Final Solution. He's the 1 who got to Hitler, really, and it's the biggest Boob of all, Christ, who's really made it tough for us.'

Art has killed men before. He did a bit in Wormwood Scrubs in the 40s, the same joint Oscar Wilde did his bit in, where you'd have to wait to shit in your bucket in the early morning, timing it so you'd come out not long after for the shitbucket line,

and I envied him for it.

But this thought is kind of strained, even though I recall it by sensations, by gestures, by smells, and it really doesn't serve to explain the Boob I'm faced with here. I have sat in my room and tried to bring myself up to date, to this moment, but there is a nethercloud that won't part, and a song of loathing I hear even in my sleep. I wonder, frightenedly, if anyone has ever hated as intensely as myself – not other men or cultures or monuments or moments,

but the sheer idiocy of living and the gutcord of Being about my throat that strangles off every flow of reason and sanity,

and the very herringbone patterns of this time that relates me to nothing but the thing of me that *thinks* and *realizes* and terrifiedly causes me to know that it belongs to nothing,

not stuff or women or ideals;

that belongs only to the next moment, and the next, like the spring of a clock,

as even the mighty dourful regularity of Big Ben belongs only to the imbecile ages.

By now I'm shunned in both wards. They, none of them, giveashit for me, but they are weak dopies, and I've been doing the bit for a longtime and my muscles are taut from angry exercise and I could beat the livingshit out of any 5 of them without halftrying. In fact, I ache for it; I've never been so finely conditioned to do violence, not even when it was my vocation.

But I find peace now, probably for the 1st time in my entire 30years. I don't have to listen to other people's voices or be obligated to answer them.

For hours I stand lookingout on the stupid snowcovered

hills into the loweringsun. I make my mind a part of all I survey, as I smoke. It affects me queerly,

and sometimes I stand before the window, so thrilled by my loneliness, so horny in my 1 *oneness*, I have an erection that strains toward the mouth of the sun, vaguely warmed by the promise of its tongue,

and I almost come in my peaceful aloneness.

2ε1/2

1 day, finally, someone decided I was only a fuckindopie, so they sent me over to the UTunit, the Usher-In Terminal, where I slept 1 beautiful night on a Posteriorpedic, then asked the whiteclad coppers at the office next morning how much they sublet the little joint I slept in. This is how so much of that futurefutureshit came about: I had a Thing with a hack named Smith who I noticed had a pepperpocked face. Cold as it was in my draftyroom, that redneck would only give me a blanket with holes in it.

'This ain't no hotel,' Mr. Smith said.

The UTunit was 2arms that stretched wideout on the browncoming taint of fading winter; it was facefilled with hundreds of funkdirty windows staring at each other.

From my 6floor window I had an unobstructed view of the brownandwhite-spotted Herefordshire cattle that came for allday grazing in the rootrich earth below, and saw them play at butting each other's nobby heads, shitting big warmsteaming turds in the acid cold, pretending 1 year short that they were old enough to fuck.

I used to show this beautiful othercreature to Tamerlane and Little Joe and a few other cons, but the Winders didn't understand it. Tamerlane was a big black dumpy dopie with cotton eyes, doing 10years for what I came to think really belonged to someone else's doing,

and hell, all the rest of them – all of us were doing bits which I added up and came to 119years. But what a God Damned Thing it is to be like this, I thought and still think, to do *this*, what 119years of confinement causes us to do—

To stand there gapeeyed and fascinated almost to voyeuristically climaxed proportions watching animals, belongs, as an idea, more to The Ages than the hand Jesus used to wipe his ass with.

But the most fascinating thing about the ward: the women's section, the Ginnybarn, was situated a mere 100feet from the UT unit – 2 big black ugly towering gates of steel that looked like the ones Kong broke through to get to the Freeworld – and me and the rest of the cons would hang around allday at our exitentrance *feenin* on them like violents, as their fat southernfed asses traveled in groups from 1 end to the other of the rattlesnake corridor, going to work or therapy groups—

and we all were prisoners with 119years, we watching ones, as the Winders watched us unbelievingly.

Doug surprised me by coming over to the unit. All the new dopie entries were standing around waiting for the unit physician, and I was leaning against the barred door leading out to the courtyard.

'How ya doin?' he said, coming in.

'Fine. What a surprise to see you. I was surprised that 1sttime I saw you through the window.'

He grinned behind his big moustache. 'The world is too small. I was thinkin about you and Joyce the other day.' He looked away briefly. 'I was locked up when she OD'd.'

'Yeah. Well. I thought you was in Marion, since you got busted in Chicago.'

'I was for a minnit, but they decided to ship all the dopefiends out, so this is how I got down here. I'm teaching math up in the highschool.'

'Well, I know about that highschool thing. You don't have to do the bit so hard, not when you're a brainwasher.'

'Who busted you?'

'That bastard Bob Trent. He entrapped Joyce for the feds, sayin he was sick and everything. You know how smooth he was. I was the 1 who finally woke up with the indictment. I tried to find im to kill im when I was out on bond, but he went to the Coast on a new job for the feds.'

'How'd you get here?'

'They sent me outta Atlanta to Danbury; then a croaker there said he thought I oughta be down here since I been using drugs for over 15 years. That's how.'

Pepperfaced Smith suddenly came out of the office and asked Doug what he was doing here. 'Don't you live on the Eastside?'

'I was just talking to a friend.'

'Well, you're Out of Bounds, don't you know that?'

'I'm an AAmember with a pass,' Doug showed him, 'so you don't have to worry.'

Smith looked at us both closely for a minnit, then he pulled up.

'I have trouble with that guy everytime I come over here,' Doug said.

'I can have trouble with him and not go anywhere.'

'Need anything?'

'I'll be all right. But I notice guys are wearing little Banlons and things around here. You got any extra shirts?'

'You're pretty big now that you got your health back, but I got some that'll fit you. I'll bring um over.'

'Beautiful. I guess I'll see you when I come out of this joint.'

'The Eastside is a drag compared to this, not as clean as over here. Try to stay if you can.'

'Well, I'll see ya, Doug.'

'Yeah,' he said,

and left.

3

But it's my newhome itself I wanna talk about—

the time I *knew* this was my place, justlike you feel sometimes when you bust a broadout, and you think O Shit I'm So Embarrassed to Think Maybe This Is the 1 Cunt in the World for Me.

Over here, to the rightside of my mind, are the admission building and combined women's unit. I don't know what it's like inside – though it sensibly shouldn't be any different than any of the rest of the joint and not have bars and grills for security – but this was the place where I came in and where even now Miss Sweet Lorraine lay in wait for some sickdopie's with mountaintattered sympathy for all yewboys, 1 mole-and-blood-speckled hand ontop of the other as though she were holding either the Hope Diamond or the used condom she found in her husband's wallet 2years ago. This place, though: it's 6long gray stories of chiseled blankeyed windows, and it watches a clustered parkinglot with southern-license-plated tails.

Sometimes they put you On Call to meet the educational director at his offices in the administration building.

To go over front you 1st head for CenterControl where you showed your pass, and turned right through the marble arches past the elevators

and a freakfaced hack everyone called Mother Gish, who guarded them,

then through the swinging doors and down the steps to the main courtyard, a footballfield of useless grass,

and arches,

lanes,

that stretched 4square under hundreds of dimwit renaissance pillars. The stone was brownly harsh, and each lane was named for some Rooseveltian henchman who held political sway in the various districts during the period,

The John A. Wallace Andrews Lane

The Peter P. Burroughs Lane

The Chesley K. Simpson Lane

The Moses J. Fetchinfield Lane,

and the natural drab music of them was such, I could tell no 1 had ever strolled them.

The admission building entrance from this side was strapped with belts of steel; it was gouged out of a tallwall

like the kind people get shot against,

and you had to show your pass to the guard inside through a little slit of nosehigh window, then wait while he made up his chimpanzee mind that it was safe to let you in. It was always like this.

Now I see the inside of my room on the 6thfloor, next to Little Joe and Tamerlane, who was out of Ohio but Joe was out of New York, and both doing 10 years for SALE – but Tam's dime was new and Joe's was old, and he only had a year left. And sometimes you hate a man simply because he has less time left than you do.

But my room. It wasn't very big, this room, and I don't know how many actualfeet

like Galileo or Caryl Chessman would be able to tell you theirs,

and it was narrow by halfaman but it had much height. It had nails in the pussypink pastel walls where guys had hung the *Playboy*pictures that are banned in all other fedjoints but this 1, and it even had 1 remaining Scotchtaped in a 2foot frame over dated souvenir pics of darkies holding the noses of winninghorses,

all pink and brushtouched around the crack of her 200-square feet of raw red ass:

This, Miss Ann of *The Clansman* and Rev. Dixon's finest-dream, her in whose name thousands of blackthroats have been stretched and a million blackballs crushed,

smiling a greatbig stupid doofus grin comparable to the crease in her crackers,

now available for only 75¢ a month at Your Favorite Newsstand.

I had 2windows (with bars over them) I had to do every Tuesday-inspection night, and I could look through these below to the Herefordshire herdquarters – the little black shed they lowered into every evening.

Next to this was the end of a brick extension of the UT building that had no windows but did have 2 huge Roman-doors big enough to drag catapults through, and above these was the chiseledin legend: THE NARCOTICS FARM.

3&1/4

There was a curiousbird I never saw before in a prison element. It is called the Winder

(because of his returnvisits)

and it is a creature who voluntarily commits to the hospital for a 6month cure, but can check out anytime it wants to

(unless they're 'under pressure,' which is often what the federal courts find best to do with their informers).

But they makeup about 400 of the 1,000population, and only about 20percent of the entire population is women. 35percent of these Winders are exactly like the black bastard who got up against me in a whiteman's court and shaped his treachery to fit my defeat. But this isn't saying anything for the majoritygroup of cons, whom I find to be *most* deadly, dressed sillily in summer in bulkyknits and japped heads and 35dollar wingtipped kicks made by JohnMcHale,

who would hiply drysnitch you off in the messhall if they saw you stealing an extra chop from the stainless-steel steamtables.

At the center

of the hallway leading down from my UTunit, a block in length or more, there was CenterControl, a longdesk that looked like some 3rdAvenue bars,

but it was presided over by officiallooking men with red-necks and big bellies with noasses wearing popart anklehigh RoyRogers boots that looked as though they were invented, with their hooks and belts and knobs, to wade through pigshit, or somebody's cakes. They, these men, were townsmen from the artificial little city 2miles away that had a street named Main and 1 called Broadway, who wore governmentgreen and drawled YALL when they meant *you-all* and stared with tighter attention at the noon-passing fatfine pussies than any con would dream of doing. And they would snicker about the 'whores' in a way I could hear from the place they 'locked off' all malepatients, the stairwell leading to the basement and Commissary,

and I heard them talking about this or that bitch and say what lousy goddamn excuses for women dopefiend bitches are,

and wish outloud in a petitionway that it was possible for the 1st hoor next to the matron leading them, the stallioned-legged Sister with blackskin and naturallypink lips, to godown on her roughblack knees and suck all their peckers.

By God.

Not far from this place, just half the gallery between Center-Control and the Ginnybarn, the office of the Headman Police was situated,

whom I sometimes saw in wonder when I 1st hit the Farm:

an energetic awesomeugly Alabaman of untender age and origins, who sponsored a singinggroup of sexually mixed black dopefiends, but the only reason I could come to was maybe he liked to hear darkies sing,

like Stephen Foster.

He had a complexion like slightlyburnt SunshineCrackers, and a voice like an alligator. He was a littleman, and every-body

but me

called him the BigOne.

I knew that sometime I'd meet him personally, as I'd met his type in the past, so I trained myself to call him nothing else but Captain Koyle.

3&3/4

Right down on the 1st floor, next to the hacks'office, there is a bulletin board whose every dopie's duty it is to read each morning and noon and night because sometimes you'd be on call for tests on Branch-5, the Psychlevel, or maybe they'd need to jack youoff for some blood, or some unbelievable madhatter of a SocialWorker wanted to talk to you,

so I did like all the rest and read the board, which was full of warnings about the things that could get you fuckedup in UT, like writing letters in the shithouse after 10oclock, or more than 3guys in 1 room, or other trivia that could knock you off with a punishment of 2hours' extra duty in the messhall,

and I counted 33things you could get upto 8hours' extra duty for doing.

But this was the Mondaymorning of the 1st week I'd been in UT, and the nightbefore I'd noticed my name on the Call List for the next day, but it was within the unit itself, which meant it was probably a SocialWorker:

But it wasn't – it was that little croaker I'd gone through all those changes with over on the gallery, and he must've forgotten me because he went through the business about the hard *v* and we both went through the routine about how I felt, and the whole thing was a little uncanny.

But now he had a record with a bigblack greasylooking photo of me at the bottomright. 'Mr. Yesyes . . . won't you follow me, please?'

This was the UT examinationroom; it had a desk, 2chairs, a medicalcouch of the kind which makes it easy for women to get up on and spread their asses for the doctor's eye, and a refrigerator.

He sat down at the desk and squinted through horn-rimmed glasses I only now noticed him wearing, and I wondered if I'd somehow thought them to be a naturalpart of his face.

'I see,' he said, flipping my jacket, stopping at the place with 8felonies, and going deeperdeeper into me until he got kind of scared from the lies and turned quickly to make sure I wasn't going for his throat. 'Ah . . . yes. Are you comfortable?'

'Are you?'

'Ah, but you mustn't ask me questions.'

'Why?'

'Because you see it's my job to ask you questions, to find out the answers to the things I ask you, that is.'

'But how can I trust you?'

'Trust,' he said smiling, and leaned back in his doctorchair. 'Trust is the thing most missing in the dopeaddict's life.'

'That's close to being a very accurate statement.'

'Well.' He beamed at me. 'I see you've been coordinating *some* things, haven't you? And I've been reading your record, going over it, and I notice a number of glaring inconsistencies that tell me you're putting on for the mostpart – that is to say, you're attempting to escape.'

I stopped being amused.

'I've been reading your tests,' he went on, and smiled, no change in his sappyseeming eyes, 'you know, the 500questions, where you have to answer all of them, the ones you took on Branch-5? that had to do with sex and whatall? And here, your answer about animals, the 1 that said I LIKE——BECAUSE, and you said Elephants Because They Don't Make War. Now what kind of answer is that?'

'What kind of question is that?'

'Why, the same sort as the others, the other 499, that is, and the ones you answered like My Mother Was BigBlackSoft and Stupid, and when the sisterquestion asked the same about your father you wrote in the same thing.'

'I don't see what's inconsistent about that.'

'No, I mean it's your flippancy in answering, because in some cases what appears to be flippancy is really the way you feel, don't you think? I mean, I do, in reading things likethis: I Would Like Most, If I Had My Wish, To——and you say Talk To A Tiger Because I'd Want To Know The Wonder Of The

World It Lives In.' He chuckled. 'Now that's kind of romantic, isn't it? I mean it doesn't make sense.'

'I don't see what you mean.'

He shook his head. 'But it's simple. This is the addict-attitude – the desire for the unobtainable, the dream. I mean things that don't make sense.'

Antman

that was his actual name

was the headhack in UT. He sat in the office in his whitesuit smoking Marvel cigarets and signing dopies' passes for the recreation area downstairs, and telling the other2 asshole hillbillyhacks what the hell to do. He was a stockyman, a blond, with skin livid the way it becomes with a Nordicalcoholic, a Jewnose over Frankishlips, and a halfassed hip hillbillyboy way of talking,

as he took me around for an interview. 'I dontgiveadamn what no doc says, since I run this place, right? If you'd been hooked up in this thing as long as I have you'd get to understand the same things I do.'

We went into 1 of the 1stfloor offices reserved for this type thing, with the bellcapped lamp common around this joint, and a desk and 2 chairs.

'Hahnah,' Antman said relievedly. He took out a sheet of form from my unitjacket and began to inkin the blank spaces. Mother n dad dead? check, n family? O you don't have 1? but that ain't what the recordsay. It says you got an aunt and kid. But that's all right. Monthdayandyear of birth. And now tell me,

'What do you expect out of the hospital?'

'Whaddaya mean what do I expect?'

'It says here you made the request to come down here for treatment. Didja?'

'Yeah.'

'Well, what do you want us to do for you?'

'Can you help me overcome my need for drugs?'

'No.'

'Then what's all the sweat for?'

'You gotta say somethin on this form here, that's why.' He scribbled in a big blankspace. 'I'll just say you want treatment.'

'That's all right with me.'

'Now, whaddaya wanna do while you're here?'

'Nothin.'

He looked pained. 'Awnaw, you gotta *do* somethin. That's the policy of the hospital, even with Winders. How you expect to go back to the Freeworld and not know how to do a damnthing? We got the powerhouse, the disposalplant and the kitchen. Which 1 do you want?'

'The 1 that gives workmen's compensation.'

Mr. Antman sat back and stared at me. 'I guess you know we don't pay any wages on these jobs, which places a greater obligation of duty on those who work on them.'

'I can see how it would.'

'But listen, how'd you like to stay overhere in UT as my officeboy? I see where you can type, and my officeboy is leavin in another week.'

'What're the advantages?'

'Well, there's the girls. . . .'

'Then you know how important that is.'

'Lookheah.' He leaned back and became himself for a moment, caught in a Take where his Marvel cigaret drooped from 2 forefingers at the bridge of his forehead like the fat oldlegs of a man with a hardon, and his mouth became sickly red around the edges, the way lobster is when it's properly cooked alive. 'I know about women, and then some. And I know about *men* and women, because I'm a man myself and I know how I'd feel if I was lockedup some God Damn Where I'd never see any for a longtime. And I got my own personal ideas about that, because there's not a man who owns um would lock a dogup without a piece of pussy, or a bitch that was hot in the ass. But here in this element, the Farm, we got both, and there's got to be a certain bending thiswayandthat, just to make sure things balance off. Now, you know well's I do that nobody's gonna let you fuck 1 of these women, but there's ways they try to make up, like letting you receive pinkmail from your girlfriend in the Barn every evening right along with your whitestuff from the street, and on Sundays and holidays you get to see her at the basketballgame or the footballgame, or sometimes during the week when the women have their volleyballgames. So you take a little and you give a little, but you don't actually give up the shonuff snatch, see? I'm not sayin this is the right therapy, but I only work here, and there's bending and twistin I do that I won't even talk about.'

I made my eyes dimout in exactly the way motionpicture cameras do, so I couldn't see his face while he spoke, and the words became more real to me.

'So what I'm sayin is I, as supervisor of this unit, I give a little and take a bit too, but you been locked up without the sight of women for quite a littletime now, and here in UT you get to see them a lot more often than you ever will over on the Eastside. Pretty soon now, you'll get a woman, and anyplace she has to go, she has to come outta those Barndoors. But you'll find out about that, and you'll find out about the Callsheet for the Women's Section and the Underground and the MessengerFolio, all that's comin.'

'It sounds like a happy way to live.'

'Oh, itis, believe me. But you'll find that out from Pineapple when you talk to him.'

'Do you mind if I think about it?'

His face became a trifle gray. 'NoNo, you take your time, all you want, and let me know tomorrowmornin. And my name is Antman, if you didn't know.'

'I knew.'

'Just plain Antman.' He twinkled. 'Sounds kinda Spanish, don't it?'

4

A man should never cherish the images a woman leaves on him. This was mostly where my main trouble was, eventhough I tried to make up by saying to myself, like *Shazam* or something, the memory *lives*, the memory was and *is*,

but it's not like that, nothing like that at all, and the way you used to make love to a woman, the way you fucked her, has nothing to do with the vacuum of being locked in now, several lightyears removed through confinement,

and the new shaft or tongue that moves her are nothing like the ones that made her runcoming 3or4 years ago. These kinds of memories, and usually all of them related to some kind of freakingoff, are generally quite selfish things.

So I'd made somekind of blackgoddess out of her, not having seen her for so long and recalling her in only the fondest aspects – not the way her early-morning mouth tasted, or the way the tips of her tits sometimes tasted stale, or the agonized, helpless-look on her face the day I walked into the bathroom and found my Venus shitting – no, only the way she bestkissed and grooved me,

and not the night I found the taste of the Thing quite foul with our excess.

So the day I saw her coming out of the Barn, standing there with Pineapple and Tamerlane at the UTentrance, it gave me something of a start. I couldn't adjust; the wrong info had been fed to my synapses; and I started off automatically, feeling in my pocket to see if I had a token for Coke when I got down to CC, where I'd better have some reason for being, and I watched the shape closely, the turn of head inches above the ones of the other girls and the yardwide ass twitching vigorously under a blue summerknit,

but it wasn't her, I could see, as they made the turn at CC

for the elevators in the front hall that carried these kinds of groups to Branch-5, and there really was no reason for me to think it should have been,

since she'd been dead now so long from the overdose.

I got my Coke and cameback past the glare of the CC duty-officer who knew I'd only been following the group to feen and maybe say something to 1 of the broads.

So Tamerlane bigman giggled at me, 'Thass the fasest I ever seen you get away from here.'

'I thought I saw somebody.'

'He thought he saw his woman,' Pineapple said. He clicked his false teeth in a keen gumpyyellow face.

'That's right': I went to lean against the bars, thinking of the way this ass moved and the way the other I used to own tricked me.

But I stayed there till the group returned an hour later, and she was in front this time, walking longlegged and wide, a tall blackSister who was no longer a youngster but still quite beautiful, with Ethiopian features and a cascade of black lustroushair, and a pelvis wide and rhythmic as her big ass. She was not quite my image but just a little bit more than my image had ever been, and we touched eyes casually as I moved up and watched them be let in the Barndoor by the matron.

The door had a sign that said KEEP OUT BY ORDER OF THE SUPERVISOR JOE ANTMAN,

his mark,

and this was Pineapple's office.

'C'mon in,' he said, and sat at the desk with typewriter and began immediately typing something on pinkpaper that began 'My dearest sweetest soul.' There was another chair, but the whole joint was only a few feet long and fewer feet wide and smelled like somebody'd been farting in it all day long. There was a window that looked out on the UT courtyard that had barbwire on the farwall, that was dinkydark from dirt, that showed only the brightmoon or lightsky.

He said, turning on me suddenly, not knowing I already knew, 'My name's Pineapple.'

'Mine's Clark Kent.'

'Wait a minnit.' He typed some more. 'Damn.' He erased. 'Antman said you was interested in this job.'

'I am.'

'Well, man, it's mella, you just take my word for it. There ain't no other place in the hospital I'd rather be. You got the run of it, the unit, and any time you wanna see your woman you just pick up the MessengerFolio and split; it's like a pass to anywhere you wanna go.'

'Oh, man . . .'

'Yeah.' He typed some more. 'I see my woman everyday. I'm supposed to go to the squaredance with her this comin Sunday.'

'Wow.'

'But I mean when you're over here you have a chance to drop your Undergroundstuff to your woman, since she can come outta the door 3times a day, if nothin else but to the messhall, and pickup and drop while she's goin.'

'I can dig that.'

'You'll dig it. The whole joint revolves around the women. There ain't nothin you want or need to get that don't come through the Ginnybarn.'

He typed some more,

then clicked his loose false teeth deliciously and grinned at me.

Mornings, noons, and evenings, we dopies leave en masse, when the airraidscreaming buzzer rings, to troop down the long hallway to the messhall. Only moments before, the women have gone to eat, and the hall is filled with the thicksweet funky odor of their passing. They eat in 2 neat messhalls on my left. There are merely 2 thick doors that stand between them and us: you can hear them as you pass, their high, chattering birdvoices raised in banshee urgency, punctuated by the chittering steelsounds their eatingtools make on the metaltrays. There is a courtyard dividing their halls from the maleside, but the windows of each are thickly boardedup, a premeditated preventive against men and women catching glimpses of each other.

Sometimes I go to eat with Pineapple. He drills me through with talk of only 1 subject, his woman Twister, a short, yellowlittle broad with the most remarkable ass I've ever seen on a woman – it is like the ass of a Sumo wrestler, defying all natural physical laws by being hooked to an otherwise fragile, unordinary network of bone and cartilage.

Each morning at8 Pineapple stands at the windows of the 1stfloor dayroom and waves and fingerwrites to her as she passes on her way to work in the garmentshop downstairs in the basement. He is obsessed with her big, unnatural ass:

'I had my fingers innit at the squaredance. Everytime we doseydoed, I got my fingers innit.' He clicked his teeth as we went to eat the evening meal. 'Man. Have you ever seen anass like that?'

'On an elephant.'

He stopped at 1 of the ashtray buckets hooked to the wall next to the women's messhall and pulled Twister's underground note off the bottom where she'd hooked it with Scotch-tape when she went in. 'I tole Twister,' he said, catching up, 'I tole her I hadda have her.' He looked at the thick pink wad of Scotchtaped stuff; it had *Daddy* written on it. 'When I get up next week, like I told her, I'm goin to Cleveland and lay for her.'

'When does she get up?'

'2months from now. Which ain't long. It ain't like the 27months I had, so I can lay for her 2more.'

'Right.'

We turned at the grill leading into the messhall at Center-Control. The hack there stood imperiously high on his raisedchair, like a fatassed Mercury, waiting to give the signal to the Eastside hacks when to cut their units loose.

We lined up on the blackside, on the right, and over to our left was the whiteline, we all waters seeking our levels;

overthere were Puerto Ricans and whities, and this mall was full of Spanish and whiteboy and blackboy talk as we waited for the hack standing at the entrance to the serviceline to give us the signal to come in. About a100 of us in each line. Faces. Hip and unhip dopies. There is an extraordinary number of peckerwood dopefiends who stare over at our blackline with something like wonder, their collective blueeye beaming with awe on us,

while we brothers and a few whiteNegroes make words and ideas that have absolutely nothing whatever to do with the moment.

Ahead of me, Pineapple is abstracted. 'You see that ass onher. With an ass like that, a broad's like the Bank of England; she can really catchum big.'

A tall blackguy bucked the line and came up to me; he wore a green Banlon and had a boil on his nose. 'Don't I know you?'

'Not unless you work for the Federal Bureau of Narcotics.'

He laughed, and there was a flash of angry curiosity about his mouth. He melted away, and I went back to listening to Pineaple:

'The ass,' he muttered.

'All I think you wanna do is pile Twister.'

He looked pained. 'No, noman, really, it's business. With the proper management, Twister'd be a dynamite ho.'

The hack waved us into the messhall. The eruptions of voices and peculiar foodsmells came close to being indistinguishable in a weird fantasiamoment, and there was something incredibly lousy about it all. A long steeltube railing divided the black-and-white lines; the steamtables branched out equidistantly chesthigh, with signs that said DO NOT EXCHANGE FOOD UNTIL SEATED IN MESSHALL. Behind the counter, dopies of all colors feverishly served ridiculously awful food – funkygreasy chops with quarterinch rings of fat, mashed potatoes only halfdone, carrots looking like orange crayon some crosseyed child had diced up, milk from a dispenser in plastic cups, and bread served with tongs by a sniffling Oyea from the Island. But the smell of it all was the most brilliant thing, like some gargantuan pipinghot turd.

Overseeing all this were the Headman Police, cigar 2-inches long thrust omnisciently over the whole eatingshow, and the dietitian, a leanboney greyeyed blackhaired figure dressed in navyblue with 4gold rings around each cuff. Her arms were akimbo and her face was grim. She looked as though she'd never been fucked by a man in her entire life.

The appointed areas on our metaltrays were filled, and we came out of this place to turn to the left and pick up silverware from the waiting cart in the middle of the hallway,

then proceed 3dozen feet down to HallOne where, in unison, we sat in either 1 of 2pews with long woodentables that made you think you were part of a Jimmy Cagney movie, and the only thing missing was a hack with machinegun in a crow'snest at the front of the hall. And we sat and ate the prepared bullshit.

'The ass,' Pineapple said, munching next to me.

And then, the din. As they came closer to being done with eating, the voices of the dopies rose to frightening decibels, until it became something like an attenuated scream of rage, and by the time you were done their voices were liquidlightning thunder that pierced the very framework of your soul and turned your bowels to solid rock. The 1sttime it happened I covered my ears, but later I learned to live with it and even eat comfortably through the babel. Around me mouths twitched and shouted, food was exchanged from tray to tray, milk was given away, and if you wanted to speak to your neighbor you screamed,

but something about this way of communication seemed most appropriate. The munchingchomping mouths instantly reduced garbage into garbage, and for the 1sttime in my life I was able to see that eating and shitting were not very different, and the privacy that is reserved for 1 ought, in the sake of good taste, to be preserved for the other.

'Yeah,' said Pineapple, wiping his mouth and clicking his teeth.

'If you was a trick, you'd turn a trick with Twister!': I smiled as I shouted at him.

He looked shocked. 'How can you say somethin like that?'

'Through this hole in my face.'

Sometimes we sat in this cacophonous snakepit for nearly an hour until the women were released from their messhalls; then some nondescript rednecked hack came to unlock the far door and let us out, and we took only our knives and forks and spoons to a portable cart at the front to drop them in with our milkcups,

and come out in the hallway, lighting cigarets and bullshittin and clinching deals for mace or 'spacers' before the hack ran us back to our units. 2hundred, sometimes 3hundred guys would be idly loitering in the hallways this way.

You could have 9draws on your cigaret, the way Pineapple and me were walking, before you got back to UT.

'With an ass like that,' he said longingly.

We passed windows that revealed in the darknight (by this time) the women's units, and sometimes a figure staring down at us as we passed. In the window I always watched, she was there, and sometimes I stopped and made myself different by standing for longmoments looking back. The gravured reaches of the Farm touched the nightsky with sillysober fingers.

As I stood and watched, Pineapple tugged at my sleeve. 'With an ass like that,' he informed me urgently, 'I could make a million dollars.'

'An assmade million dollars doesn't seem to have much dignity':

which I felt was kind of a hip thought, but Pineapple's response was hipper:

'An ass that can make a million dollars don't haveta worry about dignity.'

So saith Pineapple, and I thought he said it nicely.

4ε1/2

Joe Antman was right about the broad. Just before Pineapple got up, we were all standing around the UTgate, feening on the Tuesdaygoing groups from the Barn. And just to our right, about 20feet, a staircase led down to the basement and garmentshop. I happened to see her again, led by a dumpylittle matron to the basement area, so I was laying and rappin with Pine and Tamerlane. Certainly I was there when she showed again. But this time I moved up to follow them to the Barn, and I got my eyes in her. She kept turning to glanceback at me, which made the matron very nervous. She seemed to think we were talking, the numberone violation in the Big4: no talk, no see, no touch, no fuck,

but she couldn't prove anything, so I hung close, walking only a few feet behind them. I had a chance to check her out closely. She had on something severe and white, like a nurse's uniform that was made for less woman than what she was. Which was beautiful, all of her. She had a twitching right knee that may have been some longago injury, but her buns were spectacular and fluid and it made my guts turn over pleasantly to see them work. She walked in a flashy whorey intimidating way that drew me to watch the curve of her long black neck and spine.

At the Barndoor she turned, and we looked at each other fully. It was a whore's face, a beautiful, classicthing, with a sharply inverted curve in pouting lowerlip, brows like a witch, and big roundbrown eyes crisply defined with paint. It was an old, still beautiful, whore's face; about her long black throat I saw the rings of time. So we got hungup in each other's eyes, until hers snipped it off like sharp little scissors,

and I stood there in the instant, watching the door open and her enter proudly with a 20dollar stride. That was the 1sttime I really got a good look at Sonja.

The next day I went and copped her jacket at the Headman Police's office while he was out. The clerk, a tallwhitey with hornrimmed glasses, gave me a little static when I asked, but I casually moved over to the record plates and roughed off what I wanted. She had a mugshot that must've been done in Alderson, W. Va., a completely unglamorous thing that was probably done when she was only severalweeks off stuff. She was using a whorename, Sonja Richardson, on this bit, but her realname was Pearl Lee Smith,

and she was from San Francisco by way of Terminal Island, doing 2years in with 5out for smuggling stuff into the States. The jacket said she was 38years old, and her number was J-019-20 and she lived in KB-3 of the women's unit. She was due to go home in a few months.

I wrote her. I told her completely foolish but provocative things. I don't know what they were, but they were bound to be extremely passionate. The next day I got a pinkkite in the eveningmail; it had no stamp, of course, and it was unsealed, as all this kind of mail had to be. Her writingstroke was luxurious and confident.

Her first letter was quite formal, in a surprising way, and after reading it 16times, I decided there was an intelligent force behind it.

So it became a regular thing. We got hooked up. Every evening, she got a pink and I got 1, and gradually, through this fantastic process, we came to know each other (though so much of what we know of ourselves is such a lousy God Damn Lie),

and even make dates: She'd write,

Oh Daddy, please be at the basketball game this Sunday so I can take you off and drink you in.

On Sunday we'd sit across from each other separated by screens overlooking the basketball court.

Over there were 5neat longrows of women, a dynamite splash of colors and sizes, all trousered tightly, looking at us, we 3hundred craning necks, in the same hungry way we watched them. They were overseen by a black, fat, walrus-footed matron and 3or4 Security hacks, who seemed to be weirdly possessive of these broads, I could see as I came to know them more. Uphere you'd get shot for fingerwriting to your woman, and so could she, and her game privileges would be taken away; so you had to keep your eye on the hacks when you *did* write. After I learned how to rap, I was forced to watch them, and this is when I was able to see the kind of personal dramas they were involved in over the broads,

something kind of sleasily sick

that had them watching over these women as though they were 150unspaded bitches whose foaming asses twitched madly to behad at the slimmest opportunity. But maybe they were. Still, the personalities of these hacks were perversely significant. You could tell they enjoyed seeing us separated this way. A kind of animal control.

In this way, on Sundayafternoons, we suffered together; she would be dressed in her hippest and tightest, neutral-curveshowing colors, and I would be striking attitudes in my sensual Banlon. But it soon got to the place where these afternoons were a boring obligation;

in the midst of 300mad shouting dopefiends I sometimes sit resentfully watching her overthere with prim tight knees and that great big whoresmile, and I decide maybe it'd have been better if I'd dropped the whole business after the first kite.

I knew from the very beginning that she wasn't the girl in the window.

I didn't explain this fingerwriting thing to you. This is the way it works,

the same thing they teach the deaf and dumb:

Put your forefingers and thumbs together so they form something like a diamond. That's an *A*. Now make eyeglasses of both forefingers and thumbs and touch them at the closing points. That's *B.* For *C* you make a *C* of your fingers, just

1 hand,

and *D* is 1 forefinger pointed skyward with the other hand closed in a *C* and touched like tongues.

E is simple, with a wide-open hand and a slash from the edge of the other, and *F* is 2fingers of each hand crossed in something like a prayer.

Close your fists and strike them together like hammers to make *G*, and *H* is like giving 1 hand Skin, just a light brush across the palms.

I is like calling a waiter or testing wind direction, the little finger pointed up; use it to draw a *J* in the air. *K* is 1 knuckle against a forefinger, and *L* is the whole hand open. *M* is 3fingers bent, and *N* is 2fingers made the same way. *O* is a natural *O* with your fingers, and a forefinger against it is *P.* Hook your little finger in an *O* to make a *Q*, but you

rub 1 hand across a fist to make an *R.*

S is 2 little fingers hooked.

And any way you make a *T* makes sense.

U is like you'd suddenly screwed 2fingers into something, and the *V* is like the 1 Churchill made in the blitz. *W* is both hands patted flat backtoback in front, and *X* is the way you made the *F*, but this time using only

forefingers.

Y is a slice across 1 hand, and

Z is like you'd draw on the schoolboard in chalk.

5

Pineapple left just about 10minnits ago,

and I'm standing looking down the hall after the long-gone figure, hating him, in a very controlled way, and dismissing him altogether as I recalled this flashback:

He gave me all his best *Playboy* cutouts.

'What's the matter? You don't look too cool.'

Then he gave me a hip little portable radio and told me he didn't feel too cool.

'You still thinkin about Twister, man?'

'I can't help it.' He looked silly. 'I guess I just love the broad.'

'You love her ass, chump, and that's the only thing you ever loved about her.'

He threatened me by saying, 'That's all right. You'll get hung up too.'

'Hung up is right. Hung up in some broad's pants if I ever get the chance.'

'That's that cold thang about you, man. I don't dig you sometimes.'

'Don't disgust me.' I put the radio and other junk under my arm and started for my pad.

'I don't see what you got against me and Twister,' he said funnily behind me.

I turn, and I can feel my face going ugly as I say:

'You muss be mad. Do you realize where we are, sucker, and under what kinda conditions? I'm fed up with that love lie. The nexttime I say that to a woman, she'll know it's true and not need to have my need to say it.'

He looked at me for a longtime, clicking his teeth in a dumb way, then finally said,

'I just don't dig you sometimes.'

And maybe this was the thing that drugged me the most, because I'm easily the most digable kind of guy,

but not even in the interests of understanding would I change. And, God Damn It, finally, this was the way it was going to be, and from now on I wouldn't hide my strangeness,

because there is a black urgent thing in me that needs the room to grow.

Sonja wrote,

> *Oh, Daddy, why don't you get in AA so that on Weds. nites when they have their weeklie coffeebreak we'll be able to rap to each other for 30mins., so why don't you hit on Willie B the chairman on yr. side?*

I found Willie B down in the basement, standing in front of the evening Commissary. The long tunnelhall was loaded with guys, some waiting in line to enter the shotgun length of store area, and other guys standing in rapping groups. There was an especially irritating bunch of RocknRoll dopefiends, with 1 guy whose voice was suspiciously high.

Willie B, turning from another conversation to me, turned out to be a little sonofabitch I once did drug business with, and he went into a paroxysm of doubtful greeting, first with plenty splah, 2times, cracking the center of my palm sharply, then

'Oh, man! Wow. This is a gas. Digman, dig, you remember the last time we dug each other?'

'I'll never forget it.'

'Well, you know why I didn't get back? What happened to me? Did you know that was the time I got cracked? That the Man swooped down on me?'

'Naw, I didn't know that. You left everybody sick. 4sick dopefiends. And you got cracked, right? And we had to go through some other sort of weird changes.'

'Well, you know what that came to,' he said kind of blandly, so I went all off the wall too,

'Shadyside Cemetery.'
'What?'
'You'd never recognize it now.' The bodies surged about us; a lot of money was being spent. 'You the AA chairman?'
He looked pressed for effect. 'And it's taking all my time. I got a great big portable TV and stereo I can't take advantage of.'
'That *is* sad.'
Now he looked knowing. 'I already know what's on your mind, now that I'm connectin that broad from the Coast, and she's been pushin hard for somebody – I didn't know it was you, but you got to come down to some of the regular meetins before I can give you any kind of snatch.'
'Ohshit, man, I know what these little con front organizations are set up for. You have the power to put me in for the next AA mixedmeeting, if you wanna use it.'
'But I just can't do it like that,' he said in an agonized way.
'Not that you don't owe me a favor.'
'Listen, I could show you the records.'
'I doubt that.'
'I just want you to understand how it is.'
'After all we been through together.'
His eyes flashed 2brief little specks of hate. 'You don't haveta press so hard.'
'20year men.'
'Okay. All right. But I won't be able to do it till the next coffeebreak.'
'I thought it was every week.'
'No, every 2weeks.'
'I wonder what other coffeebreaks that broad has been goin to.'

It's funny, but it gets so you automatically bridge the vernacular idioms; 1 moment, I'm muscling Willie B in a typical manner, and the next I'm talking to a really weird little doc who had a big nose, telescope lens in his hornrimmeds, and a hole in the heel of 1 of his 69¢ socks, who is looking at me strangely and is about to speak

'How are you today?' in a voice like Donald Duck's.

'Is there any particular reason why that's the 1st question a doctor asks?'

'Well, I don't suppose there is,' he said, shrugging, with heaps of quack in his voice.

'It sounds like a cliché . . . I mean it sounds like something that's been done to death.'

'That's an interesting way to look at it.'

'Well, there are viewpoints and viewpoints. I mean, people can have a different opinion of it.'

'That's true. . . .'

'What did you say your name was before, I mean when you told me?'

He picked up a pencil and began tapping on the desk. 'Dr. Colman. I'm your new unit physician. I speak with all the patients individually when they come out in UT population, so that's why you're here.' He adjusted his glasses. 'I want to find out if there's anything wrong with you. Physically wrong.'

'Aside from being mentally sick?'

'I didn't say that. You said something I didn't say.'

'I don't want to put words in your mouth.'

'I'm always very careful about that,' he said, flicking the pencil on the desk. 'I want always to be understood, and I want to understand my patients.'

'Understanding should always feature the doctor.'

He sat back and stared at me professionally. 'Perhaps you're looking for a contest.'

'You mean I'm in for 1 of those too?'

'I can tell you you're in for a lot of things, mister,' he said sternly, 'and nobody would've had a hand in it but you.'

'You lost me right there.'

He was huffed. He sort of gritted his teeth at me as though something had stabbed him, then

got a murderhold on the leaves of my jacket, and almost tore the whole God Damn Thing apart. It was kind of scary.

'All right,' he said genially, turning around after a while. 'What bothers you?'

'You mean, physically?'

'Well, of course that's what I mean.'

'Nothing, except that I need air, plenty of it.'

'What do you mean by that?'

'I mean get out of the joint. I'm getting kind of tired.'

'And by the look of your records, you've got quite a little way to go yet.'

'Thanks for the cheer.'

He suddenly snatched his glasses off, and I was positive he couldn't see a God Damn Thing. 'You may not know it, but you've already got a chit on your institution record, 4of them as a matter of fact.'

'I like to think of them as misunderstandings.'

'And your psychologicals are inconclusive,' he said, clumping his glasses on my jacket. 'Would you like to know what the examining psychiatrist said?'

'There are viewpoints and viewpoints.'

'I'll read it to you. Here: "This patient has a high verbal facility; he answers the test questions with an almost flippant defiance. He would not fit in group therapy because he would tend to usurp the authority of the therapist. Nor is individual therapy recommended. Since he features himself an individualist, it is unlikely that he will ever change."' He put on his glasses and looked at me.

'There's something about the last 2sentences that holds me.'

'They're easy to understand.'

'I suppose that opinion was written by Dr. Uxeküll.'

'And he measures you as a manic-depressive psychopath.'

'That's a nice thought to have with cornflakes in the morning.'

'I wouldn't have told you if I didn't think you were strong enough to handle the information.'

'You said you read the test figures?'

'That's right.'

'And my records as well?'

'Yes, since I wanted to find out what kind of man you are.'

'And it didn't tell about it in the records?'

He looked puzzled. 'Tell about what?'

'That I'm a Communist.'

I've taken all the liberties Joe Antman promised me with Pineapple's going, and I've redone the little slit of office in my way. There was a lot of stuff about Jesus that Pine had in the big top drawer of the metal desk

to impress the Godagent in the hospital of his worthiness in a mixed group that included the Twister

that I threw out. There were also some nice *Playboy* shots that I kept (1 dynamite fleshy configuration from Europe that gave me an erection), and all the other essentials for clerking.

I cleaned the dirtywindow and swept the sills, and rubbed the mop from the closet next door across the grimy, pitted, agetroubled floor. It began to look kind of cool,

but you can't do anything with the slimecrying gray walls or the hardshelled waterbugs in the rims of the room,

so I hung up little pictures, little things, like clippings of Feiffer nobody seemed to understand, a youngago picture of John Ciardi, and the most devastatingly beautiful photographic portrait from *Life*magazine of Robert Shelton in full regalia with a burningcross behind him. Joe Antman didn't like it and kept asking me to take it down, until 1 day I forced him to answer my Why?

'Because it makes me nervous.'

'I don't see how': I had stopped my typing of new dopies' entrance forms.

'Because he's such a bastard' – Joe frowned – 'preachin all that hate.'

'I don't see where that has anything to do with you.'

'Well, it does,' he said a little snappishly. 'And it has something to do with you too.'

'I thought it had everything to do with me.'

'He's just like Malcolm X,' Joe said in a moodily insistent way.

'But he's nothin like X.'

'I don't mean the way he *looks*,' Joe said, waving his arms unusually. 'I mean the way he thinks.'

'I don't see how that makes you nervous.'

He declared: 'It ought to make *everybody* nervous, that's what I mean. To have things like him goin on in the nation. Why'd you put it up?'

'Because of the colors': I looked at the blues and greens and distinct fleshtones.

'Well, that's not reason enough to put him up on your wall,' Joe said resentfully.

'Maybe I shoulda put Malcolm up.'

'Listen, either 1 of um is unacceptable to me.'

'I don't know why you get so fuckin defensive about a picture.'

'I'm not defensive,' he said in a careful voice. 'I just wanna know why you got him up on your wall.'

'It wouldn't make sense.'

'You just tell me. It'll make sense to me.'

So I stood,

and I squeezed myself past my padded Lewisburg chair and Joe, and I stood looking at the photo for as long as I needed to satisfy myself that what I'd 1st thought of it was true:

I turned and told him: 'I guess I've just never seen the face of a man who looked as sad as I feel.'

Thursday afternoon, right after lunch, they busted a con patient fucking a matron on a desk in the office adjoining the PTclinic that the eyedoctor uses when he comes in from town once a week. The guy must've run his mouth off to some rat, because they were set up when they showed for countdown, her just leaving the group of women she'd brought over for physical therapy, and him trembling without a pass over here on the Westside. Anyway

busts like that just don't come off without someone snitches, and the way Security busted them was timed to the moment, so that it found her with her ass high and red and smoking for him, and him on the initial hot slickwet stroke toward impact. And I've always wondered what were the 1st thoughts in their minds when the Man stepped in.

I'd smelled the urgency that morning, coming up from exercise in the gym, and the halls were full of that funky, indescribable cop aroma, which may have to do with the way their glands run off when they're getting set to bust somebody. There was too muchmuch activity. Governmentgreen asses that rarely did more than sit were waddling all over the place, big bumpkins trying to look casual as they prowled around the auditorium and the weightroom and the trick spot the sissies used

a dark ramp next to the gameroom that led to the radio shop

where they lucked up and busted 1 guy going down on another.

This cop personality, you got to know it. It's like being in a wax museum where any moment you'll expect 1 of the figures to leap to life. They're some kind of wonder of the world, but I can't tell you exactly what. And I suppose the best of them are those who hate themselves much more than I could ever dream to.

Anyway, that was in the morning. And after exercise I'd stopped briefly to listen to Lomo the trumpetplayer and Whim the pianoplayer in the auditorium, a vast arenalike place that was invariably dark, but sometimes there was a little light from those at the foot of the stage. I got jammed there for a minnit, listening, because Lomo was doing a Milesian thing that echoed New York and her in my mind,

it almost choked me up with nostalgia,

so I got the hell out of there and went down the long-tunnel past the poolroom, and the other that went by the barbershop. Ahead of me, the basement followed the natural T of the joint, and I was now at the center of its arms. More cops ahead of me, poking around near the Chapel and Commissary and bigblue door to the garmentshop. Behind me, several stood at the entrance to the outside and warehouse area, snickering among themselves. That's when I got that helluva smell. I checked my pockets for contraband before I pushed through the swinging door and went up the stairway to CenterControl. The Headman Police was sitting, a tiny green bubble of himself, in the King's chair, burping glassyeyed ovet a (I'd swear the same God Damn) Cigar. About 4,000cops were draped around the long CenterControl desk, or enough to seem that many,

and not a 1 of them asked me for a pass as I went on by and down the long hallway to UT,

but I heard the Headman Police say croakingly in his big beastvoice to one of the flunkies,

'Well, leastways we kin thank the Holy Spirit he isn't a nigra.'

They blowed the little broad right out behind the bust, didn't even let her change her clothes had her money ready before she got to the mainhall. Sonja wrote me later that she was putting it out both ways,

and that may be so

but I didn't believe half of the dirtygossip that went around that joint.

The guy, they immediately sent to Lewisburg with a special marshal,

which always puzzled me about the sexcases,

because 'treatment' seemed to end abruptly if they caught you with a woman's ass poised in a quite natural position,

and I wondered whether it was drugs they were trying to cure us of, or just the normal human need to fuck.

DEAREST DADDY,

you never did tell me what happened when you saw Willie B about the AA coffeebreak on Weds. I've been very anxious. I want to see you up close, touch you, so badly. I'm so goddamn hot for you, and I know that isn't the kind of things ladies say so you'll probably jump on it. But I want you and you know it. This is so evil, to want somebody. I've been sitting here rereading some of your letters. Daddy, what is mons? *Oh, nevermind, I just found it in my dictionary. Oh, you. The things you say sometimes. This is why I love you most. Daddy, I have some pictures of me that a girl did and I'd like you to have them. Okay? You asked for something memorizing me, and this is all I have. I don't like to keep things, trinkets like jewelry. They make me feel so definite because I own them as though I have no other choice. I got a letter from my father tonite, whom I had begun to worry about as he hasn't written in so long. But he's okay and looking forward to me coming home in the next three months. You would love my father and I know he'd just love you too.*

You get so tired sometimes. You know what I mean? I don't bother with any of these other whores because they seem to be so emptyheaded and hung up, and they hate me for it because they think I think I'm some kind of Miss Priss broad.

Daddy, I love you. That feeling just came over me and I love and want you more than I've ever wanted a thing. There's something the same of us in each other. But whatever it is makes me kind of scared sometimes.

It wouldn't be so bad if I didn't have to get so fucking tired about the whole thing.

Yours

6

Sunday afternoon

I went down to 1 of the AA meetings in the Chapel. It was big enough to hold about 250people

(but there were only about 50dopies sitting around when I got there) and it was chickenstitched all around the windows and Sistene swoop of roof, the lightningstaggered motif that seemed to be so essential in the construction of this joint. There were about 50long sadbrown oak pews, and 20tall dirty windows that peeked in on us like the eyes of sick dopefiends.

At the front, the stage, 3feet high off the main floor and tiled with the kind you see in the respectable shithouses of fine old theatres, was wingspreaded by an intricate plaster proscenium with dumblooking little cherubs in it. At the backwall were several tallhigh oak tables, and the portable pulpit the Protestant, Catholic, and Jewish witchdoctors used.

But now Willie B was standing behind the thing, looking like something out of the Darktown Strutters' Ball with his bigeyes blurry from mace probably, and a sillydamn thick Italianknit,

red, I swear it,

both Stetsons hooked behind him as he leaned on the pew as though he dared to be *hip* about something.

Something went through me when I saw him like that. So many dirtystinking things came back to me. For some reason I even thought of a colliedog I used to have named Skippy that died of old age 1 day in my kidhood, and made me wish I could die with her. And damn it, damn me, I haven't thought about anything like that in years,

so I hated that littlebastard with a passion then. I had an immense urge to con him into the bathroom to the left of the stage and beat him to death;

it was very needful to me to do exactly that thing at that moment, and it frightened the shit out of me a moment later to realize that I'd been completely serious about the whole idea.

No. But, no, I sat at the back, and in a funnykind of moment with myself I became completely dispassionate and refused to consciously record. Their shadows faded, but only as an insinuation, in my mind. It was like being high on very-very good reefer, and I think that was the minnit I realized that no high could make you do what you normally can't do on your own. But the moment you realize that, you're completely sober,

so I guess the best high of all is complete clarity.

I saw some dopie in front of me rise and say the AAprayer:

God Grant Me the Serenity
to Accept the Things I Cannot Change,
the Courage to Change the Things I Can
and the Wisdom to Know the Difference.

which seemed to be the only bit of clarity I could pick out in the entire joint. There was a carnival atmosphere; practically every 1 of these guys was dressed up in his best Banlon or bright sweatersuit, and their ridiculous air of solemnity almost made me bust out laughing:

'Now, I thank,' the prayer guy said (he meant Think, but this was being hip), 'that all really we got to do is thank about this whole question.'

'Right.'

'So I see this Godquestion, you know? But how can you argue with it, I mean God's been aroun so long, you dig? So that's what I mean, about I don't care what a cat thanks unless he's defendin himself.'

'You dig?'

Willie B grinned, Right.

'So if I have to take my faith from anything, I don't really care, you dig, as long as it's goin to *help me*, you dig? which is what I mean about notever usin no drugs no more, but I don't need a God for that, you dig? I mean, but thass me, you know? and another guy might not go along with it, but I don't giveashit, as long as I know that what I thank is right. You dig?'

'Right.'

Another guy stood up. He was a chubbyfat worthless-looking kind of cocksucker.

But he:

'Don't think you right, man, see what I mean? See, where you comin from is cool, but I don't think you've really given it the kinda thought it oughta have. Mean? See, drugs is drugs, but not givinashit about another guy who might not go along with it, I really think you're not really *thinking*, mean?' He had buckedout kind of teeth. 'Which is what I keep sayin all the time, and I been comin down here for 19months, man, sayin the same thing all along. Cause AA is my Life, You Dig It? and I just don't agree about what you said for somethin like that, mean?'

I said: 'Right,' going along with the gag, it had to be a gag.

'Diggit?'

Everyone agreed.

'Jesta second.' Somebody else's bastard sprung up. 'Now, I been listenin to all this. And Willie B you know I have very little to say about anythang that go on in this group, now. And that's the way we gentlemen will keepit, cool?'

'That's cool with me, Johnnyboy,' Willie B said.

A whitey stood, a tall sissylooking guy whose pants stayed plugged up in the crack of his ass. 'Something essential is going away from here. I would, you know, like a definition. So that's why I see something being lost from here.'

Willie B raised a gavel I didn't see before and waved it with a disparaging grin at the whitey. 'I don't think you were listening to the gentleman, Claude.' The sound of his language had changed.

Claude abruptly pulled the plug of pants out of his ass,

which is always an unsettling thing to see. 'No, Bill, I was listening to the gentleman, Mr. J.J., who always has something nice to say. And generally I generally agree with him, but I must take an exception tonight.'

'Well,' said Willie B out of voice, 'if that is what you muss do, Claude, that is what you muss do.'

'Thank you.'

'I will cede the floor to you.'

'But this isn't parliamentary.'

'Then why don'tchu say what you gotta say?'

Claude put his hands on his hips and turned to those of us in the back,

but I saw in his darkeyes, though, that he believed in what he was saying.

'Diggit?' he said. 'I mean . . . FUCK THAT SHIT, MAN!'

'Now, that's *saying* something.'

Everybody rippled.

'I got somethin to say. . . .' somebody hollered.

'Waitaminnit, Claude's got the floor.'

'But even Claude said it wuddn't parliamentary.'

'Ohshit, man!' Willie B flared, 'can'tchu wait justaminnit?'

'Fuck that lousy shit, man,' Claude said quietly. 'See, fuckit. Now, they can take me and stretch my arms too, and put me on the rack, but fuckit. See. You. And Other People in my Life, you know? See? Who gives them the right to think we're any worse? because we don't do anything they don't do on another kinda level. I MEAN, FUCKIT, MAN, IT'S SO GODDAMN CLEAR TO ME, see?'

'Right.'

Claude's hoteyes swept over us. 'That's why I say a stud who doesn't dig actually what Addicts Anonymous is, he really doesn't want anything done about the way he is. You know, it's so fuckin simple. Just livin the program from daytoday, that's all anybody needs, so I don't see where you came up with this shit about God.'

'I never said anything about God,' Willie B said, 'you can't blame that on me.'

I had to get in – I pushed to feel it – I had to make them feel what I was feeling then. I exploded into laughter because it all seemed so unreal.

They're still after me.

This morning I got a special pass from Antman that sent me to the Branch-5 level–

down the long corridor from UT, past CenterControl to the right and the recordroom and dispensary to the left and up finally on the automatic elevator handled by a sleepeyed goateed con brother–

the 5thfloor.

As you left the elevator, you faced businesslike swinging glass doors, where, inside, a male receptionist, a civilian, with big yellow horseteeth, sat grinning at you from behind a Lewisburg desk. He was halffat and pale in a tight bluesuit,

and sometimes when he smiled he looked like an asthmatic BugsBunny. 'Mr. . . .?'

I gave him the pass.

'Oh, of course,' he said briskly. 'Won't you have a seat?'

There were about 3con guys sitting where he indicated on hip pseudoDanish furniture reading stupid *Life*magazines,

while across the room all sorts of women sat on the same kinda furniture under the ArtGroup pictures they displayed on the walls up here

For Sale,

hooked up beautifully, most of them, their thousands of whorescars vaguely concealed under paint and hip hairdos, and tightbright assclinging skirts. But I'd missed this crowd the lasttime I was up. So I sat down watching them with a deephungry feeling in me.

At about that time, the matron came to pick them up, and I saw the guys suddenly come to life, feening on the juicygoing fatrumps,

and it was 1 of those funnythings for me you just can't understand. It seemed most important that they were not *discovered* peeking.

'Dr. Cambridge has a patient.' The guy smiled at me. 'It'll only be another minute or 2,'

and when he smiled again I got that little electric feeling of discovery when you suddenly realize a guy is a faggot.

This was the most modern part of the hospital, the showfloor, and it teemed with funnylooking little guys in whitejackets and big baggysuited Outsiders with briefcases who looked like salesmen,

and a surprising number of young pinkthings looking flush and collegey, wearing firm juniorsized foundations over firm little asses. I didn't even know all this was happening.

To my right of the couch, a long doorbracketed hallway stretched back in an awkward L and out of my vision. Right next to the guy's desk was the WOMENroom, so the door at the end of the hallway, in my shotgun line of vision, must've been the Little Boys' place. They'd never make us neighbors here.

Then I looked up and saw Sonja coming from the other end of the hallway with a tall, distinguishedlooking white-haired whitey in a whitecoat. She was rapping so hard with him, she didn't see me until she was almost at the guy's desk.

'Oh, *Daddy*,' she said in a voice like colored streamers.

'Oh?' the tallguy said curiously.

I stood and tried to get close enough so I'd have an excuse to put my hand on her. She was erotically redclothed. I could smell the musky stuff she used 5feet away.

'This is my Daddy,' she told him in a naïvely breathless way.

'Your Daddy?' he chuckled,

but the guy at the desk got up and told Dr. Cambridge who I was, and he beamed in an infuriatingly pleasant way and caught my hand. 'I've got to apologize for being so long.'

'That's all right.'

'Oh, oh.' Sonja stared at me, smiling, running her eyes over me as though they were tongues. 'Are you for therapy with Dr. Cambridge, baby?'

'No, dahling.'

Her big eyes showed the God Damnedest Pain then. 'Oh,

Daddy, if you could only have him like I have, and maybe he could treat us together.'

'Well, now,' he said reluctantly,

but I helped:

'Really, since I don't have much faith in therapy, it doesn't make much sense.'

'Oh, *Dad*dy,' she sighed mournfully.

'You're not supposed to talk,' the guy at the desk tsk-tsked at us.

The croaker didn't act as though he knew what to do with himself. 'So, Miss Richardson. I'll see you next week, sametime.' I couldn't get close enough without them seeing. I was going to get a handful of her ass. But she went to sit on the women's side of the room, blowing exquisite wetred kisses to me as I followed the doctor to the place they'd just come from,

a long blueroom with about 1,000windows and a cash-meresweatered black con patient with a thick moustache typing on an electric in a casecluttered anteroom.

But his office was nice and warmfeeling, with a deep-masculine temper to it, cattycornered with 2high bookcases loaded with treasures

Reik, Menninger, Freud's letters and a collected Freud, Jung, Proust, Joyce and Sartre, at least 400others

and disorganized in the way gifted, or demented, men live in a place.

'Sit down, please,' he said, so

I pulled up a chair and got hungup in the titles.

'You like to read?'

'Why not?'

He sort of chuckled and went over to his desk, and sprawled with his whitecoat open in a looselyjointed way. 'Is that a natural response?'

'Are you asking me a question?'

'No, no, just remarking to myself.'

'You get a lotta manic-depressives who do the samething.'

I got that big candid grin again. 'Now that *is* good.'

I stopped looking at the books.

'I don't know why I'm here.'

He put his hands behind his head in a relaxed manner, and his long elbows swatted the air reflexively from timetotime, like wings getting set to fly. 'Because you were referred to me by Dr. Colman.'

'What about Dr. Flexcool?'

'You mean Dr. Uxeküll?'

'I have trouble with *v*'s.'

'Of course he had a hand in the referral.'

'Feels like a fist.'

'Maybe that's really what you want,' he said quickly.

'I'd rather have the ax.'

'You'll probably get it.'

I pulled up and watched this guy. 1st, I took what seemed important about him; then I sent out vibrations. I made myself as sensitive as I could, but I couldn't detect any evil about him,

and I guess this was when I was really amazed, because I'd only met 1 other person – no, 2: 1 being my old Choctaw grandmother who lived with us in Bedford-Stuyvesant for a while when I was a kid, who looked like the head on a nickel everytime she gave me 1; and the other was a white pianist named Kurt in Manhattan who I burned 1 day for a typewriter. Only these 2 till now,

and they're very difficult people to livewith because you're always clashing in some hideous way with their damnable purity.

'I don't know why I'm here.'

'Because you interest me. I've read your liferecord.'

'It's an unauthorized edition.'

'It told about your wife.'

'It couldn't have done her justice.'

He frowned around the eyes. 'You were locked up this time 20months when she OD'd. Your institution record went from bad to worse at that point.'

'How do you explain that?'

'How the hell do *I* know?' he said. 'All I know is, you've been using drugs for the last 15years and your obvious intelligence isn't substantiated by that fact.'

'My obvious intelligence tells me this is turning out to be somekind of hassle.'

'The record says your wife, Joyce, was your accomplice in dope sales.'

'The record is wrong.'

'It says you assumed the blame for everything.'

'They had me cold.'

He blinked at me. 'There was a government informer involved, wasn't there?'

'Isn't there always?'

'I'd like to think not.' He waited for a minnit. 'The FBI report says his name was Bob Trent.'

'Well, the FBI should know.'

He waited again. 'How do you feel about him? This Bob Trent?'

'I don't feel anything about him.'

'You know he's a professional informer?'

'I do now.'

'Suppose he should show up while you're here? How would you react?'

'I wouldn't know him if I ever saw him again.'

He laughed. 'Oh, c'mon now—'

'I don't know why I'm here.'

'Neither do I, to tell you the truth, but when things like that happen to me I think they're the things that should. Do I miss you?'

'No.'

He batted his elbows again. 'As soon as I read your tests I realized there was something ... different about you.'

'I . . .'

started to say something, but that would've shown that he'd touched me in some little way

'. . . don't know why I'm here.'

He pointed. 'There's the door. You can leave anytime you like. Mr. Wallers out front'll sign your pass.'

'But this doesn't guarantee I won't be called again.'

'Not unless you request it.'

'I won't': I stood. He stood.

'Oh . . .' he said. 'Miss Richardson speaks about you all the time. That was 1 of the things I'm interested in, since she's 1 of my patients.'

I looked at him. 'I hope you're not gettin ready to say what I think you will.'

He smiled that way again. 'No. No, I wouldn't interfere. I just.' He put his hands on his hips. 'I've been here 5years now, and I've seen a lot of pinkmail affairs.' I was bigger than him. 'I have faith in this girl.'

'She's a 38year-old woman.'

'No,' he hastened, 'I didn't mean "girl" in that sense.'

'She's not a girl in any sense.'

He was finding it hard to be nice now. 'No, What I mean. You naturally exercise a lot of influence over her, and a lot of her present therapy will depend on how you impress her.'

'Now, you listen. You. Just leave *me* alone. If you want her therapy to go on the way it's been going, you just leave me alone.'

It wasn't nice, but I left.

LISTEN, BITCH,

don't you ever again in your unnatural mind tell 1 of these fucking psychiatrists a God Damn Thing about me. He doesn't have a thing he can provide me with, and I'm beginning to wonder whether you have. What I do with my brain is my business, and how the fuck do you, can you, imagine that a whiteman would be able to tell me 1 actual thing about myself?

I am by myself. Dig? I need you only for what you can furnish me with that will provide the kind of groove of living that I'm accustomed to when I have my full senses about me. This *is the thing that makes love, the things you give your loved 1 that make him happy. At your age, I certainly don't have to tell you what this process is about.*

In future, remember that I have the lowest sort of opinion about the operation you're going through with your goodsmiling doctor, and I'm not pleased with it.

So don't ever in life take me through these fuckedup sort of changes again.

You'll make me do something real and horrible to you.

ME

6E¾

Strange, ain't it?

but today, Saturday, I got high on mace, 4packs for a do from an Oyea over in K unit,

Oscar Pieta, the joint dopeman, who had connections with a couple of the staff. He was a chubby yellow Chineselooking Puerto Rican with hair like Brillo. Yesterday I told him to cut me out 4spoons of mace for the weekend.

Mace hits me in the eyes 1st. I was able to see this while I stood in front of the wide mirrors digging that sickening paste out of my skin

(but it hit me fast, considering I'd only done it about 3hours ago with coffee, when sometimes it takes up to 6or8),

and it was only then I noticed how much my moustache'd grown. This was the only fedjoint you could grow them in. The mace made me contemplative. And it also made me very anxious to *do* something, in the way reefer had,

something meaningful,

it didn't make any difference or not whether it was evil.

So

I roamed around UT heckling dopies, feeling heavylidded and gutwarmed. I was in a firm, moisthot state for a woman. I was showering when the mace hit me, and by the time I'd come out I was turned on wonderfully, thinking about her,

thinking of 1 miraculous sex episode.

This herb gives me a queer toxic effect, a potential deep nausea, as though you'd eaten something wrong and couldn't quite control the urge to shit.

I'm going to bed on it, but awake 3hours later soothed and Christlike, who, according to Matthew, didn't care so much about things like pussy. I am thinking fabulously highly. The covers warm my body almost in the way of a woman, and I hear the Herefordshires mooing into their leanto. I haven't seen a piece of beef on my tray since I've been here.

Voicesounds come into my room from the dayrooms, the TV and guys playing bridge,

and I've drawn the shades over my windows so little light comes in, and the 1 on the window of my door is like a polkadotted friend mellowseeing on me.

But I drag myself up for some reason,

naked,

and stand for a longtime looking at the rawassed Miss Ann grinning back from the long frame on my wall. I feel insane for a moment with the need for a woman, and I'm encouraged to masturbate,

but I resist the urge and drag my ass into my newpressed con grays and a soft little shortsleeved green sweater from Scotland that Doug had given me along with 4more. And go around to the widewhite washroom, where I have the most soulstirring expellation,

and wash and dry before the shining mirrors. This was when I noticed the moustache. It is like the ones of villains in those old allnigger gangster flicks starring Ralph Cooper,

and my wide forehead makes my eyes look as though they're pleading.

Sonja hasn't written in 2days,

When I came out, Tamerlane was standing in the hall in front of our rooms, lookingout on the parkinglot, a greatbig hulk of man in a blue turtleneck sweater, with browneyes sadder than I've seen on a hounddog.

'Hey,' he said, noticing my eyes 1st. 'I see you took the top off.'

I am at the top of my mind. 'You gotta let the rocks out sometimes. They grow like kidneystones.'

He knew what I meant. 'Yeah. Nothin's supposed to hurt anybody like that.'

I reach for my doorknob, but he says,

'Just been lookin today.'

'Ohyeah? Whaddayou see?'

'Not many cars out there today,' he said in a smiling way. 'Not many come in on Saturday. I wonder sometimes why it takes less on Saturday and Sunday than any other time.'

'Everybody gets a day off.'

'But us.'

'We're not supposed to.'

'I guess that's the reason.'

I start in again, but he says,

'You don't play bridge, doya?'

'I don't play any cardgames.'

He pulled a shelf of window out and leaned on it, facing me. 'Oh, I just wondered. I notice you don't do nothin much but go to the gym.'

The bottoms of my feet feel funny. 'I'm in training. When I'm strong enough, I'll kill myself.'

So he laughed, but he said,

'Sam won't letya till you're done with the bit.'

I got interested. I came over to the window where he was. A mild breeze choked idly through the slant. To our left the extension that held the women's units clung like a parasite to the ass of the main buildings.

'This is my 2nd bit on the Farm,' he said. 'The 1st time was in '53, but the Price Daniel Amendment came in in '56, which made me do a dime for this time.'

'Sale?'

'Uhn. But I didn't *have* to come.'

'Nobody ever does. They didn't want you.'

'Right. They wanted my connect.'

I spit, and watched it fall in a fluffy puff toward the ground. 'The Proposition.' I turned to him, saying,

'The Proposition they gave you – 'You buss *him*, and we'll let you go' – it'd be like gettin piled in the ass, if you did.'

'Yeah,' Tam said with a little wonder, 'ain't that right? They done took everythang they possibly could, right at the beginnin, and the last part is takin your right to be a man.'

'Or somethin like that.'

His eyes became distant. 'This is a hard thing to explain. I tried to tell my wife when I got this dime, tried to explain. But all she could say was, "What about us, What about *us*?" Her and the kids. Women can't understand things like this.'

'They're more practical. Maybe it's good not to be able to think in abstractions.'

'Whad you say?' he said, when I lost him there, but I said,

'Just you're right about what you mean.'

He squinted at me in a warm way. 'You sound high.'

'I very much am. But getting high don't disqualify my right to think.'

'Nobody said it did.'

'Or even to think thinking is unnecessary.'

He shook his head. 'That's a little too much for me. See, I don't have much of an education.'

'Neither do I.'

'I came out in the 8thgrade,' he said.

'I came out in the 10th.'

And his eyes got big. 'But you don't sound like it.'

'I don't know how you're supposed to sound.'

'I mean, you sound sometimes like you mighta been to college, but then in a way not.'

'College is nothin but another kind of school': I turned and looked at him.

'Now,' he said laughingly, 'I'm not no intellectual, but I know an education when I run into it.'

'It's just something I trained myself. Words.'

'You muss write?'

'No.'

'Then you muss, if you don't.'

'Ohshit, I'll see you later.'

'But you ain't seen the sun,' he said behind me.

'I already know what the God Damn Thing looks like.'

'Not this sun. C'mere.'

All right, I went back over.

'See' – he pointed – 'this is a southern sun.'

'I can see how it's different from a northern 1': And it was.

OJesus, it was the most beautiful thing I've ever seen in my life. The mace must've stirred the imagery. My brain cackled with the color refractions. The profile of the hills, and the road 2miles beyond, were lashed to weirdgreen definitions in the mad spatter of dying light. It touched my heart.

'This is the only time of the day I get sad,' Tamerlane said.

'Then why do you watch it like this?'

'To *make* myself sad, I guess – make myself pay, you know what I mean?'

I didn't say a thing.

'A man knows when he's to blame for something,' he snorted, remembering, 'And there's really not much to complain about when the hammer falls. Right?'

'Right.'

'So, much as it hurts me, I look at this kind of sun that's almost like the 1 I used to look at with my son DeeDee. He's almost grown; you oughta see him; I got pictures

'and it hurts me as much as a time a guy buss me in the center of the head with a winebottle full of piss.'

'I know how that musta turned you around.'

'Well, that's 1 way to look at it,' he agreed, 'but I'm talking about the *hurt*, that toothpullin kinda hurt. You know what the judge told me? The judge told me that in view of my family and all, my 4kids and home, he was sorry he had to give me time.'

'They all are. Sorry they can't give you more.'

'No, but for real,' he protested; 'this guy didn't wanna give me anytime. It was just I didn't cooperate, and the prosecutor wouldn't prosecute me under the Boggs Harrison Act.'

'They told me the same shit.'

'You see guys come in here everyday with 2years for Sale.'

'And they're all rats.'

'For 1 thing, I'm too old . . .'

'For what?'

'For this dime. I'm 44now. I'll be 50 when I get the dime done.'

'I was 27 when I started the bit. I'll be 31 when I get up. It's all relative; it's all time.'

'Naw,' he said. 'But time is more than time. Time is time with your family. Time with your son to see him grow, and your daughter with her first boyfriend. You know?' he said, turning earnestly,

but now I say, to cut all this shit off before it goes too far,

'You shouldn'ta been fuckin around with drugs. You shoulda cooperated.'

And I went ashamedly to my room.

DADDY

I've tried to keep from writing you, but you knew I wouldn't be able to. You have become my man. You are *my man, and angry as I might get at you I know I'll have to do what is your will. Daddy, you don't ever have to be so harsh with me. I know all about the Devil. But I just figured, without asking you first. I never said much to him about you, except I thought you were the most wonderful man to happen to me, and the way you think in my letters. I don't dream this made him go and pull your jacket. Please, Daddy darling, forgive me. You are so good for me. Each day not receiving your letters has been a deep pain. Please write, please tell me you know what I mean. You say you don't know whether I'm right for you, but I* am *right for you. There is nothing you want I can't give you. But you said more about love, and that's what I feel too. Women search for the man they need, but sometimes a long time ago you stop searching. Daddy, I didn't ever think you would happen to me, because the time seemed so late. I'm so tired. And I need you, you know that.*

But you seem to know everything anyway there is to know about me. I'm so burning for you. The way you stand. The way you stood while we talked to the doctor. Obaby, if you could only fuck me that would make things so much easier, because I

love you so. If I had that piece of you in my vagina.

Oh, I love you, Daddy. Write me please.

Yours

Coming back from the basketball game that Sunday, where I saw Sonja,

I ran into Doug. I got a fatherfigure kind of feeling from him. My father gave me up for mentally retarded when I was 12years old.

We walked back from the gym. 'How do you dig this joint?' he said.

'It's pretty cool when I'm high.'

'Hooked up in the Barn yet?'

'I got a broad named Sonja.'

'Oh. Ohyeah, I remember her dancing on 1 of the con shows. That's a goodlookin broad.'

'For her age.'

'She had a whitey from the Coast before you showed, a bassplayer. But I think he was mostly keepin her smoke habit up.'

'I don't believe in the broad.'

'Maybe because you believed in another broad.' He knew about her,

and I got kind of drugged about what he said:

'Yeah, well, fuck all that.'

Doug laughed. 'Well, that's just the way it is, man, and you can get mad as you want to about it. It won't make no difference.'

We came up the long ramp from the gym. The staircases were lockedoff because of the women, who had to descend by a Westside ramp. The muscles in my legs tingled with the pull.

Here, at CenterControl. I stop to drop a token in the Coke machine. I have to buy Doug 1 too.

'This is a strange joint,' he said, walking along with me past the CenterControl desk.

'Won't you get busted?'

'I have a councilman's pass.'

'Oh.'

'But about the joint. I've been here 20months already. This is an unusual place.'

'I see that.'

'The women figure in it more than anything else.'

'I've seen that, too.'

'Guys get real serious sometimes about those God Damn Pink Kites.'

'I don't even use them.'

'If you hooked up with a broad,' he said knowingly, 'you use um. I stay away from that kind of thing.'

'Right.'

'But I know you from the street. I know you. I know how you are sometimes.'

'I've changed a lot.'

He looked at me in a fishyeyed way. 'That's saying a lot in 2seconds. Remember, I been knowing you since you were 15.'

'That was 15years ago.'

'Well, I was a man when you were 15, and I can remember the time when you and Joyce were kids.' I could see him remembering it. 'Being a kid is the crazytime for making mistakes, like you and Joyce did about usin drugs.'

'Yeah? Well, Joyce is out of it now, so we don't have to talk about that shit. Nothing came of it.'

He looked hurt. 'Joye came of it. You can't say nothing came of it.'

'Maybe Joye is some trick's baby.'

'You know she's not,' he said in an angry voice. 'You can look in her face and see she's nobody's kid but yours. That's a helluva thing to say about your own kid. Just before I got busted, I used to stop by all the time—'

'Yeah, thanks for the crumbs. You shoulda used um for a good lawyer.'

'Look,' he said as I walked away, 'I'd do 10bits to cure that kid's clubfeet,' but I tuned him out and went down the long corridor to the place where I stop to watch sometimes. When I saw her shadow in the window, it stayed for only a few moments,

and I went back to the unit with an angry drugged feeling in my guts.

A storm came up tonight

a swirlyblack frightening thing as I see it through the barbwire of the courtyard wall from my office window. The heavens are alive with light, and I try to say to myself,

Fuckyou, God,

but I can't quite make the words have significance in my mind, and I have a dairyfreeze moment of fear

in which I'm told that He *is* there, so don't fuck around and say something It might take offense to.

I tried to get away from it, but it was raging now, the way I've seen sexcouples come toward climax in dirtyfilms, so I gave myself up to amazement and deliciously rubbed the bones of my butt where sitting had crippled me.

It was highly erotic. It rolled back, the wholeround black ass of the sky, and farted beams of angry brilliant light. The pussy of it grew red in something phosphorescent, then closed its milelong slant of eye to the tongue of a horizon. I cheated watching, 1 eye at a time,

and focused closely on the jagged tits of storm. It was coming fast, a huge lightscattered tidal skywave.

In something like bravado, I opened my window to the night, where it surged anticipating, and the gusting flowergarden made small mewing sounds, like all the sighing little cunts of women who have married Christ.

I saw it sweep over a hill not many miles away, gathering black momentum. A nigger freed. And suddenly all sound ceased, sucked into its mighty force, and it laughed like a woman screaming just an instant later, slamming into the great walls of the manmade place and shaking it to its very asshole.

But that wasn't the time I was most afraid.

When it began to recede, when it had muscled this joint down to its core and fiber, when it had torn windows through and uprooted the guts of the flowergarden, when all the hearts that knocked as mine had, had quieted and stood grateful that the wrath of Something simply had not *cared* to rip us off,

and I stood raindripping and trembling in my demolished little bit of space,

in that 1 moment I was frightened toward the boundaries of death.

7

I got drugged with myself today;
(it's Monday)
because Joe Antman and Pepper lounged around in the office making cracks, some of them about blackbroads over in the Barn when I came in with finished work from my office
Joseph Barnes/remit/Kenneth Walker/remit
for the files. And I stood at the big populationboard long enough to hear Pepper say,
'I woodn't dirty my cock on 1 of them hoors,'
and I got drugged about it. But that's when I said, when I shouldn't have, to start it all,
'You'd spend your whole little 2week governmentgreen check for 1.'
Pepper had a little hole for a mouth, and his watery blue eyes looked as though they were rimmed with frost.
'What?' he asked me.
'I said you'd buy pussy from her as long as you could get a hardon.'
He chuckled as though something foul obstructed his lungs. 'I gotta check this boy out.'
'Oh, don't pay no tention to this guy,' Joe Antman said. 'He's doin a 50year 5year bit.'
'It's *my* bit.'
Pepper coughed out his laugh. 'It can get hard when you do it like that.'
'I didn't get any instructions on how to do it.'
'Maybe I can give you a few lessons.'
So there it was,
and I knew it was going that way, so I couldn't really give you an excuse. I felt an urge to knock the guy out, though, and I had to be careful about that; they'd give you another 5 for that, and

Oh, my insides! I burned to swell his lips up! The 4big black knots of my righthand just *tingled* for it.

He said, a little nervously, 'I s'pose cause you peck a bit on that machine and read a lotta funnybooks, that you can't get a shot.'

Joe Antman sat back, out of it.

'What would you shoot me for?'

'Well, for Insubordination,' he said, looking around to Joe for help. 'Mr. Antman heard what you just said to me.' He started working himself into the idea.

'Whad I say?'

'You said I'd buy pussy from one of them dirty hoors over in the Barn, that's what you claimed with my own ears.'

'You've never stopped.'

'Do you see what I mean?' he invoked Joe, who was beginning to look uncomfortable.

'Oh, just dropit.' Joe laughed.

'But, Joseph, I cain't drop this, not the way he's been talkin to me. It's a matter of principle.'

'Then shootim and sendim upstairs,' Joe said pettishly, 'and that's the end of that.'

What did he wanna say that for? Pepper leaped over to the file cabinet and pulled out a shotform,

which had to be typed, and there wasn't anybody around who could but me,

and split out of the office.

He found someone who could peckandhunt, and came back a little later with the whole business. *This man*, I could barely read over his hiding fingers as he showed it to Joe,

arrogant attitude later down the page.

Insubordination finally in the little box headed CHARGE.

'Ohlook, why don't you just dropit?' Joe said. 'You got the right to shoot a guy and all, but he does most of the typin around here. Who's gonna do it? You?'

'Listen to me, Joseph,' he said, pointing at me, 'we know about this patient's attitude, right from the start, when he asked about *rent*in his room, and nobody likes him, not even the doctors.'

'Doctors ain't supposed to *like* nobody,' Joe said.

'I'm just talkin about our jobs as psychiatric aides,' Pepper insisted.

'You don't have to tell me about my job – I been around here years longer than you.'

'No, I was just sayin it was our job as psychiatric aides to minister corrective treatment, as the case may have it. You know what the Manual say.'

'Better than you,' Joe said snappishly now.

'Bout establishin new Patterns.'

'Ohshit,' Joe Antman said in agony. 'Sendim upstairs, I don't giveashit.'

So they did. Pepper escorted me warily down the long hallway to CenterControl, where he turned the shotsheet in to 1 of the hacks there, and left me,

almost in an apologetic way.

But not before I had the chance to tell him quietly:

'You'd still buy it.'

This hole isn't so bad,

not anything like the sewerhole in the otherjoint, where you had to crawl up on a 4sided pyramid of a shitjacket, looking like Buddha with ballshung as you took off. And these lousybastard government screws who tend the holes all have a thing about toiletpaper

and none of them will give you more than 4to8 sheets at a time,

but I've always believed that men who work as basically as this with other men were some kind of anal freaks.

Nextdoor to me, a littledopie is actually crying because he's in the hole, a Winder, 'under pressure,' who said the only reason they put him here was

'Because I refused to work.'

'That's enough to get you a holebit in any joint.'

Then he goes kind of psycho on me, talking about things

like pride and the bad picture they got on the TVset in his dormitory,

and I knew then the guy was some kind of little prick.

I nutted on him for a longtime, making myself conscious of the cell. The bare ironbunk we wouldn't get nakeddirty mattresses for till 8pm,

the scummy seatless utility conproof toilet bowl, and the silt and soot on the floor that entered through the window and screen 7feet above the backwall. I was shoeless

they sent you in here barefoot

and wearing only shorts funky with the smell of 1,000-asses. Filth is an important part of hole therapy. It's no good if you don't feel debased afterward.

'You still there?' the guy said from nextdoor. I can't see him, but I know he's a brother from his voice.

I stood very still and quiet for a long time.

'I know you're over there,' he said. 'I can hear you breathin.'

'I bet breathin's not the only thing you hear well.'

I went over to the front of the cell and strung my arms through the bars. 'I bet you hear a lottashit you got no business hearin, and that's why you're up here now.'

His voice got a whine in it. 'I don't know why you'd say somethin like that, man.'

'Because you sound funny to me. You tell a funnykind of story.'

'But it's the truth,' he swore. 'I ain't got no reason to lie'

'Tell it to me again, and don't cry this time.'

'I just refused to work.'

'Naw, naw, that's too light.'

'Well, I *did*,' he said, 'you can ask the police when he comes back in with the food.'

'I'm askin nobody but you. Where'd you work at?'

'On the Shootinggallery.'

'And you just refused to work, huh?'

'Awman, I just got tired of that shit.'

'How long you work there already?'

'2months – some days and 2months.'

'And you just now gettin tired?'

'It just all come to a boil, the headnurse Miss Harvey, she's *always* in yer ass about somethin.'

'What's your name?'

'Charles Nicholson. Why?'

'Because I want to remember it. Somethin's wrong about that name.'

'Awman . . .'

'A guy just don't get tired on the Shootinggallery – it's a good gig. You pulled up for somethin else. I bet.'

'You musta heard somethin about it,' he said in a slightly accusing way.

'Yeah. I heard *all* about it. Now, why don't *you* runnit?'

'Well, it ain't true to start with.'

'They say it is.'

'These guys from Canton don't hardly know me; I just saw um sometimes when we copped at the same joint.'

'And you busted um?'

'*Nawww*, man; see, it was a mistake. I cut the guy I used to cop with into them, and he turned out to be a federal agent.'

'You set um up.'

'I swear it wasn't nothin like that.'

'I know better.'

'Believe what you want, then,' he said huffily.

'You got cracked by some guy who probably cut you into the same agent, and you went and copped 2or3 pills for him, and then *you* had a Sale. So they propped you, just like they propped the guy who cut the agent into you, and you had to go crack them other guys. And they probably got nickels and dimes, and you got an "Under Pressure" 6month cure.'

'Ohman, I wish you knew better,' he whined.

'So them guys just came in on the Shootinggallery, sick and fuckedup, and you just pulled up because you were afraid they were gonna grind your ass. But that's all right.'

I laughed when I heard nothing but silence from him.

'But that's all right, man. If it wasn't for little ratbastards like you,

'I wouldn't be able to see myself so clearly.'

I do pushups
which leave my mouth dry and sodatasting,
and I watch the accumulation of dirtyscum on my flesh that makes patterns in gradations, like the scarred face of a weatherstripped landscape
and take long thoughtfilled craps.
I cut the little rat completely off, but they came and got him early the next morning, leaving me the only con on the longdirty rock
doing holetime.
But about 12oclock I heard keys shangling against the grill up front
(but I thought it was chow)
and in a moment Dr. Cambridge came.
I was sitting crosslegged and funky on the floor, next to the shitbowl.
He had that pleasant smile; it didn't mock. 'Well, how're you doing?'
'I want out, naturally. I've found all the reasons I can for it.'
He frowned. 'For what?'
'Just the simple idea of being here.'
He was finding it hard to understand. 'Well, it's certainly not the most pleasant place in the world to be, but it has a purpose, don't you suppose?'
'No, I don't.'
And he looked uncomfortable until I said,
'I've just never taken the time to. People like me take things like this for granted.'
'And just what sort of people are you?' he said carefully.
'Ahn': I rubbed a gooey blob of dirt off my right forearm into a tight little black ball and flicked it at his shadow on the floor.
And he said, 'Ahn,'
and came closer to look in on me, where our slant of angle

at each other caused an eclipse of light in the dimdark place. The only thing I could see were the edges of his whitejacket, and a forehead of torpedoed hair with fine, sharp edges to it. 'What happened?' he said.

'Have you gotta know?'

His dark blankface nodded. 'I'm the Officer of the Day today, so I've got to know your story in order to make a decision in the case.'

'Didn't you talk to the cops?'

'No, but I read the report Mr. Smith put in on you, and I find it hard to believe.'

'Ohyeah?'

'The charge is *Insubordination*, which can get you up to 72hours in the hole.'

'Ohfuck, I've done 24 of that already. I've done too many of these things. Just gimme the whole shot.'

'Sure, sure, I can make that easy, but that's what you want, isn't it?'

I cocked my ear: 'Whad you say?'

He said, 'You heard what I said.'

'Waittaminnit, you're gettin an attitude.'

He stood 1step back from the bars, face surprisingly involved. 'I don't think I can afford to get angry with you.'

'Not under present circumstances, anyway.'

'Well,' he chuckled, 'at least you haven't lost your sense of humor.'

'At the risk of you losing yours.'

'I see you enjoy this kind of fencing. You mind telling me when you developed it, the ability?'

'You mind telling me what the fuck you think you're doin, giving me therapy or something?'

'No,' he said thoughtfully. 'I'm curious as to what makes you operate.'

'You know what you can *use* on me? a lotta *si*lence, that's what you can use. What's this? I never seen a campaign like this. I'll vote for ya; you don't have to press me. What kind of pictures do I have to paint for you, man? I mean, isn't it simple? I'm sittin here in this filth, but I'm not bitchin about anything – you, it's you the 1.'

'I'm talking about *symp*toms—'

'You sound like a preacher.'

He put his hand in a pocket and jingled some keys. 'Somebody's got to say something, about this Thing.'

'Now you sound like a martyr.'

'Oh, *c'mon*, now, let's play fair. It's *you* who thinks I need to help. That's why I'm getting all this static, for 1 thing – you think I want to help you, and you're afraid *you* might need it.'

'Ohshit.'

'All right, I'm not preaching.'

'Really, man, I don't see why we're goin through all these changes. If you'll look in my eyes you'll see what I think, and that's nothin. You don't have to harass me this way. I have nothin to offer you, and you have nothin to offer me, so that makes it simple. Isn't that simple?'

'Of course.'

'Then that's fine. So all you have to do is get in the wind and let me do the next48 in something like peace. I don't ask much of the world.'

'Then you're cheating yourself.'

I didn't look up as he walked away.

About 2hours later

Joe Antman came and stood before the bars, fingers digging slowly at his blond scalp. 'Whachu doin sittin on the floor?'

'I never thought about it.'

'Well, you oughta,' he said. 'That's not accomplishing anything.'

'How do you figure to accomplish somethin in the hole?'

'Well, it gives you time to think,' he said solemnly, 'and that's probably the best thing anybody can take out of life.'

'Ohhell, 1st the doctor, then you.'

'You know,' Joe Antman said seriously, and stood back with knuckles on hips, 'maybe you needed this. I coulda stopped it.'

‘Then why didn’t you?’

‘Cause it woulda made a case with Smith, for 1 thing and it wouldn’t hurt your ass to store you away for a night.’

‘72hours.’

‘Naw, you’ll be goin out of here in a little while now. Dr. Cambridge told um to let you out. Anyway, it didn’t hurt, did it?’

‘So I’m expendable whenever necessary, right?’

‘Listen, I work with you, but I *live* with him, understand? I appreciate your understandin,’ he cautioned me; ‘maybe that’s the thing I like about you best. Our understandin,’ he said with a little bow. ‘So don’t go makin me think I was wrong. You,’ he pointed at me,

‘got to come up for air sometime. A whole lot of other things are goin on.’

‘Oh, myGod, Joe.’

‘Look, I think you bust your head open on purpose. I been readin the record, and you get so you see patterns.’

‘Mine is a concentric circle.’

‘You know what I’m talkin about – the way you go around wearin your ass on your shoulder. Yeah,’ he said in a breath, ‘I deal in diplomacy, ignorant as it might seem, because I’m lookin out for somethin in the end for little ole Joe Antman. Now, all that is, is a magic formula.’

‘For me?’

‘If you wanna use it. Whad I tell you about bendin thisway-andthat? It’s because you won’t bend that you’re doin such a hard bit, boy.’

‘Oh, God Damn It.’

‘You know what I’m talkin about. . . .’

‘Joe, I didn’tever think I’d get this kinda shit from you.’

He came and leaned an elbow in the bars. ‘It boils down to a simple mathematic: if you unhappy, then I as your supervisor will eventually feel some of your unhappiness. And I don’t wanna be unhappy, if you know what I mean.’ He hacked his pants up over a gelatinous paunchiness. ‘I like you. I don’t really know ya yet, but I like ya. And I wantcha to stay over here in the Usher-In terminal.' He waved. 'It's all right with me if you bitter or something, because at least you're *feel*in something.'

'You talk a lot.'

'Sometimes I got a lot to say,' he said apologetically. 'And since you're somethin like a captive audience, I might as well say it all.'

'Go ahead, get it off.'

'All I mean to say is, This is a big joint, and it has a lot of people in it. A bunch of people doin a lot of different things. Some of it's good and some of it's bad.'

'But all of it's real.'

'It don't take an Einstein to figure that out. What's important is, You figure a way to get into it.'

'For what?'

'Well, just to be a part of it,' he said. 'Who's gonna know what you *think* even if you are part of somethin? You know what I'm tryin to say?'

'Yeah, I know.'

'Well, that's all I'm tryin to say. So you get a hardon for Smith – or any of us, me maybe – but you don't let what you feel get you put out of the club.'

'Waittaminnit . . .'

'Just think a second.'

'You're makin it sound like a plot.'

'Well, that's the principle this place operates on, so you'd better get used to it. Get your eyes open. Get to seein.' He stepped back, gave me a snappy little salute, and left me where I sat.

It had to be a conspiracy, but don't dream it was. Him and the doc reading from almost the same script. I just can't get away from them.

The screw came grinning and jangling his keys, acting like a niceguy,

'Ready?'

And I say, already tired with the idea of going out,

'Ohshit.'

8

The coffeebreak.

All day I been getting myself together for tonight. I got high early off mace, and now I'm standing in front of the bathroom mirrors in early evening, shaving with great precision, all warm and brownfeeling. No 1 here now but me, and that's always the way I prefer it,

I don't know why.

Outside, it's raining through a deepblack overcast, and from both of the slightly pulleddown windows next to the urinal I can hear the pigeons who live in the marble lightningstrokes flutter around nervously as the force of the rain increases.

Little Joe came in and slammed the door.

'You goina coffeebreak tonight?' He'd just come from running; he was short and wellmuscled, and sweat ran easily down his lemon skin.

I said yeah I was going.

'Me too, I'm supposed.'

'Oh, your woman in AA?'

'Rosey Hernandez. She empties the garbagecan outside the Barndoor every mornin.'

'A pale-lookin little redheaded broad?'

'That's something.'

'What?'

He started to strip for the shower: someone'd almost carved his left shoulderblade out a longtime ago.

'Right,' he said.

'You mean that's her?'

'That's the 1.' He leaped in the shower. The water coughed. He leaped out of the shower.

'Damn, you got it down to a fine science.'

'Naw,' he said, blowing water, 'I just ain't got that much time left. See, you started gettin ready ahead of me. It starts at 7.'

'Well, that allows you at least another 2½ minnits to wash some of that funk off your ass.'

'You know what you are?' he said, toweling himself briskly. 'You a complainer. I had an uncle once the same way, and he wound up dyin.'

'Somebody killed him?'

'Naw. He just died.'

'What's that got to do with complaining?'

'Well, how can you prove there ain't a connection?'

I just didn't try to answer.

We milled around the Commissary in front of the chapel for a longtime, till after it closed,

then 1 of the hacks let us in, checking our names off with the passes we presented,

then onebyone we squeezed past him and down the steps into the Chapel.

The broads hadn't come yet, but Willie B had it all set up. Tonight he had on another thickknit, but this 1 was white,

and he was assisted by 2henchmen from the AA Steering Committee, a whiteguy and a blackone, who strongarmed the pulpit to the center aisle and put the *God Grant Me the Serenity* AAprayer in front. Claude was there, sitting right on the 1strow. I went down 4rows from the front and sat down on the outside next to Doug.

'Well, well,' he said. 'Didn't think I'd see you again soon.'

'"Well" yourself. I thought you said you didn't fool around.'

'And I don't. I just happen to be a member of the Steering Committee, so I gotta show up at least once a month. I get enough laughs outta what these foolass dopefiends have to say to last me till next month. Little guy talkin tonight, I specially wanna hear him. Little Junior, the dancer.'

That's when Little Junior came in, decked out with a chintzy-looking little blue tie and concoat cut like an Eisenhower dinner jacket, plenty gold in a couple of front teeth,

dragging along some of his Washington homies, including 1 special loudmouth named Barry Guyse.

'A getup and coffee,' Little Junior said. 'What a wise 5years.'

'Awman,' Barry Guyse giggled, 'you'll have your head on your knees tomorra night thistime.'

'Oh, Yes,' Little Junior said. 'but I'll be *free.*' He did a neat little softshoe shuffle in the aisle.

I never did like Brothers who danced much, right from Bojangles.

'Where's the broads at?'

Somebody called, 'Hey, Willie B, who's speakin tonight?'

'Claude and myself on the 1sthalf,' Willie B said, 'then Johnnyboy and Little Junior last, since he's goin home in the mornin.'

Little Junior's Washington group sat down up front. They were all rough young dopefiends, some doing 5's and 10's, nickels and dimes. I could hear Little Junior croaking over and over,

'Free, Free.'

I got kind of drugged.

'Where's the young ladies at tonight?'

'Man, you got 5more minnits before they get here. If I had the kinda action comin like you got, I wouldn't be in such a hurry.'

'Did you hear that? With that scumbag you call your woman?'

'How you been doin?' Doug asked me.

'All right.'

'Need anything?'

'Some smokes, maybe. I don't have any bread, and the broad is as poor as I am.'

'What can you possibly need with a poor broad?'

'I need her the same way I need those cigarets, not at all.'

His salty moustache smiled. 'So why the attitude? I'll send a box of Pall Mall tonight.'

I told him thanks, but I could feel he was going into another thing about the streets and some sessions we had together, so

I cut it off by running down my holebit and the thing that brought it on,

and by this time the guys – about 75 of them – had quieted to whispers, so I knew the broads were about to show. Each hack at the doorways of the raised staircases stood quite rigid, bodies hunched as though listening,

and I could feel the whole joint straighten up, all heads left, Willie B posing at the pulpit:

Now here come the Mamas, led by a tall slim dark Sister matron, all 45of them, a rash of gaudy pleasedanxious whore smiles and protruding buttocks and spiked heels. They clack together down the aisle,

heads raised, spines straight,

like fine horses. Here and there are monstrosities, torn from the outside in, but even they have dignity in their colorful caricatures of sveltness.

Stepping high among them is Sonja. She is wearing something black and 1piece with a deepslit in the throat, and I see her eyes leaping over all the menfaces until she finds mine,

then she flares warmly, like salt sprinkled in a fire.

She blew me a kiss,

and I watched them file in demurely

(and everything was absolutely quiet!)

and be seated, with 1 matron at the front and another at the back. The hacks had pulled up. We sat across from each other, blinking back and forth and looking dear. Fingerwriting was a bust here too, so

the most you could do was feen on each other, you and her, until coffeebreak time.

Willie B stood high now. At a little table to his right, the female chairlady, a darkskinned young broad, sat in an orderly way, feet crossed in front, showing only a little thigh. She had very big beautiful lips, and she had painted them pink and drew darkrings around the little slants of her eyes.

'Well, ladies and gentlemen,' Willie B said with a huge smile, 'we are up to our old tricks again on the Wednesdaynight AA Coffeebreak Meeting, which is why we are here. We have a very good program for you tonight, includin a number of speakers who might have somethin to say.'

1 of the Chapel doors opened and 2guys came in with a big Thermos, the steel tank, full of coffee, and wheeled it to the front rightside of the Chapel. They did a lot of snorting and snotblowing to get it set up.

'Well, I see the refreshments have arrived,' Willie B said, 'so I won't detain the proceedings any longer. Buttermilk, will you lead us in the AA prayer?'

Everybody stood up. I never got to see who Buttermilk was.

Then we sat down. Then a childwoman with sandyhair and sharp little tits under an orange sweater came up to the pulpit to read the 12Steps,

then Willie B came back grinning and posing at the broads.

'On behalf of Rub, who is in the hospital suffering from an operation, I want to thank you ladies who sent cards up last week, and especially ONE who might understand where I'm comin from.' I saw a heavilypainted broad swell up and get conspicuous. I happened to look over and find Sonja staring right at me; it must have been for a longtime. She was smiling, but that was bullshit.

'Now,' Willie B said, 'I'd like to turn the chair over to our chairlady, Miss Rhetha M. Rhetha?'

She uncrossed her legs and came juicily over to the pulpit. Her voice was tiny and soft and puton. 'Thank you, Willie B. And I'm glad you gave me this opportunity to express how happy I am to be here again, since I happened to be too sick to attend the lastmeeting. But I'm disappointed, ladies, in the closed-meeting attendance, and I'm sure you know what that means. AA is full of obligations, which is 1 of the reasons it's AA. But that is something I'll discuss with all of you later. Miss Carrie G. will be our 1st speaker.' She went back and sat down. She was a musclebitch, and I got a little hint of jasper.

Carrie G. trembled up and told about how she just couldn't keep her house in order without stuff, and how she was so strung, and how long her money used to be, and how AA made her see what a mistake she'd made.

Then Claude got up and said something wild about being the only ofay cat in AA, even though there were a number of ofay broads,

and how he didn't dig being rejected:

'So you can ask me – maybe tomorrow if you want to – you know, *how* I feel. And I'll tell you I don't feel any different than I do right now.'

A lot of guys thought there was something scientific in his speech.

And now Willie B.

'I really hadn't intended to say anything tonight, but 1 of my speakers became ill so instead of him I put myself in as a last resort.' He spread his hands casually, humped grinning at the broads over the pulpit. 'I just want to say a few words on a thing that I feel is timely and worthwhile, and that's Brotherhood in the Fellowship. A lot of guys are forgettin about that, and maybe some of you ladies too.' He stretched out. 'Now, there's never been a day in my life when I couldn't go to 1 of my main mellows and get some help. I've always maintained my life like that, and I seriously believe it's because of Brotherhood.'

He happened to look just then and see me, and his face changed.

'And responsibility, responsibility to the Brotherhood. Otherwise, there's very little you can do in AA without it, and I think it's a thing that should be emphasized.' He mumbled some other things I couldn't understand, then smiled suddenly and looked devilish. 'I think at this time we might be able to go into our coffeebreak period.'

There was a scramble. A matron went to each end of the Chapel, so they'd be able to see everything that went down.

I stood up, and Sonja was waving me over to the corner where the organ stood. We got hooked up there with another couple, a tall Brother and a little blonde broad. We were breathing hard over each other.

'Oh, Daddy.'

I touched her hand. I saw the matron watching us.

'Oh, Daddy, I got so many things to say I wanted to tell you, and now I can't remember any of them.'

'Stand closer to me. Here.'

She shifted over. 'Daddy, I don't know why you get so mad at me sometimes, but I really tryhard to dig you. I've never tried this hard with any man.'

'I'm going to touch your arm, but nut on it, then turn a little to your left, on a 3quarter angle, so both matrons can see your hands in sight.'

She turned as I directed, talking all the while. 'You said something to me once about being tired, remember when you wrote that? You said you want to get Out of It, and I do too, Daddy,' she said, catching my hand, 'I want Out of It more than anything.' I touched her spine. It looked as though we were just talking. Her heat filled my fingers. I luxuriated over the hearty fire of her big rubbery ass, tracing it contour by contour and crack, to the place where her stockings began and the traces from her garterbelt pulled them tautly up. 'I want *you*, Daddy,' she said, and her eyes were full of water. OJesus, she felt so good, and smelled so wonderful, and I could feel her ass twitching in my hand, and I hung there trying to look blank, while she whoresmiled all the while and said,

'I'm crowded now more than ever. I'm tired of these little bits.'

'You want to become a housewife?'

'If it means *peace*, yes.'

'Then what happens to the years?'

'Aren't there more years? More time?'

'I'm not sure.'

She sucked her breath in and closed her eyes. 'Oh, feel me, Daddy,' she whispered, 'feel It. Touch It, please.'

'I can't. Your ass is too big.'

The matron was looking at us. My finger worked around that ridged little spot in the seat of her panties. I'm looking right in her eyes as I do it.

'Do you want me?' she said. 'I mean really *want* me?'

'Didn't I tell you about asking questions like that?'

'Oh, Daddy, I'm not after you or anything. It would just be so sweet for me, you know, something I could have.'

'Yeah, I want you. But I want more than what you've been.'

She shook her head. 'All you have to do is tell me how, Daddy. There're so few things I know. I know how to obey, when I've found the kind of understanding and everything else I need in my man, my 1 man, my alwaysman.'

'Ladies and gentlemen,' Willie B said from the front, 'that will be the end of the coffeebreak.'

'But that hasn't been 30minnits!' I said, a huge piece of her rump in my hand. She drifted away from me. There was a scurry to the maleside and femaleside. I dragged numbly back through the pews. She was still thick in me, and I felt veryvery angry.

'And now,' said Willie B, 'we'll have Mr. Johnnyboy M., with all the latest news from Chicago interraveled in his narrative.'

I sat down, staring over to her. We just watched each other. I didn't hear a thing that doofus little guy said.

I wrote on my fingers to her when the matrons weren't looking:

I am going to fuck you.

And she wrote back quickly:

Hurry, Daddy.

About this time Little Junior came on. 'Evenin, ladies. Evenin, gentlemen. As you know, my name is Little Junior McFee, and I'm from Washington, D.C., where everybody knows how to do somethin. I know how to dance.' He did a little twirl. 'And I been dancing my way through this 5year bit for the federal Government of the United States.' Something was happening to his mouth. He was high, he looked like. 'But really, yall, I wantcha to know what a deep feelin I'm leavin in my heart for AA, and for all of you whom I probably won't ever see again in life after I leave here tomorrormornin.'

Somebody snickered.

Something was happening to him.

'What did I learn while with AA?' Little Junior asked. 'Well, that's a very good question and I'm happy to answer it. I learned a great deal from AA, particularly about myself. And when I heard other guys tell almost *my* lifestory, then I knew AA was the thing for me.' He was grinning, and whatever it was was getting worse. A couple of the broads giggled, and he thought he'd said something pretty hip,

so he stirred his fires:

'But there's somethin here in AA for those who want it, but you know it's just gotta come from the heart and not lipservice.'

His whole mouth was turning white.

Incredibly, it deepened and made him look like he was in blackface. I began to laugh, really open up, and got a cramp in my neck.

It was like seeing magic.

But I swear, the more that guy rapped idiocies,

the whiter his lips got.

The Two Part

1/4

That was the time I started looking around the hospital,

because of what I told Sonja I was going to do. And I hadn't begun to realize how isolated I was. Neither why I should tempt the facts the way I had by telling her some mad shit like that. I never could figure out how I chumped myself off on something like that,

but I had promised more in these circumstances than I should safely, properly promise. She understood what I said, and I understood what she said, completely.

For long hours I cased the place. I took the Messenger-Folio and made all the runs Tam used to make when he was done with his Orderly assignment in the morning,

and I got to check out the dispensary area that could be reached from UT, the branching arm and thin corridor that led around to the Male Waiting Rooms, and the bigthick door with 3locks that led into the women's unit.

Then the day came when I had to decide whether or not I was bullshitting about what I planned to do,

and my answer said No.

1

Uxeküll does a lot of harm over here, I was able to see for the 1st time today. Somebody read his orders to him wrong,

but anyway take a look at what this guy did:

Yesterday, Friday, a little whitey came in from 1 of the deep bigfoot countries, a doctor himself,

a fragile kindof, Germaniclooking, man. I'd been wound up in some sort of plot during the earlymorning and didn't notice him till I came in from lunch.

Dr. Uxeküll, looking fat around the ass because of the toosmall whitejacket he always wore, was lecturing the other doctor like a judge.

The man must've been 65or70years old, looking across almost 4decades to the simpleseeming face that bobbed above him now.

I remember him mumbling something about Demerol, but he looked like a dopefiend to me,

I mean real scroungy dopefiend,

the opiate addict.

But whatever. He was beautiful, I could see that too, with a face full of anxious lovely things to be remembered, a completely alien personality to me,

but anyway

Dr. Uxeküll was telling the guy:

'It's something you'll have to control on your own. This is what *hap*pens when you take goofballs, you ought to know that, Doctor.'

'But my God, man,' the little doctor said, 'surely you know what I'm going through now.'

'Well, of course I do.'

'And you mean to stand there and tell me I can't have medication? You can't be serious. I had 1 intravaneous injection of Demerol in the time I've been here, almost 60hours. How dare you tell me,' he said, getting red, 'how dare you tell me that Benadryl every 4hours will be enough to aid my withdrawal? Surely you're joking. . . .'

'Boy, I wish I was,' Dr. Uxeküll said, grinning, 'but we have certain programs here, you can understand that, and it's not that we don't care about making an exception, but you can see how any exception would alter our treatment procedures, even the minutest bit. I'm afraid you'll just have to make it the best you can. My prognosis is usually right. A few sleepless nights—'

The doctor was trembling. 'Do you realize how old I am, man? Don't you read your own records?'

'Well, of course I do, or how else would I be able to form a prognosis?'

The little doctor looked at me blankly, as though I had the answer, then back to Dr. Uxeküll. 'But this is unbelievable,' he said. 'I can't believe this. I am an addict. You have everything you need to know about that. I have been an addict for over 25years. Knowing this, surely you know I need some sort of medication. In consideration of my age and infirmities.' He looked closely at Uxeküll's unmoving face. 'I'm a Luminal addict, Doctor. Even if I were 30years younger, I could easily die from this sort of withdrawal.'

'Oh, believe me, Doctor,' Uxeküll giggled, 'You won't die.'

The little doctor was wearing a USNrobe; he pulled it up closely about his throat. 'I want you to listen to me, Dr. Uxeküll. At this very moment I am in a secondary stage of withdrawal. I was sent down here much too soon. I can hardly bend my back, and I'm beginning to get skintrembles. Now, I don't know how you diagnose that, but I diagnose it as a very sick man, or 1 who is about to be. If you won't treat me, then please make it convenient for me to leave here at once.'

'Oh, sure, we can do that,' Uxeküll said, 'but you must remember that I advise against it. Just see Mr. Antman.' Joe Antman was watching with Pepper from the office. 'You can sign the papers for WDA, Without Doctor's Approval. And you'll be able to leave Monday.' He grinned.

'*Mon*day?'

Uxeküll shrugged. 'Well, we won't be able to clear your records before then.'

'You *do know* that today is Friday, don't you?'

'Sure, everybody knows that,' Dr. Uxeküll said.

The other man trembled. 'I will be in complete withdrawal by that time.'

'Oh, well, you should have with*drawn* by that time, shouldn't you? I mean, the worst part of it will be over.'

'On Benadryl?'

'We've found it very helpful. . . .'

'Doctor, Benadryl works on the sinuses.'

'Ah, but it's also a depressant; it'll calm your nerves.'

The little doctor clutched at the collar of the USNrobe. He must've worn shorts underneath, and had thinspindly old legs with jagged, cracked blue ropes of snaky veins. He had genteel feet in worn blue bathclogs

that were probably his most holy feature.

'I understand you are the doctor in charge of the withdrawal unit,' he said.

'Rightly so,' Uxeküll said.

'You determine, then, the medication policy. Is this an experimental policy?'

Uxeküll cupped his white elbows. 'I'm glad you asked that, Doctor. No, it is not. It is the result of a complete screening of narcoticaddicts over the years, and it showed us How, how to treat them medicinally. I wish you could see what we've compiled on it.'

'I'm sure it's interesting.'

'You couldn't guess what we found out,' Uxeküll said. 'Which applies specifically to what I'm saying right here. We can't give you any medication because our studies show relatively cold withdrawal is the best in the long run.' He shook his head, and shrugged, grinning. 'That's the best deal I can offer you, Doctor.'

The little doctor pulled himself together in a dignified way, but he trembled a bit. 'I would like to remind you that this is not a used-car lot and you are not a salesman trying to sell me anything. This is allegedly a hospital and you are allegedly a doctor. For years I've labored under the delusion that this place was set up specifically for the *relief* of the addict – I've even referred patients here. And you tell me that after committing myself, I am now a prisoner until Monday morning and you will do nothing in that time to relieve my illness? I simply can't believe it's happening.' He had a spasm that seemed to shake the eyeballs around in his skull.

Uxeküll was smiling and benign; he held his hands together in front like a priest. 'I'm afraid it is. Happening, I mean. What I strongly suggest for you is for you to take your prescriptioncard around to the dispensary and get your Benadryl medication, then return here and go promptly to bed.'

'And what I strongly suggest for you, youngman,' the little doctor said in careful choking fury, 'is for you to go off to some secret place and cut your God Damned Useless Throat.'

So today

Saturday

Little Joe happened to be prowling around on the 1st floor looking for any new faggots who might have been sent in lately

(this was the only floor in UT we put them on),

passing by and looking through every doorwindow, when he noticed the little doctor tied all up in his sheet and blanket, bed rolled up in a mattresstangled position that made it look like a V. He was having convulsions. His eyes had rolled back in his head.

and he'd bitten off a piece of his tongue and drooled a bilelish blood all over everything. His smooth feet pointed bonefrozen in arch ballet rigidity.

Joe knew 1staid, so he got something to put between the guy's teeth after he straightened him out on the bed, and raised his head.

Today was Antman's day off, so the unit supervisor in his place, a dumpylittle broad named Miss Silman, who had a complexion like owlshit, came steaming in to handle the operations.

And there was chittering and chattering around about who had what authority between her and Smith

(who didn't have enough seniority not to work Saturdays)

and the headnurse Miss Gifford from 0-3.

The little doctor was dead by the time they got him to the hospital.

The nexttime I saw Uxeküll was early Monday morning when I came to get the moves into population from Joe Antman. He looked kind of sick,

trying to look professionally somber,

and he was trying to con Joe Antman and Pepper to go easy in their reports about the little doctor's kickoff.

'It was unfortunate,' he grieved, 'but medication was *not* indicated.'

Joe Antman was slouched back in his chair, looking at him. 'Me and Smith heard everything last Friday when you told him he couldn't have any.'

'That's right,' Smith said in an uncommitted voice, leaning against the cold radiator under the office window.

Dr. Uxeküll put both hands in both whitepockets and smiled understandingly at them. 'Naturally, I'd want you to put everything you heard into your report.'

'I'm kind of accurate with my reports,' Joe Antman told him.

'Me too,' Pepper said.

I asked if they had 1 for cons, but nobody heard me.

'There's no reason for us to get confused about this,' Uxeküll said.

Joe Antman demanded to know

'Who said anything about confusion? Maybe I *am* only a G-5, but I know what I hear.'

'I don't see where ratings have to come into this.' Uxeküll grinned.

'It was just the way you said what you said about confusion,'

Joe Antman said, bouncing the heel of his rightshoe on the top of his desk. 'I think we know what our jobs are down here.'

'I think so too,' Pepper backed him up.

Like an announcement, Joe said, 'We don't have to be analyzed to know what our jobs are.'

Uxeküll laughed sociably. 'Well, I certainly wouldn't attempt to tell you what your job is, Mr. Antman, and I haven't suggested that you need psychiatric treatment. I was talking in terms of professional agreement. We all know the unfortunate fellow was on some kind of LastLegs when he came to us.'

'I don't know what kind of condition his legs were in when he got here,' Joe Antman said. 'He was an addict; that much I do know. And it's my unprofessional opinion that he needed somekind of shot, or maybe a series, to tide him through his withdrawal period. I'm not as young as you,' he pointed out with a darklook; 'I've seen a lot more over the last 20years than you will in your 2. At least I've come to know what a dopefiend needs.'

'Well, that's interesting,' Uxeküll ha-haed. 'Here we are looking for the Cure, and you have it all the time.'

'Yeah,' Joe said, with a little vehemence that was out of character for him, 'I've got it. But why should I tell you? You raise my rating to a 10; then I'll tell you. But it wouldn't do you any good, and it certainly wouldn't do me none. The Joe Antman Solution for Narcotics Addiction.'

'Why don't you let me decide that?' Uxeküll smiled.

'Because that's all you're good at,' Joe Antman said, 'deciding. Like a butcher dividin ½pound of ribroast, that's what you deciders are. You decide and slice, and you still ain't got no answers. Naw. No. Doctor, I can't let you decide my way of thinkin for me, so I'll just put in my own report about what happened to that gentleman you said had LastLegs.'

Joe put in a bomb. I had to type it up.

Uxeküll was gibbering ineptness when I got through, and Joe signed it.

Pepper wrote up something in longhand that sounded like the paper from 2B of a grade-school essay about WHY I DONT

LIKE MISS ANGELUS THE GIM TEACHER BECAUSE SHE HAS MUSCLES.

But nothing came of it.

The guy was dead.

I didn't know there was that much friction between the psychiatric aides and the professionals. Joe Antman ran around for days,

trying to see Mossler, the Medical Doctor in Charge,

in an attempt to jam Dr. Uxeküll.

But he was rural and far from the politics of the hospital.

And the guy was dead.

Today

Saturday

I got so high off mace I lost consciousness.

When I awoke it was night,

and something stood in the shadows of my room under the *Playboy* picture next to my clothes rack. My hair stood up at the back of my neck, and for 1 terrific moment

I was urged to cop out. I almost screamed. Then I saw it was nothing but a sweater I'd hung on the wall and forgotten about, and my eyes burned to the point of tears,

and for 1 hopeful, exquisite moment

I thought I'd be able to cry for the 1st time in my life.

2

Where I live,
on the 6th floor,
I get a lot of extraordinary action. A lot of young dopies live up here, with 1 or 2 who are undercover faggots.
Sometimes in the middle of day
the whole floor takes on a funereal mood, and I find this time best,
with all others shirking,
to go to the bathroom and rest.
I was this day when George Prospectus came in, with a newdopie grin and a Lewisburg toothbrush.
I was sitting there, on the leftmost john, when he came in to groom himself.
George is a guy you'd have to see to believe. His pale white skin is like a shark's belly, but his eyes are like those of a dove or hummingbird. I can never get the order of them.
But I dug him for mellow right away, and I
stopped my straining to see what he said.
'Hi.'
'All right.'
'I just came in today.'
'Yeah, I know. I made your card out.'
He turned blue things to watch at me. 'How's this place?'
'In what way?'
'Oh, you know – every way. I was just thinking.'
'So far as I know, it's cool.'
'Oh.' He soaped his face to shave.
'Been here long?' he asked my mirror's reflection.
'I never think about time.'
'Oh, you know,' he said, turning, 'I didn't mean time like that.'
'You just meant In This Place.'

'Yes. Well.'

'I've been here something like a month. When I really think about it.'

'Are you doing a bit?'

'5years for Sale of Narcotics': I rubbed my nose when I said it, and rubbed the place that was numb on my thigh.

'I guess you think I'm kind of nosy.' He grinned in the mirror.

'Yeahinnaway.'

'What I want to tell you is about myself.'

I looked up in the eyes of his image. 'You don't have to tell me anything.'

'Oh, I know that.' He splashed water and drew the blade over his skin. 'But there are things people need to tell other people, you know?'

'Okay, if you want to.'

He dushed his face and looked kind of boyish. 'My wife is over in that place they call the Barn.'

'Ahn.'

'But she's got some hangups. She says they're after her.'

'Who's after her?'

'The Lesbians.'

'Oh. Well, this is a penitentiary, ya know, and you should have taken both of you to a private hospital if you didn't want that kind of complication. People need to come when you're locked up in a joint, so you can't blame them too much.' I shifted on the toilet seat. 'Specially if she's kinda fine.'

'She's beautiful,' George said. 'I've got her picture you ought to see.'

'I wouldn't care.'

'I'll get it for you.'

'You don't really have to.'

'But I want to,' he said, and left right away to go down to his room on the tier and bring back the flick and 2 cigaretpacksized others.

'That's her in Connecticut, with the trees behind.'

'She *is* kinda fine.'

'Dora.'

'That's a maid's name. But she doesn't look like.'

The broad was long and willowy, with thick blondehair and

a popsicle kind of nose that gave the lowerlush features of her

face a heavy sexcurve,

and she was standing in the foreground of what looked like a greenago campus,

wearing a stupid pair of Mr. Moto-type glasses that showed she was blind as a bat.

But her physical hookup made up for all that

the way her biglines licked into themselves, with warm summer in all her flesh, and I got the overall impression that

all you had to do to make her come

was grab her by her greatbig python ass and bite her right in the middle of that astonishing nose.

'Yeah, she is somethin.'

'I thought you'd like her,' George said.

'You don't know how much.'

He started shaving again, and I looked at the other 2flicks. 1 showed her in an ignorantblue bathingsuit, the crack of her buns peeking through, in a grotesque Monroe pose.

But the other was nicer and formal, a capandgown thing done on some FinalDay. And though she was freshsmiling and cleareyed on all of them, you couldn't get around the nose situation.

'So the butches givin her a little trouble, huh?'

He tried to look casually at me in the mirror. 'Dora's had that kind of trouble before. She used to be in a girls' school. Her father and mother are divorced, so you can see how she'd come in contact with something like that in a girls' school. I met her at Harvard.'

'How'd she get there from the girls' school?'

'She came down for a Soph prom.'

'Are you a graduate?'

'Oyes,' he said.

'And you're a dopefiend too, huh?'

He sort of bobbed his head with sad affectation; it made me stop believing in him. 'I've been hungup with this problem for 4years, Dora and me.'

'I've been hungup with it for *15*.'

'I've been using ever since LawSchool.'

'I've been usin ever since DaySchool.'

Then he sort of pickedup on me and cooled out.

I squeezed my ass around on the seat to make it more comfortable. I still had the pictures:

'You want these back?'

'Oh, no,' he said, 'I'm all wet here; I'll be done in a second if you're not going anywhere.'

'It'd take a whole new operation to get ready and leave now.'

He suddenly slashed a greatbig patch of skin out of his face with that governmentissued soiltiller they give for a razor,

and began to bleed all over the God Damned Floor.

'Ohman, Tamerlane's gonna be very upset about that shit; he has to clean up in here.'

'Well, I wouldn't go around cutting myself on purpose, you know.'

'You did if you shaved with that God Damned Ax they give you downstairs.'

'I'll buy some at the Commissary tonight.'

Blood was all over the floor.

'With the kind of plastic surgery you already done on yourself, you won't ever need razorblades again.'

'I suppose you think it's funny,' he said, daubing around and bleeding to death.

'You'd better get the fuck out of here and try to get a transfusion as fast as you can.'

He didn't think that was funny either.

He bled so much he slipped up on it and fell on his ass. Then he got real excited and ran out of the shithouse, flinging blood all over everything. In a moment he came back with his head twisted up in a towel like the Mummy, and he 1eyed it around until he finally got most of his sloppy bright-red life up off the floor. By now the towel he clenched at his head was bloody.

'Say, man, maybe you're a hemophiliac.'

'I don't think so,' he said calmly; 'I think it's just because I've got thin skin.'

'Well, I got a sneakin suspicion you oughta check it out.'

'Ohno, my bloodlines don't even indicate anything like that.'

'Your bloodlines won't even indicate themselves if you don't find some way to stop bleedin.'

'I've had a lot of trouble with blood,' he said, going over to the sink again.

'Your problem will be solved in a coupla more minnits.'

'You seem to be making fun of the wholething,' he said resentfully.

'Naw, it's just that I never seen a man dyin right in front of my eyes before.'

He filled the basin with hot water and dushed his head up and down. It looked like where somebody'd killed a hog.

'God Damn, man . . . you better go see about yourself.'

'Oh, I'm all right,' George Prospectus said.

'I figure you got about 45more seconds before you're all wrong.'

But that just made him dush his head up and down harder.

'I'd better get the hack ready to go over and break the news to your old lady.'

'Now, you stop that, damn it,' he said, slashing

bloody water around at me. 'You sound like somekind of psychotic.'

'The manic-depressive type. I think I'll go over to my depressive side until you finally fall out and die.'

He ran the basin full of cold water, and did the same damnfool dush, but it seemed to be working this time,

hair slashing and sloshing a clearer red mixture now.

I got up.

'I better call the emergency medic.'
'No, don't do that,' he sputtered out.
'You mighta cut your throat and didn't know it.'
'If I cut my throat, don't you think I'd know it? Just don't be pushy, will you?'
'I wouldn't want to push you in anything right now but a greatbig plasticbag.'
'All right, okay, you've had your fun.'
'Not until I've seen you fall completely out on your God Damned Head.'
'Say,' he said, turning and squinting, 'what is it with you?'
'I'm anti-Human.'
'You know.' He turned to look at me now. He wasn't bleeding somuch now, and he wasn't really injured, you could tell. 'Maybe I know what it is.'
'What?'
'Would you answer me a question truthfully?'
'If it didn't interfere with anything I had going at the moment.'
Then his whiteness came out when he said,
'Do you resent me because I'm white?'
And I say, thinkingly,
something like no in Just this way:
'But I'm drugged with a system that requires you to ask me a question like that.'

2ε1/3

I began to concentrate a little more,
  I don't know why.
  But I began to feel something happening to me. Downstairs 1 day at the Commissary
  I even said hello to Willie B, and you know how I despise that little asshole.
  But some people call these things transitions.

&1/3 MORE

The physical character of the joint was very important to my plans. You see

there's hacks all over the place. There're 4Male units and there's a cop in each of them, sicklyfaced-looking guys from the hills, all suffering from somekind of congenital abnormality,

like humped backs or cottonsack bellies, and it was surprising when you think the government oughta have some sort of health standard with employees engaged in this kinda work. I began to get superiorityfeelings when I came in contact with them,

and that's a bad thing to get when you're doing a bit.

But all you have to do is look at them.

It's easy to understand, though:

Freakology is common in the family of bureaucracy.

I got hooked into something the other night at the AA closedmeeting, which I certainly didn't want,

but it happened anyway.

With 1st this guy standing, a tall bluelooking kid someone introduced to me as out of New York,

and I was sitting in the back.

But there was some kind of hassle, because the air suddenly got warm, and all the dopies got intense, because the guy was talking about stuff in relation to race, and there were a few whiteyfaces scattered around in the audience, like little

bits of cauliflower.

And an argument developed between him and a Puerto Rican fella, 1 of those specialtypes who think and look white. And Willie B mumbled around like a fool at the front, trying to end the thing gracefully.

'Now I thank,' he said, 'that you guys just oughta be cool.'

But the blackguy said,

'And I think you oughta shut up, Willie B, 'cause I got the floor right now.'

'Well, you will always have to give the Chair respect,' the Chair complained.

'It's my opinion,' Montenegro said

(and isn't that a paradox of a name?),

'that you're being prejudiced about the wholething.'

'Ohman, listen,' Matthew told him (that was his name), 'don't give me that discriminationshit. All I have to do is look at things the way they are. Do you think I'm blind or something? Don't you think I have sense enough to know stuff is nothing but a plot against the black ghettopeople?'

'Now you're sounding like a Black Muslim.'

'Oh?' Matt's big white eyes got wide. 'Because I bring out racial factors that make you feel shitty, I have to be a Black Muslim?'

'I don't see what you mean by that,' Montenegro said. 'I came out of the same ghetto situation myself—'

'And you're a dopefiend, doesn't that prove something?'

'Not the whole way, and you should know that.'

'I don't see where race has anything to do with it,' Willie B said from the front.

'And I don't see where you have, either,' Matthew snapped at him. 'The argument is between this Oyea and me.'

'Well, 1thing I don't like to do is argue,' Montenegro said modestly. 'But you have to be wrong, Matt, because there's just as many whitekids using stuff as Negroes, so how could you call that a plot?'

And that's when I got in

for some foolish reason I can't understand right now. Because I began to laugh, and when you laugh in an unlaughing group, attention is naturally focused on you.

Willie B shuffled around uneasily at the front. 'You got somethin you wanna say, man?'

'Yeah. Bullshit.'

'Should the Chair take that as a statement?' Willie B said.

'Bullshit is what the Chair is composed of anyway, so I don't care how you take it.' I stood in the pews. 'You dopies make me sick. Don't you realize you're products, just like Campbell ChickenSoup? A cop busted me in the mouth when I was a kid and called me a Lousy Product.'

'I think we're gettin away from the question,' Willie B said falsesoundingly.

'This *is* the question, you God Damn Fool; Matthew was only tellin you the way it is.'

Willie B's eyes flashed. 'You don't haveta get disordered.'

'Just pretend you're a Chair, and keep your mouth shut while I'm talking. Why is it you can't find a place to live, a place to work, a place to exercise what makes you think: but you can find stuff without even tryin?'

"Product" is the word,' Matthew said out suddenly, looking toward me. Then told the group, 'We're products, and all you have to do is look around at these faces to tell who is the valid dopefiend.'

'That sounds like an anarchist way of thinkin,' Willie B explained from the front.

'What the hell do you know about anarchists?' Matthew snapped at him. 'You never revolted against anything but an intelligent idea.'

Grievedly, Willie B said,

'More and more you make this sound like a personal thang, man.'

'Ignorance always is.'

Then Matthew turned and told me, 'You're right.'

But I was very surprised at myself for opening up the way I had, even for being interested, and I resented the thing that told me Matthew might think we had something going together, now that he felt he understood me.

Later

Willie B came moaning around my office on his AApass

talking about I shouldn't have said this and that and that we should have no racialfeelings in AA because the hospital wouldn't dig it, and it might interfere with the Broad Situation,

but I told him to get the fuck out of my face or I'd beat his ass.

Matthew Paine was the guy with the boil on his nose, remember?

but I didn't recognize him till later, 1reason being he didn't have the boil any longer.

Anyway

right after that AA set I was looking around for someone I could trust and I ran into this guy in the basement corridor coming back from exercise,

waiting in line to get his clothes at the laundrydoor. This was Thursday, the alternate day of Tuesday, to do things like this. And I suppose I had something in there too, but I didn't know for sure, since I'd been beaten out of my congrays by somebastard who worked in that criminal mill

and had to wait another week to get others.

But I was passing, very sweaty and tired from only a few benchpreses and pounding the bigbag, and some selfproclaimed blackbelt artist was teaching me karate. When Matt saw me.

'Heyman.' He smiled.

'How ya doin?'

'Trying to get through this hassle.'

'I suppose I got something in there too, but I don't know for sure.'

'You didn't come to AA Sunday,' he said.

'Fuck that shit.'

'Yeah, I feel the same way, but I feel like I've got some kind of crusade going.'

'Well, if that is what you muss do, that is what you muss do. But I think Crusades went out with Richard the Punk-hearted.'

'You know, there's a lotta talk about you in this joint.'

'Just like there is in any police station.'

'Naw, nothing like that.'

'I don't see how it could miss otherwise.'

'No, but you're somethin of another kind of guy, like we had Tadd Dameron once, and he was something like you.'

'Tadd Dameron could be nothin like me. I don't play music.'

'But you *do*, in your way.'

'I don't like to see people get all mistaked about something.'

'Im not gettin mistaked about a God Damn Thing.'

'You are if you think about me like Tadd Dameron.'

He looked around him. 'Ohman, this line ain't moving worth a shit.'

'C'mon down, I'll buy you an icecream at the Commissary.'

'I ain't got no dough.'

'My village aunt sent me some, so I'll treat you.'

We walked down to the place, because Matt could come back in about an hour to get his stuff,

and I didn't have anything anyway.

Inside, the Commissary is like a rule of thumb, because you measure from the front to the back, a long graything, like everything around here is. On the walls are implorations for Salem and Pall Mall filters, and 1 sign says,

You bastard buyer, don't you buy a thing until you buy Philip Morris KingSized. Or something like that.

But we went in anyway.

Now this is a strange place.

Over to my right is a kind of paint that makes the walls seem funny, like they're made of Softskin Toilet Tissue or something, but I'm sure they didn't intend it this way. The other windowedside is wirescreened, to keep dopies from stealing: they had a clue about that.

You stand in line with the other dopies at 3small windows like those of banktellers, buying your stuff from 3tall grayguys who looked like bankrobbers. And what you used for money

was a longthin book of scrip that you signed out of your

account at the window upstairs next to CenterControl.

Matthew stood on the side while I ordered the cream,

but I really never liked it myself,

and rapped casually to me as the line moved along. It was noisy as hell in there, as it always is,

and if anything recommends stuff for dopefiends, it's the horror of the inhuman noises they make when they're off it.

'I remember the 1st time I saw you,' Matt said. 'You looked like a guy I know in New York.'

'That's where I live when I'm not doin bits. Madison and 112th.'

'DopeCity.'

'All of um are anyway.'

'That guy you look like,' he went on. 'He had the same kind of intensity too.'

'Intensity? That AAshit's all a hype to get to the broads; I know: I got a broad there.'

We stopped at the window, and the guy took my scripbook and savagely ripped out 50¢ for 2little pasteboard cups of CherryVanilla and Vanilla icecream,

and we came back to stand in the long corridor, eating it,

and watch the screaming dopies stream through and bubble around us.

The Oyea crowd stood in the lockedoff ramp leading up to the Eastside, the 1 the women used when they went to the movies,

shouting at each other in pidgin Spanish.

and you heard a lot of *maricóns* being pitched back and forth. Most of these Islanders were out of New York,

but a few came from the mountains, the hillbilly Oyeas, still wearing family amulets of firedwood and pictures of the HolyVirgin looking all sweetly pious up to Heaven.

Matt said, halfway through his CherryVanilla,

'I go to a group every Thursday. A divinityteacher from town runs it. About 6other guys with me. A couple of them think.'

'That's hard to believe.'

'Well, you'd just have to come up to see.'

'No. If it was true, it'd throw my whole philosophy about dopefiends off.'

'I know you'd dig some of the sessions, man, and it's only about for an hour in the afternoons around 3.'

'I do a lotta readin in the afternoons.'

I threw the rest of my icecream away, right over in the corner under the radiator like everybody else.

'Well, it'd be nice if you could,' Matt said. 'You'd dig it.'

'I doubt it.'

But I had another thought just then: 'You said on Thursday at 3?'

'Right.'

He was surprised when I told him I'd think it over.

'If you make up your mind you want to,' he said, 'just use your officephone to call me down in the woodshop where I work, and I can arrange to have a pass sent to you.'

'Yeah, if I make up my mind.'

He seemed kinda pleased. 'Well, I'm gonna take a run back to see if I can pick up my stuff. I'll hang on till I see ya again.'

'Okay, me too.'

He left rightaway, but I stood around thinking for a longtime, my heart swelling a bit.

MOMMIE:

I'm sure you remember the statement I made to you at the coffeebreak before last, and I'm sure you know I was entirely serious about it. I really think it's only a matter of being in the right place at the right time.

I know how you tend to be frivolous when it comes time to obey your Man, and this is a trait I'm determined not to let interfere with my plans. You will have to listen closely and do everything precisely the way I tell you, and I'm emphasizing precisely.

Write me back directly everything that occurs to you on days you go to see your therapist, also send me an outline of what the ladies' john looks like inside. When you have your next set I'll intercept you. At least we'll have a chance to see each other.

Send back the information in the same way I've sent this to you – by Underground.

And don't sign your name to anything.

But that not fair: You're frivolous, but not a damned fool.

ME

3

So that's how I got hooked up in
Reverend Kleague's class.

I was drugged to have to go through the wholething, but I didn't see anyway around it. I'd gotten obsessed with the idea of taking Sonja off.

I arrived ahead of the female group she came with, but she wasn't there, and I wondered what kind of shit she'd gotten into now.

Me and 3other guys sat on the left of Mr. Wallers' desk,

where he sat chittering around and making sure nobody talked to the broads,

and looked stupid for a while; then the other guys starting trooping in with their passes for Mr. Wallers, stumbling around in front of the desk, trying to get off a smile or a message to 1 of the broads, but

Mr. Wallers was all sharpeyes: 'I wouldn't if I were you, dear; you know I can give you 4duty hours for that.'

Then Matthew came in with a strange little whiteguy in a shinyblack suit

and saw me and said Hi

and we all stood up to follow the whiteguy down the corridor to 1 of the big conference rooms with wickerchairs and a big 2way mirror in 1 oakpaneled wall. Somebody said it wasn't hooked to operate just then, and they always asked you for permission before they observed you like that,

but I told him I didn't believe it.

There were 7 of us now, so 1 guy was missing, but the littleguy smilingly bade us sit, and another guy said something about not letting 1 monkey stop the show.

And I was starting to get irritated already.

Reverend Kleague introduced himself to me and another

guy who was pimplyfaced and Spanish;

then everybody started to unlimbering, taking out cigarets, preparing to get as selfcentered as hell, and I've been through these kinds of sessions planning stickups with guys: it gets completely incoherent after the first 20minnits.

The Reverend wasn't a badlooking guy, kinda chubby-cheeked and red but smoothskinned. He had purple hair. He told us he was from some Church of Jesus' Perennial Agonies, but he wanted us to know that he wasn't selling religion: it was just a Study in People he wanted and he was glad we'd consented to go along with his program.

A lightskinned guy with gold in his teeth took over as something like a moderator. I couldn't remember having seen him before, but he spoke with nicegutty inflections.

'Reverend, I've been listening to you for 3weeks now, and there's just 1question that keeps crossing my mind: You've told us what *you* want, but what is it we'll get out of it? There's always somekinda test going on around here where the dopie is used but isn't given a damnthing for his use. I want to know what *I'm* going to get out of coming up here for an hour a week, when I could be playin pingpong or pittypat down in the gym.'

'That's a good question, George,' the Reverend said.

'And there's more I'm gonna ask.'

'Well, that's practically the main purpose of this wholething, George, to ask questions, because I'm sure, your having been addicts, that you've formed a lot of them.' He crossed his shinyknees. 'I don't want you fellas to mistake this for therapy or anything like that, or a revivalmeeting. But I do want to tell you that I believe, for the purpose of selfhelp, intelligent men should come in contact with others.'

'Then you been selective about us, right?'

'That's right, I've read all your records; your consent to come gave me the right to do that.'

'Then you must've selected us on a racial basis too,' George said, 'because I see only Negroes and 1 Puerto Rican.'

'It wasn't anything like that, believe me,' the Reverend said.

'I tried to enlist whites right along in this group, but all of them said they'd rather not – it's not compulsory, you know.'

The Puerto Rican's name was Jimmy De Soto, and he said,

'This is the way the whole hospital is hooked up. Keep to this side, keep to that side. It's easy to see in mixed-therapy groups.'

'And I've seen hacks make Brothers go to the blackside of the messhall,' another guy said.

'I think we should make the racialfactor secondary to our own experiences as men together. [I guessed him for around 25.] As you know, this is the South, and the people who come to work here are Southerners and they can't help bringing along all their old attitudes with them.'

'There's only 3 Negro hacks on the staff,' the guy who spoke about the messhall said, 'and only 2 who're Spanish.'

'But I've seen them on staff all over the place,' the Reverend protested.

'Yeah,' the guy said, 'as painters and plasterers and laundry-men. But why is it this hospital that employs over 500people only employs about 25black?'

Matthew said something for the 1st time:

'I think we're getting into another sort of problem; I think it's the hospital itself is the real bitch. It's kinda hard to condition yourself to humanity when you don't have any here. The whitedopies suffer, but in another kind of way.'

Jimmy De Soto said:

'My whole bitch is against the psychiatricstaff, because they ain't even equipped to handle the Spanishspeaking people. There ain't 1 Spanishspeaking psych here. So what is this? I say. As ratio against ratio, I mean. It don't work out fairly. You got kids outta the mountain from the Island, and they even have dialects.'

'You know,' Reverend Kleague chuckled, 'you're all using me for a soundingboard about your gripes against the hospital. I've been here long enough to know practically all of them are true, but what ought to be more basic is not what the hospital does for you but what you're able to do for yourself.'

‘If you knew half of what you think you knew, you’d really see what *was* basic,’ Matthew said. ‘Because this place isn’t set up to really *cure* anybody. Look what a business you’d shut down if dopies started getting well.’

Then George came in again:

‘There’s kickback going down all over this joint; that Commissary monopoly for 1thing. TV’s, radios, record players.’

‘Fellas, fellas.’ Reverend Kleague laughed. ‘I know you have gripes, and I’ve never been antigriper, but you’re firing all your shells at the 1person who’d be *least* able to help you. I’m not saying anything has happened like that exactly like that, the way you tell me. It’s interesting to see I have selected a group pattern advocating the overthrow of the hospital.’

‘*Vio*lent overthrow,’ Matthew straightened it out.

I was thinking about why he said I’m Not Saying Anything Has Happened Like That Exactly Like That, The Way You Tell Me,

but I couldn’t figure it out.

‘What we’re looking for is an Objective here among ourselves,’ the Reverend said. ‘I mean, it doesn’t mean much to gripe about anything if you aren’t willing to initiate the change yourself.’

‘Let that be the Objective then,’ Matthew said: ‘Initiating change here in the hospital.’

‘Believe me, if it’ll help us come closer together,’ Reverend Kleague said, ‘then I’m all for it. But I think our Objective ought to take everything into account. For instance, you’re all prisoners and not in a very good bargaining position, but there’s a thing already set up here for that—’

George interrupted,

‘You’re talkin about the Patients’ Council.’

‘That’s a puppet organization,’ Matthew said, ‘all handpicked by Security. Nothing ever gets done there.’

The Reverend uncrossed his knees. ‘Then there ought to be somekind of changes made.’

Jimmy De Soto said,

'If you're talkin about serving on the council, forget it – it's a clique. Nobody out of the Clan can make it.'
'Well,' said the Reverend, 'if you're going to revolt against anything, that's the place to start.'

Just as we were leaving
after Reverend Kleague shook hands all round
Matthew asked me what I thought.
'Okay, I just don't like bein observed.'
'The group is new, but there's a few of the guys who say a little something. It's kinda like my own idea. I suggested it to the guy when he came down to an AAmeeting 1 night, and this is how I got to feel about you the night you said something, and I thought you'd kinda dig it.'
'It's all right; I never said it wasn't. I just said I don't like bein peered in on. Do whatever you want; I won't get in the way.'
'I know them all and they're pretty hip.'
'Maybe hip in the sameway the CIA is.'
We'd just given our passes to Mr. Wallers for signing, when a new group of women came through the doors,
and I got a little start when I saw Sonja was with them.
The browndressed grayhaired matron gave me a hard look, so I nutted up on myself right away.
'Well, men,' Mr. Wallers said briskly, 'you're ready to leave, scatscat now.'
So I had to get out without saying a word to her, her all yearning and dribblyeyed and pouting sadkisses at me.
At the elevator I told Matthew what I'd decided to do
but not in detail,
and he agreed to help me, saying,
'It's been done before, but not anything like what you got in mind. 1 time a bunch of guys had keys to the Barn.'
I got a little shock of warmth from him when I watched him thinking of the trick, and I didn't have to go any further to know I could depend on him.
It was the 1st time in my life I'd ever been friends with a guy.

In a note I got Underground later that day, Sonja wrote:

Daddy I'm so sorry I couldn't make it today, but they changed my job over to the garmentshop and I'll be going down there from now on.

But I was too drugged behind it to care, so I didn't write back for a week.

4&1/4

She was back again for the 1st time in weeks. I'd even stopped glancing up as I passed. She didn't move, just as never, and I could see the curve of her elbow.

I stopped and hooked my fingers in the screen. It was night and dim, but I could always tell.

It's hard not to know about things like this, the way you can't help what you feel.

They had a general-population stageshow last Saturday night. Let me tell you about this:

About 8o'clock we all went down,

dopies foaming at the mouth and running like madmen. Even hacks hid behind things to get out of the way. Then we got down to the auditorium where you had to sit 900seats back if you didn't have somebody strike out ahead of you and snatch off a couple of seats. Sometimes dopies got to fighting about that.

Same madripping noise here,

but I found George, the guy from the group, holding a seat for some guy who didn't showup, so I took it.

When I sat down, the lights were starting to dim behind the big funkdirty curtains of the widestage,

and guys were beginning to bust open potatochip and popcorn bags. The buzz went down a bit.

Then the broads came, and there was almost absolute silence:

2hacks stood at the EXITstairs at each end of the stage.

The broads all sat in the balcony, a storyhigh above us, sitting reluctantly at the 2matrons' snappy biddings, blowingkisses and mouthing words,

and there was Sonja, I saw when I turned around. But she didn't see me, hard as she strained looking over the crowd.

Then the lights went out.

'Goodevening, ladies and gentlemen,' 2loudspeakers said, 'my name is Whim and I'd like to introduce myself and our show to you tonight, but not before I tell you how I got the name I just told you, because I don't wantchu to think I'm an accident or anything. It's just that my old lady didn't have time to name me, so she gave the job to my older brother who had a hole on the inside of his nose. My name is *Will*iam.'

The band slammed in and the curtains parted, and Whim, a shortred man, pigeontoed over to his organ at stage right and struck the ComingChord: It was a bluesmarch that sounded original, and it was very angry,

the way Whim slashed at his 2keyboards. The band, 3headed totempoles of 15 and a drummer sittinghigh on a special podium, was infected with Whim's fury, and everybody couldn't help but arrive right on time.

The music was excellent, but all the dopies started grumbling after a fewbars about

'Bring on the bitches,'

and you missed both the tenor and alto solos because of their complaining.

'*Dame las putas!*' some fool screamed on the Spanishside.

But finally the band intro was over, and they struck up a Latin theme for a littlegray girl in blacktights and a curly haired little Oyea I've seen chasing faggots in the hallway.

All the dopies started stomping their heels on the floor when they imagined they saw her crack in a spin. The broads upstairs raised almost as much hell. Guys were snorting and pounding seats all around me.

'What the hell is this?': I turned to George.

'What?' he said with real curiosity.

'All this hollerin and screamin and shit. What's the matter with um?'

'I guess they just doin time, man.'

'Yeah, theirs and everybody else's.'

'This the 1st time you ever been to 1 of these conshows?'

'Yeah, but I think I'm gonna take a raincheck.'

'Oh, you can't leave now,' he said. 'The hacks have locked the doors.'

'You mean I can't get up and go back to my unit?'

'Not after the show starts. You just gotta tough it out.'

'Awman, shit.'

Now a number of Oyea and blackbroads, with 1 white, came out to do an ensemble thing, but their timing was all off,

and 1 of the Oyea broads looked like somebody'd slammed her right in the middle of her back with a sledgehammer 1 time.

They all had on blacktights with little crepe balletskirts, and they stiffassed it around up there for I'll bet 20minnits.

But the dopies around me seemed to be all out of their minds in paroxysms about what they saw;

they were kicking their heels and screaming and completely insane with delight.

'This Player'll take Miss Puerto Rican Sunset,' Barry Guyse screamed a few rows ahead of me.

'It gets kind of frightening,' George said next to me.

'You ain't kiddin.'

'But after you do almost a pound here, like me, you get so you can stand it.'

'All I wanna know is, What's wrong with um?'

'I figure it's the only way they get a chance to come out of themselves,' he said. 'Dopefiends are really very passive people. The doctors try to say it's the other way round, but that's a fraud.'

A tall lightskinnedguy came on to do a very lovely tenor solo,

and Lomo did a nice 16bars,

but all the dopies grumbled upstairs up the right EXITside to the men'sroom, and that gave the rest of us a chance to listen.

But they all stampeded back when they heard the theme change. This time it was a skinnylegged little blackgirl in a verynice blackdress and veryred lips who tried to do a ballad, but the dopies sucked around on their tongues so slobberingly you couldn't hear what she sounded like.

Then uptempo: A guy who'd become Little Junior's successor,

till the dopies got tired and screamed up at him to get the hell off the stage. It was mostly his own Washington friends.

Now that funnyformed troupe came back, and the dopies couldn't be restrained. The broads had changed clothes behindstage and now they wore filmylittle slavegirl suits.

I sat in the din for a longtime trying to figure it out,

but the answer didn't come to me till muchlater, long after it was over and everybody was bubbling back to the units,

and I didn't hate them as much.

I was out for a little feening with the MessengerFolio 1 Tuesdaynoon, and I'd just passed a group of broads returning to the Barn at the precise moment I made the right turn toward the elevators past CenterControl,

when I ran into Robert Leroy Trent facetoface.

We could only stand there staring at each other like 2statues in some freak of a Roman's garden. My hands leaped out involuntarily, I guess, toward his heart, but I had no control over them, and the psychiatric aide from the Shootinggallery who accompanied him couldn't figure out the gesture, and stood frozen and stark in the same way as we2.

I stopped breathing.

Trent is a dumpy sloppylooking blackman with a receding hairline and a moustache like a plucked chicken's ass. His teeth are small, even and white.

I made myself move away, watching him as they passed. He kept looking over his shoulder. The only thing changed about him were his clothes; now he was wearing conpants too small for his fatass, and a white USNtunic.

Mother Gish was watching me suspiciously from the front door, a puffed little glob in governmentgreen,

so I turned left at the elevator and followed the other2 down to CenterControl where they turned right for the dispensary and I turned left down the hallway to UT.

My heart was pounding like I'd been sledged in the chest.

Tamerlane was hanging out front when I got back. 'I hear Bob Trent come in today.'

But I didn't say anything, and went into the office to throw the bag up on the radiator and go out just as Pepper called me from the desk where he was relieving Joe Antman.

I went into my office and sat there breathing very hard until Pepper came busting in, claiming I'd ignored him.

'That's hard to do.'

'Didn't you hear me holler?'

'Yeah, I heard you.'

'Well, that meant you were suppose to see what I wanted.'

'Okay, whaddayou want?'

Pepper squinched his eyes up. 'You better come into the office.'

I got up and followed him in to where he sat down and began sternfacedly to write me a pass.

Before he tore it off the pad he looked up and said,

'Boy, you gonna have to do somethin about your attitude.'

'Maybe you got some suggestions.'

'The ones I got,' Pepper said, 'they wouldn't go along with.' He snatched the pass off when I didn't say anything. 'This is to see Cappin Koyle, and you better get down there to see him rightaway because he's been waitin on you.'

'What does he want?'

'I don't know, but you better get down there and find out. Maybe he wants to give you some suggestions about your attitude.'

Tam still stood by the UTgate when I came out.

'I hear Bob Trent come in today,' he said.

'That's the 2nd time you said that.'

'That's the 1st time you answered.'

'What's so important about it?'

He hung 1 bigfoot in the bars. 'Well, everybody's heard about Bob Trent the Informer. The feds send him down every 6months or so, so he can clean up for more jobs.'

'Yeah, I've heard about him.'

'He's busted a lot of people, ya know. He's even got a few guys in here right now, and he just got through bustin 4people in Chicago.'

'Yeah, I know all about the bastard.'

I went on down the hallway, trying to figure how to handle what I knew was going to happen, and by the time I got down to the Headman Police's office, where his clamfaced clerk told me to wait outside for a minute, I had all my rage by the throat.

Captain Koyle's voice croaked out of proportion to his size and shape; I'd never seen him up this close before. He was a frog of a man with lizardcheeks, and he had long white hair that looked like some kind of vegetation.

'Siddown, boy.'

I sat next to his desk. The office was a long slant on the Westside of the building, with President Johnson's face looking down on us both.

'Wal.' He had my jacket there and was looking at it. 'You doin 5years for us, huh?'

'That's right, sir.'

He was chewing a cigar, a blackstub unlit. 'Ain't got much leff, I see; 10months more, maybe. Been to the hole once. But you wuz in the hole in our last institution Up Noff and you went to the 1 in Atlanta, which is not a very good attitude.'

'You can't deny I've had adjustment problems.'

'Wal, I'm here to tell ya you won't have none on the Farm becuz I won't hesitate to put disciplinary action on ya. And I'm tellin you like I tell any of the rest of ya.'

'I perfectly understand that.'

'I hope you do; this is a warnin about that.'

'Do I understand I'm being warned?'

'You understand right. We get a lot of you people who come in here Hot, and you know what I mean by that. It's our job to protect ya, whether you Hot or not, whatever you mighta done. Even if you might be stoolpigeons. You understand what I'm talkin about?'

'Yes, sir. You're talkin about stoolpigeons. Informers.'

'And you know the 1 I'm talkin about, becuz the grapevine has tole all about it by now, and you know I'm talkin about Bob Trent.'

'Bob Trent?'

The cigar looked like a big blackbutton in his mouth. 'Don't go playin the fool with me. It's all right here in this book on you: Bob Trent testified on you for the Government of the United States, and he has requested our protection from those of you here who he did his duty against.'

'Ohyes, sir, I do remember him now.'

'I thought that would influence your memory.'

'But I really don't understand. You can see how I feel about Mr. Trent: I didn't even remember his name. I doubt if I'd know him if I saw him now, since it's been a fewyears.'

'All that's a nicesoundin songndance,' Captain Koyle said, 'but I want you to put this interview on your mind anytime you might get the idea you got some accounts to settle with Bob Trent. We'll hole you absolutely responsible fah anything that happens to him.'

'Perish the thought.'

'You touch any government employee on a government reservation, be he a stoolpigeon or not, and you can get another 5years. It says here in your book that you Predisposed to Violence, and I want you to know that's somethin we ain't gonna tolerate.'

He chewed on his cigar and looked at me as though it were all over. 'You got anything to say?'

'Not a thing, sir.'

'All right, then. Ole Bob's just here for the Cure and won't be around but for only a couple of months, so it'd be wise for you to just stay clear of him, considerin the Goodtime and everything else you could lose if you made a ruckus.'

'You can be sure I won't make 1 of those, Captain Koyle.'

'All right, then. You can get on if you want to, 'less you got somethin else you wanna say.'

'Ohno, Captain Koyle. You've made everything so clear, there's nothing else to say.'

When I got back to UT

Tamerlane still had Bob Trent on the brain:

'He's a rat from the Old School,' Tam told me. 'An Entrapment Specialist. If somethin happened to him, the whole narco bureau'd be handicapped. I don't see why nobody kills him,'

which was 1 of the things that shook me for a second,

because I was trying to decide when and where to kill Bob Trent.

5

I happened to be standing by the downstairs window early 1 morning after Bob Trent came in,

watching the women going to work in the garment area through the windows of the basement floor, looking for Sonja,

when I saw Pepper go through some very suspicious changes.

Since he's a UThack, it's part of his job to go out in the morning, noon and evening, and lock off the grills as the women pass through.

Sometimes the broads take a longtime coming up,

and some of them stop off to rap with fingers through the windows of the upper landing or drop off Underground stuff they brought from the Barn.

This morning it was purely by accident I saw Pepper hook something in solidly behind 1 of the radiators

then he hustled on down to the grill at the Barn out of sight as the earlyleaving woman started coming upstairs.

She must've been the broad,

a ravenhaired little pinkthing,

but somewhere they'd gotten their signals crossed, and she passed by the place without knowing.

When the halls were cleared I went out and picked it up and locked myself in my office.

It was a bottle of haircoloring with an alcoholic content that was contraband around here, and a note on regular padpaper that I recognized as Pepper's handwriting. I sat down and lit a cigaret and made myself comfortable.

My Darling,

I have been verry worried since I didn't get you note the other day like I supposed to. But here is the thing you ask me to get so I bet this shows now how I love you becuase I could get a lot of truble out of this. You say that you are goig to signed out well I want to tell you that I will have a place reddy when you come to town so you dont even have to worrie about that. You know I love you. Just you hole on to your end and I will mind. Just dont you worrie that I will do what I say and I will bringe the earrings next time.

YOUR SWEET LOVEDED ONE

It seemed like sciencefiction.

I hooked the note in the falsebottom of a book I kept

and put it back on my shelf, and the rightleg of my metal desk has no bottom in it and is big enough for me to shove the bottle right in the socket. It's too heavy to move if you're just fooling around, and they didn't make shakedowns on this side like the East 1.

At lunch I was watching him again,

and I saw when the broad went past him alone, and I saw them say something to each other;

then Pepper's face got kind of pale with panic and he stopped what he was doing to run over to the radiator and rustle all behind it in a frantic way.

As he turned around stricken with fear,

he happened to see my face watching him from the other side.

Pepper went out of hisway to be friendly,

but I always nutted on him.

But 1 day I needed supplies out of the storeroom, and Joe Antman wasn't around, so

I had to get Pepper to open it up for me.

'I don't see why you workin so hard.' He grinned. 'You could let that staffingstuff go over till tomorrow.'

'Yeah, but I'd still have to do it tomorrow.'

'There's no sense in workin the hell out of yourself.'

It was about 2o'clock, and nobody was around: most

unassigned guys were On Call and the rest were down to the gym or the afternoon Commissary.

Pepper followed me right into my office, but I turned and stared at him.

'I'm tryin to get this work done, Mr. Smith.'

'I won't get in your way.' He grinned. 'Just stand around a minnit. Just ain't got nothin else to do.'

'I could tell you what to do.'

'I bet you could,' he said in a sly way, something like the way faggots get coy.

'If I did you'd only put me in the hole for it.'

'Listen,' he said sorrily, 'I'm so sorry about that; I don't know how to tell you. I hope you don't hold it against me.'

'I'd be somekinda freak if I didn't.'

'You just go right ahead if you want to; don't let me bother you.'

'But you do bother me; I have no control over it.'

'Well, I always figured,' he said philosophically, 'that a man ought to let go those kind of feelins.'

'What are you tryin to tell me?'

'Well, mainly that a man shouldn't hold grudges, because of the way it makes you feel inside.'

'Who do you think you're talking to?': He flinched a bit when I said it.

'Why, I'm talkin to you, who do you think I'm talkin to? There's nobody in here but me and you.'

'Just what is it you're tryin to tell me, man?'

'Why is it you have to think I'm tryin to tell you somethin?'

'I hate to think I can't even communicate with *you*.'

'Awnaw, it's probably the way you feel against me.'

'Me feel against you? Because of that holeshit?'

He tried to look remorseful. 'That, and maybe other stuff I can't remember havin made a mistake about with you.'

'It don't fit, you havin a guilt complex about me.'

'Well, my Daddy always said,' Pepper said, 'that The Worst of Us Are Innocent and the Best of Us Are Guilty.'

'At least your oldman had a clue.'

'You can believe that.'

Then I sat down at the typewriter and tried to nut on him, but he wouldn't cut it loose:

'You know, you fixed this place up rightnice since Pineapple left.' Then he tried to giggle goodnaturedly. 'I gotta come in and give you a shakedown 1 day.'

'You probably did already': I turned and looked at him. 'But you won't be able to find it.'

His face fell. 'Find what?'

'Find whatever it is you'd be lookin for in here. You think I'd be foolish enough to put somethin where *you* could find it?'

'Oh.' He looked hard at me, not knowing how to tell whether I was serious or not. 'Ohwell, if I *did* happen to find some contraband or somethin in here, I think we'd be able to keep it in the family, right?'

'Whose family? yours or mine?'

'Ohhell,' he said, waggling his hand stupidly, 'you know, after that mistake we made about the hole, I'd just be inclined to be lenient with you if I caught you with anything.'

'Just as lenient as I'd be if I caught you doin something you weren't supposed to.'

He really didn't know what to make of that,

and he still couldn't tell whether or not I was the 1 who took him off. 'Well, you couldn't do anything to *me*, now.'

'I know all about it.'

I saw him tremble a bit. 'Know all about what?'

'Exactly what you're gettin ready to confess to me.'

'But I wasn't gettin ready to confess . . .'

'You might as well. I got the opinion government employees should be made to go to confession just like Catholics.'

'I don't see why you'd say anything like that,' Pepper said.

'Because you're all a dirty snakepit of bastards, and you can never run into the samekind twice. Now go ahead and bust me for that. That's what you really call Insubordination.'

'Well. Oh. Now, that really wasn't anything, and I'm not a good aide if I can't understand what makes a man say things.'

'Then you oughta have a good idea why I'm saying the things I am.'

It had gotten too much to believe in, so he
started backing. 'You and me oughta have a talk sometime, so we can really get to know each other.'

'I've already scheduled it. I'll let you know when.'

He was shook up when he left, but I could see the why's too clearly:

His whole future rested on a doofus note and a bottle of haircoloring,
and for the sake of these he could blow his job
all his children and his hayseed wife and home
and probably get 5years in Atlanta for bringing contraband onto a federal reservation.

He wasn't the only 1 here who was doing it:
It was just my luck to catch him.

6

The broads went on a rampage in the Barn last night:

they've got a lot more guts than their dopiecounterparts, and Security had to go over and subdue it, but it wasn't an easything for them to snap off.

It 1st started in the girls' messhall about food, somekind of garbage so sickening nobody ate the stuff.

All the guys did was roam around and grumble about the God Damned Dietitian,

but the girls started a riot on the spot. Security was so stupid they thought it was a fight because a couple of the women got cut on the edges of trays. When they finally got them all muscledback to the Barn

the riot continued.

All the matrons ran for cover,

but somebody called out the GoonSquad, who, all4, look exactly what they're called. But they didn't live up to the name, because 2 got seriously hurt and a jasper cut 1 on the arm with a bottle,

a whiskeybottle.

That's when everything got closed off like Red China. They called in extraduty forces and gave the whole Barn a shakedown.

I don't know whether it's true or not, but this is what Doug told me they found

the next day:

2fifths of OldGrandad

amphetamines and heavy tranquilizers, the CIBA kind

2 bottles of Chanel Number5 (you can *drink* perfume)

and a footlong dildo attached to a sanitarybelt; it had a core of steelwool, an outside of foamrubber,

and was covered allover with 6Trojans someone took the courage to count.

When Bob Trent came into UT

I pretended to nut out on him completely. He didn't know what to make of it. They kept him on the 1st floor next to the office because of his rat status, and you could always find him in the office sucking up to Joe Antman and Pepper and drinking the coffee they brewed up everyday.

Trent had a limp, and was infirm in many ways from using bad stuff. His hands were swollen like hockey gloves, and twitched all the time. I watched everything he did very closely.

There were 2 otherguys he'd busted out of Chicago who were doing nickels here,

but they all3 walked around together just as cozyasyouplease.

Everytime he got a pass from Joe Antman or Pepper to go down to the Recreation area, I'd get the bag and follow him down the hall, staying well back of his

hippityhop.

He was always rapping with guys, and he was on excellent terms with all the known rats in the joint. There used to be a floor in the hospital during the early 50s where they kept all the informers isolated, but now

since there's a taint of informer on every dopefiend

they've opened the whole hospital up to the trend.

Trent always wound up in the Chapel, which was usually empty during the day, where he sat around attacking the organ with big blockchords while he sang spirituals with another informer friend, a twisted little blackwisp of man. They were getting ready for Captain Koyle's group.

I could watch them simply by pulling the Chapel door open a little. I kept thinking about the toilet at the rear of the stage, and how quiet everything was, with little traffic, during this part of the day. There was only 1 hack on the whole basement floor, and he was down near the laundry and exit to the storeyard.

I'd already figured out 1 way to do it.

2days later

the guy had nerve enough to come into my office and plop down exhaustedly in the extra chair.

He caught me off guard, and I trembled a bit.

'Don't you see the sign on the door?'

'OhGod,' he said in that slimygenteel voice that made me think of the night he'd set me and Joyce up. 'I've just been walking *all* over, I'm so tired.'

'Get outta here.'

'Ohman. I don't see why you feel like that. Why don't we let bygones be bygones?'

'You're pressin me. Get the fuck out of here.'

'You know how it is with the feds, what a slave they make outta ya.'

I turned around to face him: 'I'm a ½second away from putting an awful hurting on your ass.'

Fear flashed in his eyes and twitched his mouth. 'Waittaminnit, waittaminnit. I never had no hard feelings for you when that thing went off. It was pure entrapment – I asked *you* to go make the Sale for me. Any good lawyer could beat that.'

'Mine was federally appointed.'

'But they cut your old lady loose, didn't they, when you took all the weight?'

'That ½second was up 5seconds ago': I stood up, and he jerked up from the chair.

'Don't do nothin, now,' he begged me.

'I won't be able to help myself.'

'All right, I'm goin,' he said, backing out. 'But I want you to know it wasn't my fault.' He tried to smile before he left. 'You know what the Game is, man.'

The only thing that hurt after he'd gone was

I *did* know what the dopegame was.

My Dearest Nephew:

Please do find enclosed another $5 dollars which should help you with the things that need to be done. Im sorry to be so short, but you know what it is when you are alone *and dont have anyone but yourself. This is why you and me should try to stick much closer than we have in the past. There is really no one else but you and me. I guess this sounds churchified like you say, but God meant for us to be together since he took everyone else away from us, like your mother Rosiland and your daddy Jim. Jim and me always understood each other while he was alive and Im very happy about that. And that's the reason for you and me to try to make something of the family we are. I know your moods better than anybody. Jim used to leave you with me when you were small and him and Rosiland was on the offs. You have always been a strange child. But so was Jim a strange man. No one knows a brother like his sister, or knows her brother's son just as well. I've watched you go through the reform school and prisons with not a breath of peace until you became a man, and even now you don't have any peace. I've taken your child in as my own and I love her more than I love life because I know that even out of evil and pain something good has to come. There's nothing you can do that will surprise me, and I yearn for the day when you are tired of trying to fight life. You have always blamed yourself and Joyce about little Joye because she came into the world twisted, but these things are always an act of God and Joyce would tell you the same thing if she were alive just like she used to tell me when she was living. Joye is healthy and getting along just fine with me. Her legs will get their last treatment next month. Your friend Douglas helped out a lot with that.*

Please tell me how you feel about this new place you're in, and try to rest your mind and soul as well as you can. Please write me more often, dear. Except for Joye I have no one else in the world but you.

Your loving aunt,
CYNTHIA

I tore it up like I do all her letters.

In the dark
from my bedroom windows
I can look across the nighthills and black traceries of roads snaking toward a towered bluelight in the farfar distance.
I get a funny feeling when I watch it. Like the shutters of my mind are open in a wind, and I can't close them.
This light I see is cold, like the inside of a freezer where the carcasses of animals are stored,
and it makes my very eye go cold inside, as though I am about to go blind.
Sometimes I wait till everyone on the tier is dead with night; then I watch this light, this frighteninglight, till my eyes grow dim as my insides,
and the only thing left in the world to do is sleep.

6ε1/3

Thursday came again

but this was the day my plan was supposed to go off.

I alerted Matthew in the messhall at noon;

he sat on 1 side and I on the other, and I wrote to him on my fingers while the dopies screamed like madmen:

'I plan it for after our set. We all come out at the sametime.'

I looked over to see some rat reading my letters, so I froze it out.

In the corridor we synchronized again, but I must've acted kind of nervous, because he said,

'You don't have to test me. I know what to do.'

Then I went back to UT and stripped and got in a shower, then shaved and brushed my damp head hard with Royal Crown. Then I put on a nicelittle sweater Doug had given me,

with nothing underneath my congrays but a jockeystrap.

I had irresistible images about her and how she looked under her clothes, and the way all of her would fit and feel in my arms, andGod the way her mouth would taste, I could taste it,

astringently warm with the smell of what she'd eaten for lunch, lips like grapes that wouldn't burst no matter how hard you sucked them, and the raw red ribbon of slick warm tongue:

I got dressed quickly and went right downstairs.

'You look like you goin to roll in the hay,' Joe Antman snickered when I went past the office, and I had a start of heart for a moment.

But he couldn't know anything.

I went on down to CenterControl with my pass,

and for some reason there were an unusual number of cops out this afternoon. I didn't hesitate in going by.

Then up on the elevator to Branch-5. Mother Wallers presided. 'Just have a seat overthereplease.'

And I sat, and strangely enough I was the only guy who'd arrived yet. But the wallclock said I was late. Mr. Wallers didn't give up a clue, only grinned and vamped outrageously since I was the only guy here, and I fully expected him to ask me to run back with him to the men's john so he could give me a quick blowjob.

Then the guys started trooping in, and I got hungup in a conversation with George about something, then

Matthew came in with Reverend Kleague, and everybody got up to split. But I didn't move. Her group hadn't come yet.

Mr. Wallers didn't notice me for about 5minnits, gossiping on the phone with some fagfriend who worked over on the Shootinggallery. But he jumped when he finally turned.

'Oh. Are you still here? But didn't you belong to Reverend Kleague's group?'

'I had a cramp and couldn't move.'

'Oh,' he said in distress. 'Is there anything I can do?'

'No, I think if I sit here another minnit it'll be all right.'

'You know, cramps are not to be played with.'

'It's not me who's playing with them.'

'Nevertheless, you can't be too careful,' he said sagely.

'You couldn't argue with that idea.'

'Is it in the rightleg?' he said, looking.

'No, the leftone.'

'Your muscles seem to be all bunched up.'

'No, I seriously think it's getting all right.'

'But they need some sort of manipulation, don't they?'

'My muscles? Yeah, I think I'll manipulate them a little. Awyeah, that feels good. They're gettin better all the time.'

'Just be careful with yourself.'

'Oh, I won't hurt me.'

'You know,' he said, 'we're sworn to report all injuries as per the Manual.'

'Well, I don't think you could call this an injury, Mr. Wallers, it's just a cramp.'

'Why, it's the same thing, I'll have you know. Anything that hurts the body is an injury. We're not going to argue about definition while you're in pain.'

'But the pain is going away.'

'You've *had* it; that's the important thing.'

'It's practically all gone right now.'

'You can't lightly brush off attacks like this.'

'There's not much else you can do if it's not attacking anymore.'

'You're *sure* you feel all right? Do you want me to take your temperature? I have a thermometer.' But I thought the only thermometer he could have would be a rectal 1, so I said No.

'This could be some kind of virus,' he said thoughtfully.

'Virus?'

'Well, there's always an interconnection of symptoms, you know, and this is probably just 1 of those, your cramp.'

'I hope it isn't 1 of those.'

'1 must make the best of what 1 has.' He smiled gently.

That's when the broads came. Sonja was out in front expectantly, wearing a tight, impractical little flowered skirt, and fear lightspeckled her dark eyes when she looked at me.

Mr. Wallers' attitude changed abruptly as the matron delivered the group to his desk. 'Since your cramp's so corrected, you can go right down to Reverend Kleague's group.'

I could only tell her, brace her, ease her fear,

with my eyes,

but I think she understood. I'd gone over the whole plan with her through the Underground after I got her penciled layout of the women'sroom directly behind Mr. Wallers' desk,

so there really shouldn't be any problems.

I got up and went on down to the group. All the guys were sitting around not saying anything, and Reverend Kleague looked as though he were suffering from the crabs.

'Well,' he said, 'I'm glad to see you've arrived. We've been waiting on you.'

'You shouldn't ever wait on me.'

I went over and sat down facing Jimmy DeSoto.

'What's happening?' he asked me.

'Naturally nothing.'

I tried to see what Matthew was thinking, but conversation suddenly bubbled up, and all I could see was how pink the rims of his eyes looked. But I didn't take that for a sign.

'It might sound sometimes like I'm riding this joint to you,' George said, 'but it's only because it's such a God Damn Fuckedup Thing, I mean the way people have been deluded about it.'

Reverend Kleague rolled his eyes in a humorous way, 'Here we go again,' he despaired.

'But just look at the lie of it,' Matthew said, excited with an idea. 'The sexual quality is the big thing. Everywhere you go there's sex. You see it on the policefaces everywhere you go. They need to get hooked up worse than we cons do.'

Anotherguy, with eyes like Nietzsche, and very smooth black skin, said:

'There's sex goes on around here all the time. But it's not the cons coppin; it's the staff. My roommate walked into some funnyshit when he made a records' delivery over at the photography shop yesterday. That's where most of the broads work.'

'That's no rumor, Jim,' George said. 'Mr. Hazel, who runs that place, has been screwin the broads for years. Everybody in the joint knows it, even Mossler, because broads have been coming out of that place all knockedup.'

'That's almost inconceivable,' Reverend Kleague said. 'Certainly nothing like that can exist and nothing be done about it.'

Matthew said: 'You mean, does Washington know? Naw, they don't know. Mossler hides everything like that. Nobody wants to upset a perfect game. Broads are always getting knockedup around here from the staff. How do you think all the contraband comes in here? It comes through the Barn. The women give It up, and staff brings it in.'

'Anyway, what my roomie saw was Hazel split into the women'sjohn directly behind 1 of the Spanish broads.'

'Maybe he suddenly felt the urge.' Somebody else laughed.

'But I can hardly believe that,' Reverend Kleague said. 'I know Mr. Hazel, and I'm sure he'd never dream of doing something like that. He's a respected citizen in town and has a fine home with 3children.'

'He's probably a Rotary member too': Everybody looked at me.

'It's those mostrespected guys who do most of the dirt around here,' Matthew said. 'This joint couldn't stand any kind of investigation. But federaljoints don't get investigated; everybody who works in them cooperates to coverup any funnybusiness, because it's *their* institution, and it's only the dirtiest kind of federal goon who would rat on his buddies unless he could get kicked upstairs if he did.'

'But, Matthew, listen,' Reverend Kleague said in a holy way, 'what you're saying is, The whole complex is evil. But we can all see that it's not completely so. There're goodthings to come out of the hospital; there has to be, because there's at least 1 true person working here who really *does* give a damn about what's right and wrong, and *does* dedicate himself to the drugaddict. What about Dr. Cambridge, for instance?'

'We're not talking about him,' Matthew said; 'we're talking about the other hundreds of purebastards who work here who nullify everything good Dr. Cambridge can do.'

'He has colonel rank just like Mossler,' George said, 'but he doesn't do a thing unless he talks with Mossler 1st.'

'I don't see why anybody thinks the hospital is set up to cure anybody,' Jimmy DeSoto said. 'It's been here so long it's like a city. Cities never cure themselves unless something like a volcano erupts on them.'

Reverend Kleague was caught again. 'Matthew, did you consider what I said about the Patients' Council? If the hospital is as evil as you say, repairs can only be initiated from your side. As a council member you'd have every right to protest. How could they stop you? You complain about the food and lack of psychiatric care and the Commissary gyps and the phony shots from officers, and things like the sex scandals, but you've got to complain in a way everyone can hear you.'

'You could fry me for lambchops if I got up and hollered about things like that,' Matthew told him.

'Then do it as a *group*,' Reverend Kleague said. '1 agitator is no problem, but it's a little more difficult to remove an organized group of demonstrators.'

'Not if you have firehoses and policedogs': They all looked at me again.

'Maybe you'd want to sponsor us as prospective council members to Captain Koyle,' Matthew said. 'That's who runs the group.'

'I certainly would,' Reverend Kleague said firmly. 'I'll do it today, as a matter of fact. I'm supposed to see Captain Koyle later today.'

'It won't do any good,' Jimmy DeSoto said; 'he's gonna say no. The council is his rubberstamp, and it runs everything around here.

'Listen,' Reverend Kleague said, 'most of you guys have a little over a year to do yet. You're all 5year sentences for precisely the same charge, Sale and Possession. Now, this means you've all got something in common, and you had it even before you came to this room. George said something not long ago about me selecting you. But, you see, you've really all selected your*selves.* I'm not talking about individual idealism or anything like that, Matthew, because that's an abstract you're always pouncing on. What I'm saying is, The power to Reform rests in a common corporate cell.' Then he smiled nicely. 'Nobody can say Lenin was wrong about that.'

Matthew and I timed ourselves coming out. The Reverend was shaking hands all around and looking forward to next week,

but me and Matthew hung around, talking with him about inanities, until he got hungup on some sort of solipsist theory about God, and I

got kind of worried I'd miss Sonja. She knew what she was supposed to do, anyway.

Finally, we came out, but we had to give the Rev time to get on out himself. He had an appointment, he said. He was in a hurry. Smile. Shake. Byenow.

We trailed him out, some distance behind, and I was glad to see through the windows another of the constant storms around this place, coming,

and everything was dark in the corridor; no 1 had thought to cut on the houselights yet.

Her group was there waiting for the matron; I could see dimly the short flowered skirt. And she saw me immediately. She got up and went over to Mr. Wallers' desk and told him she had to go to the john, which he handled keys for,

and she looked over his shoulder at me as he let her in. Now.

Matthew went on ahead of me, timing himself to arrive just as Mr. Wallers sat down. More dark it became in the corridor. A Spanishbroad in a tight blackandwhite-striped dress and white 5inchheels seemed to be watching me as I moved silently.

Through slowmotion I saw Matthew pull Mr. Wallers' attention with something about the fishbowl behind his desk, and how he had some of his own fish over in the unit. Which made the guy break up in all kinds of smiles.

'Oh, how wonderful,' he said. 'But you do know about blue fantails, don't you? Their sexhabits, I mean?'

Sonja was just closing the door to the john behind his desk. No, but she mustn't close it.

I still moved darkly. My throat was tight. I saw the way her hip and thigh and 1 longleg disappeared into the john.

Mr. Wallers nearly turned in an instant, but Matthew had him very uptight, like a magician or a torero,

and I began to think again about how she would feel in my arms, and my body against and inside her, and how my hips would move against her and me upfront stir her pussyliquids. The sense of it hurt my heart. The Spanishbroad still watched me.

I've never liked time; I realized that then. The way it imposes.

Why should anything take *time*? It's like the funkiest monkey in the world has a hammerlock on you.

And just as I had the knob in my hand the houselights came on all over, but it was perfect for the moment, everybody blinking,

and I twisted the knob, and as I twisted the knob

I felt the most furious surge of anger I've ever felt in my entirelife, and it was as though I'd suddenly generated all the uncovering light with its brilliance.

I'd instructed this fantastically stupid woman not to close it.

The God Damned Door was locked.

The Three Part

1

I was sitting in my office

trying to figure out some things about myself, and it was a Saturday, early in the morning, about 10, I think,

when a moment later Dr. Cambridge came around and peeked in, just after I'd recapped the dream I'd had the night before. To myself:

It was my dead mother sitting on something like a throne, smiling at me with the big marvelous falseteeth she'd done daywork to buy from some exorbitant dental shyster where we lived in the slums, and she had 1 hand held out,

like Justice,

but she never said a word to me, only grinned in a stupid dead way, waxfigured in my memory,

and I woke up very angry because I'd almost cried.

'Well, hello there,' Dr. Cambridge said, cutting in.

'I didn't know you guys worked on Saturday': He saw something in my eyes when I looked up, and gave a little start.

'Psychiatrists are like mailmen.' He laughed.

'Salesmen, is more like the word.'

He came in and sat down in the other chair, and I turned around aggressively with both legs widely parted in almost sexual invitation, because I was getting a little drugged that I couldn't drive this guy off and it seemed the only other way to do it was insult him.

'Nice little place you've got here,' he said, looking around.

'It's not nice. It's a cell.'

His eyes got wide on me. 'I'll bet it's an improvement over the others you've been locked up in.'

'A cell is like a whore: nothing changes in it except the shape of the key.'

'I ought to tell you I wouldn't be so interested in you if it weren't for Sonja. She says you haven't written her in a week.'

'And I ought to tell you that's our problem, not yours.'

'You *could* be working an injury on her,' he said warningly.

'Not in precisely the manner I'd like to.'

'I sincerely believe Sonja's in love with you.'

'That should set some sort of precedent for Sonja.'

He looked at me quietly for a long time after that. Then he said suddenly, 'Listen, would you consider undergoing therapy with me?' And before I could say fuckno, he added, 'And Sonja? You know she's due to go home soon.'

So, in a flash, I decided Yes, because this would give me another shot at her, but I didn't tell him so, and I stared at the grinningyoung picture of John Ciardi a long time before I answered.

'Why would you need me for therapy?'

'Because it would help Sonja,' he said. 'I don't usually make a practice of pairing couples, unless they're married and are volunteers, but something stands out about you2.'

'Probably our ignorance.'

He smiled and nodded. 'I know you're suspicious of me.'

'I'm suspicious of everybody.'

'I know that too. But you're not as cynical as you'd like everybody to believe.'

'There you go with that religious shit again.'

'Religion of any type isn't wrong. What've you got against it?'

'God, primarily.'

'Oyes, Oyes,' he said, and smiled, and I started feeling violent about him. 'Do you mind if I smoke? You don't smoke, do you?'

'Only occasionally.'

'You smoke pot?'

'By the pound.'

'Ah.' He lit up. 'But it's too soon to ask you that question.'

'I probably wouldn't answer it any God Damn Way.'

'Listen,' he said. 'Have you screwed Sonja yet?'

I got took back. 'They got laws against that kind of thing, even when you ain't locked up.'

'No, I just wondered. Her feeling for you is very sexual, I've noticed. I wondered whether you knew her in the World and whether or not you'd been to bed together.'

'What would that get you if I said Yes?'

'A better understanding, obviously.' His eyes got very blue. 'We're not going to completely fake this thing. I believe Sonja is at the stage where she wants to reject drugs once and for all, but you came along and involved her with another factor. I don't know about you. I think you might be tired of drugs too, but I'm more concerned about Sonja than I am you, let me admit, because you're an independent factor. But in order to help my patient I've got to know both of you, together, if it's possible for the willing 1 to be saved.'

'What's that got to do with me fucking Sonja?'

'That should be obvious,' he said blinkingly. 'Sex is control, you know that – you've used it before.'

'Not recently.'

He flickered ashes on my floor, so I gave him an embarrassing ashtray.

'Thanks.' He puffed once more, then put it out. 'But you know what I'm talking about; you're not ignorant.'

'Not right at this moment.'

'And you know what I'm saying.'

'Of course I do. You're saying you want me to help you assume complete control over my woman.'

'Not in exactly those terms—'

'Then you want my woman to help you assume complete control over me.'

'That hadn't entered my mind at all.' He looked at me again for a longlong time. 'You know what you're doing to Sonja; it's all very calculated. You've filled her mind with your words; then suddenly you cut it off, everything.'

'Have you been reading my letters to her?'

'No, I've never seen them, but she's told me about them. And I could've seen them, you know, simply by having your mail sent up to my office.'

'You wouldn't care for the ethnic jokes I write.'

'You still haven't answered my question.'
'What was it?'
'Whether or not you'd laid Sonja.'
'You haven't given me reason enough to answer that question. Ask Sonja.'
'She'd only say what you told her to.'
'I really don't giveashit what she says.'
'Were you in the army?' he said, on another track.
'You've read the records. You know. The only service I've done is institutional.'
'I just wondered – in your *own* words. The opinions of others are usually very unreliable.'
'Is my telling you this part of what you call a Better Understanding?'
'Yes, part.'
'Well, okay, then; well, I was ready for that Korean shit, but I was a dopefiend then and the army didn't take them. But you've got all that down, and you know all that, so I'm beginning to wonder whether you think I'm some kinda trick.'
'Of course I don't.'
'And you've read all that other stuff. About my wife Joyce. You've got the whole package. Either you buy it or you don't.'
'The decision is up to you.'
'Then you buy it cold. You can't cure me of anything no matter how much you know. You keep after me this way I'll think *you're* the 1 who's fuckin Sonja.'
'I knew you'd probably say something like that.'
'If you knew I'd say something like that, then you know what I'm about to say, and that's That I Believe This Whole Psychiatric Bag Is A Bunch of Bullshit. But it's a plot, and I can't help digging plots.'
'I don't think you really believe anything like that,' he said. 'You've read enough to know better.'
'No, I've *lived* enough to know better. I've seen enough of The Murphy and Drag and The Knot to know a hip congame when I see it go down. Nobody wants to give you anything for nothing.'

Now he relaxed and leaned back and began to waggle his elbows in that funny way he had.

'You *like* living alone with these convictions, don't you?'

'I wouldn't share them with anyone.'

'I wonder how many of them are purely tones of self-pity . . .'

'Only the ones in B-flat.'

'Up till now, I've noticed, you've had a lot of trouble doing time.'

'It's funny I never thought so.'

'The time in Attica, and Rikers Island: you spent a lot of time in the hole.'

Then I stood, but the office was so small I couldn't move away in it:

'Life is a hole. Nobody's heard me complain about it.'

'But you *do*,' he said, looking at me. 'Everything you say or do is a complaint.'

'The only thing is, you can never find the Complaint Department.'

'And the time in Atlanta—'

'That was the time the hacks came to the hole in umpire-suits to beat me up. My only complaint is, they didn't belong to the major leagues.'

I saw some unrelated pain come across his face

and it twisted me suddenly and gave my guts a turn. I got drugged with myself for talking so God Damn Much. It was only then I noticed I had been.

I found him smiling at me. 'You realized it, didn't you?'

'Realised what?'

'That we've been communicating.'

'No, that's just the expression I get when Nature calls.'

That pressed his Go-button. He stood up and stuck out his hand, but

I ignored it.

After a moment, he dropped it, but he was still smiling.

'Suppose I put you on call for next Thursday, at Sonja's time?'

'That's the time I go to a group, Reverend Kleague's group.'

'Oh. Well, we can arrange something. I think my schedule's clear at 2o'clock. We could have that hour together before you went into the Reverend's session. Is that all right with you?'

'It's your schedule.'

'Fine, then. I'll tell Sonja.'

'I haven't said I would yet.'

'Oh,' he said, and rubbed his bottom lip with a finger. 'Well, will you?'

'Maybe I will. It might help to break up the bit.'

'I'll take that to mean Yes, then.'

'You could also take it to mean No.'

'No,' he said. 'I'll take it to mean only exactly what you mean.'

I suppose it was the way I'd suddenly became sensitive to lights and shadows, and the way the texture of his paleskin seemed to reflect me in a kind of truth,

and the other things I'd done to drag him that gave me a sense of guilt:

But I hated the bastard for becoming a part of my life the way he had:

The whole bit fucked up the rest of my day.

2

I don't know how he managed it

but Reverend Kleague arranged to have the whole group sit down with the Headman Police, Captain Koyle, in his office at the main building the following Monday.

Somebody called my pass over the phone, and it took Joe Antman by surprise in the same way I was.

'Now you listen to me,' he said before I left. 'I don't know how you greased up these politics, but it's done now and we can't ignore that fact. You been doin time long enough to know how these things go. Koyle is a funny man, but he's fair – him and me come here at the same time on the same day lookin for jobs, and we got um. But he's a G-10 and I'm only a 5, so that tells you about his ambition. When you go over there, I don't want you to say *nothin.*'

'Nothin at all, Joe?'

'Right. You know how you are with your mouth. Sometimes things come out, and you don't even know they're comin out.'

'But I never say anything, Joe.'

'You're a God Damn Lie, so don't you try tellin me anything like that. Koyle can make it hard for you if you talk to him the way you do me. I'm from Alabama too, but I was so far back in the sticks I didn't see a blackman until I was 20years old.'

'I knew you were suburban, Joe, but that's ridiculous.'

'Now, just cut that shit out,' Joe said snappily. 'That's exactly what I'm talkin about.'

'Well, you don't have to worry. I've talked with this guy before.'

'But I am gonna worry,' he said in a way to make me feel warm inside. 'Because you're such a God Damn Dickhead about the way you think life oughta be.'

On the way over

I met George Prospectus in the hallway.

'Hi,' he said in a bleak way. I noticed he'd been chopping himself up again. 'I just came from my analyst.'

'You gotta watch sexhabits like that': But I could see he didn't dig.

'We see Dr. Uxeküll, my wife and I.'

'Ohman, I know that's a drag.'

'No, you're wrong – Uxeküll is very good. We get a lot out of him. He doesn't work from a Freudian aspect.'

'Naw, he's more outed the Mickey Mouse School.'

'I don't see how you can say that.'

'If you'll look around, you'll see they all have certificates of merit from the Walt Disney studio.'

'My God,' he said, looking at me hard, 'what's the matter with you?'

'I've had a sheltered life.'

'That's no reason to be so cynical about everything.'

'It's really happiness: I was raised in a Father Divine mission.'

'Ohell, you can't be serious about anything.'

'The last time I was serious about anything, I got a federal indictment out of it.'

Then,

dammit,

before I got past CenterControl, I ran into Doug, who had gotten to the place where he was looking out the sides of his eyes at me.

'What's happening, Killer?' he said.

'Nothin. Where're you on your way?'

'The meeting in Koyle's office. I see by the Callsheet that you're down too.'

'What're you doin, goin over?'

'Didn't you know I was a politician in this joint? Koyle don't move unless he talks to me 1st.'

We were there by that time. We had to go through the

main building once the guard had let us in, then down to 1 of the basement conference rooms. This was the biggest. It was laid out in fashionable and surprising style, complete with electricdoors that could cut the whole big square in 2 in soundproofed teeth.

All the guys were there

and some I didn't know but recognised as someone others had told me belonged to the Patients' Council, sitting around in plushlittle theatretype seats. At the front was a shinymahogany roundtable, where sat the Headman Police chewing his stub of a cigar in a peaceful way,

and Dr. Uxeküll, Dr. Cambridge, and 2blackguys, the chairman and vicechairman of the council.

Me and Doug sat down in the back.

Then the chairman stood after we were settled. 'Good afternoon, gentlemen.' He had a fine voice, wore redtinted hornrims over a big lushblack moustache. 'I think everyone knows everyone, but I'm Ralph Jefferson for those of you guys who don't. Well, at this time I would like to turn the meeting over to our sponsor, Captain Koyle.'

Reverend Kleague came in suddenly, looking a little winded. His purple hair had boiled up on his head. 'Sorry to be late.' He hurried up front and sat down next to Dr. Colman.

'Well,' Jefferson said, 'as I said before you came in, Reverend, I'm about to turn the meeting over to our sponsor, Captain Koyle. Captain Koyle?' He sat. Captain Koyle didn't even move. But in a moment, he belched, and it seemed like all the bones in his face had disintegrated:

'Wal, yall know,' he said, leaning forward with his elbows, 'that as sponsor of the Patients' Council group, I am very proud of it. A lot of things have been done by this group, and I like seein the attendance like I see here today, becuz it shows a lot of you people are innarrestin yourselves *in* yerselves. This is always a good thang to see.' I thought I saw heads bobbing up and down all around him. 'Now, I talked to Reveren Kleague about 2weeks ago about possibly havin those of yew people up here today who make up whut is said in the patientbody. I like meetin Complainers facetoface, becuz some of yew feel like the hospital ain't doin a goodjob about the way it does thangs around here. And that's why I'm here to listen atcha.'

He didn't say anymore, just kept sucking at that stub of cigar.

A lotta guys started looking at the tops of their shoes, nuttingout completely.

Jefferson stood up again, playing with a long yellow pencil with the point broken off. 'Well, thank you, Captain Koyle.' Then he looked around. 'Is there anybody else who wants to say something?'

Everybody was asleep.

Then Matthew suddenly popped up like a God Damn Fool and said, 'Yeah, I got something to say.'

Some guys had taken on fetal positions. All the acey-doosies and heavytalkers. Everybody dressed in his best, rakish pseudopimp colors.

'I was under the impression,' Matthew said, 'that this was supposed to be an open session before the council, but the council isn't fully represented. And I thought also we were supposed to air views, not complaints.'

'Well, it looks to me like that's exactly what we're doing,' Jefferson said. 'If you have a view to air, you go right ahead and air it.'

'Is this to be a frank and openmeeting?'

'Sure, it's going to be frank and open, because you can say anything you like.'

'That doesn't reassure me.'

'Then you're not listening.'

'Oh, I listen,' Matthew said, 'all the time I listen. And I see, too.'

'Those are things you can't always rely on.'

This was growing into some kind of fuckedup duel between these guys.

Onstage, Reverend Kleague broke in somehow and began

to set the scene. 'Thank you, fellows. I know a lot of you fellows *do* have a lot to say, in general. I think Captain Koyle will agree that Nothing is perfect.'

But Captain Koyle didn't look like he agreed.

'It's my feeling that the Patients' Council and the patient-body really should come together and get acquainted with each other. Because there are misunderstandings and complaints among you; I've heard them myself. The most constant is the 1 about food. Will anyone talk about that?'

Captain Koyle said, looking at us,

'Oh, they don't like the food, do they?'

'I've eaten so many carrots since I've been here,' Doug said to me, 'I feel like I'm in the middle of a rabbitfarm.'

'The Dietitian told me herself it had all the nutrunts anybody would ever need in a day,' Captain Koyle said. 'I think her menu is right delicious.'

'If you take away the potatoes,' Matthew said, 'what've you got left?' I knew him: I could see him reach his safety-whistle point. 'I notice next week's menu has pork on it 12times.'

'Has anyone else got something to say?' Jefferson said.

'Waittaminnit, I'm not done with what I want to say.'

'I'm sorry, Matt, but we have just so much time, and we'll have to get right around to someone else, so everybody gets a chance.'

Matthew looked at him hard; then he smiled and sat down, saying,

'Ohyeah. Yeah, I diggit.'

From then on it was the Reverend's show. Everybody stayed shut right up. Dr. Cambridge's face vanished and became a flatwhite pancake: I couldn't see anything there.

Dr. Uxeküll stood up to say something I still don't know what he meant, and announced he was taking over the female-unit as Doctor In Charge. All the guys were kind of drugged about this, because Uxeküll never made it a secret that he was against coeducational servitude, against the pink mail, and against the whole idea of women in general.

'Mark the end of Fraternization,' Doug said then.

And I could see by the looks of many confaces around me that they thought so too.

Then Dr. Cambridge stood in his wrinkled whitejacket: 'I know it's hard for you fellas to come right out and talk, on an initial meeting like this 1. But I think we ought to have more of them, so once or twice a month we can sit down and really hash over some of the problems in the hospital. And maybe we can put our heads together and come up with solutions. Most of you have got to remain here for some unspecified length of time; some of you will check out WDA. But the rest of you will be here for a while, and since you belong to allied sections of family units you've got to *live* as a unit. And that means 1guy's problem is everybody's problem. More than anything else, What narcotics is primarily is an antisocial disease.'

Then I dialed him out because he seemed to advocate everything that had been said by his cohorts, and I could look in his face and tell he was afraid.

Jefferson's hatchetman, the vicechairman, a blue-Banloned little blackguy with a penitentiary konk and features like the sharpeyed crows that eat garbage, sprung up and told us:

'The Patients' Council is proud of its achievements. They're a lot of those we have. You can take for example, the dance we got planned for you on MemorialDay in the gym. And Mr. Strainer, the gym director, is going to arrange for refreshments. This is only 1 of the things we accomplished.'

'And don't forget the ChristmasDance we had,' Jefferson prompted him.

'And don't forget the ChristmasDance we had in the gym last year – that was another of the things we did under the sponsorship of Captain Koyle.'

Captain Koyle sucked quietly at his cigarnub.

Then Jerfferson stood up again and expressed his thanks to all the honored guests Particularly Captain Koyle, and we got up and trooped our asses out of there just as we were supposed to,

but I heard junkies grumbling in a way they grumbled only when someone has viciously burned them for the last essential dollar.

2ε1/2

Matthew managed to slip past CenterControl 1night 2nights later when the women were putting on their volleyballgame for the entire population,

and come over to UT to see me.

Most of the guys were gone to the game, so my door was open. I don't know how he got past the evening hack, but when I looked up from reading *The Divine Comedy* he stood grinning in on me.

'What's happenin?' he said.

'Nothin. What's happenin with you?'

'Just thought I'd come over to rap for a minnit.'

'Yeah, well, that's all right with me. Come on in and sit down. You must've been Invisible Man to get way over here at this time of night.'

'Nobody pays attention when the broads are out. They got 200broads to look out for down in that gym, so that's naturally where all the heat is.'

'Sit down, man.'

'Yeah, thanks.'

'Want some coffee?'

'Well, yeah, if it won't put you out.'

'Justaminnit.'

I got 2plasticcups out of my bottom deskdrawer, and the pound of sugar I'd bought for a pack from an Oyea who worked in the messhall, a spoon, the Borden's Instantcream and 2cup pads to lay on the wing of my desk.

'Waittaminnit while I get some hotwater.'

I got some steaminghot from the mopcloset next door.

'You want much sugar?'

'2spoons is enough for me.'

I like mine sweet. We stirred up, the coffee smelling fictitiously brewed, but I couldn't help getting a groovy sense of freedom about it all.

'What brought you way over here tonight?'

'I guess you heard about the 2broads gettin busted down in the garmentshop this afternoon.'

'Naw, I haven't heard anything.'

'What? You're sittin right on top of all the news, man. Didn't you see the female Callsheet for tomorrow?'

'Naw, I didn't see that, either.'

'Well, let me be the 1st to tell you that your woman was hooked up in it. She got shot into the Barn with the other broads.'

'Sonja?'

'Yeah, but I don't think it was anything *she* did. I got an Underground from a friend who works with Sonja, and she said your woman just happened to be on the scene when the sexaction went off.'

'Then why'd they send her in?'

He shrugged. 'Material witness, I guess.'

'How'd all this shit go down? Sonja is short – I'd be very drugged if she lost goodtime about some dyke production.'

'1 of the matrons went down there on a run this noon after Prado Reyes' woman, and caught the broad going down on 1 of the ladysupervisors in the women's john. The matron got all turned around and ran upstairs to tell all.'

'They're writin better scripts than that around here.'

'No, man, that's exactly the way it went down.'

'Where the hell was Sonja?'

'Don't get excited. I told you your woman wasn't an accomplice – she just happened to be in the right place at the wrong time. It's Prado's woman, and the broad who was lookout for her, who're up tight, not to mention the supervisor.'

'What's gonna happen to her? the supervisorbroad?'

'Well, Mossler called her over for a chat, but he cut her loose with no action.'

'You mean she didn't blow her gig?'

'Am I talkin to a deadman? I said Mossler sent her right back on the job.'

'That don't sound to me like the correct kind of science': I sipped my coffee, trying to fix Sonja's position in the midst of truth.

'You oughta hear the hacks gossiping about it.'

'Yeah. It's somethin to say Wow about.'

We sat round, chewing it over for a while, and I was drinking too much coffee, I knew, to sleep that night,

while Matthew ran on about the evils of the joint and the way the broads are induced to give up cunt for contraband, and I got drugged about Sonja again, and said,

'Don't tell me anything about the image of a whore, my wife was 1. The way this shit happens here is the way it's supposed to. If you're gonna change it, it's not gonna be with Patients' Councils or any other God Damn Thing. Wait until you get to the world to shoot your mouth off about reform.'

'Ohshit,' he said, getting up, 'I can see how I'd get hung up here. I just wanted to tell you the news about your woman, and the fact that I put your name down on the twicemonthly meetings like the 1 we had with Captain Koyle.'

I called him a sonofabitch as he left.

Sonja came by Underground early the next morning. She stashed a note for me, I could see, in the underground passage that led to the garmentshop. It was Out of Bounds, but I made a creep down the stairway to pickup, and read it later in the privacy of my office:

Dearest Daddy,

I know you are bound to have heard the latest, but I want you to know that all the vicious things are not true. I was just squatting on the toilet when I heard all this head action going down in the next stall. I didn't dream it was Miss Ann and her sweet girl taking off. Please don't think I did, because I didn't. But I got busted right along with everybody else, and I didn't get cut until I ran it to Dr. U., who you know is not easy to convince, so they sent me back.

Daddy, I know you are bound to hear a lot of things about me. I won't deny my first man didn't teach me to have relations with other women because he thought I ought to know everything there was to know about life, but, Daddy, I haven't bothered myself that way for a long time now. I'm meant to have a man, and that's all I'll have from now on. I love you and need you. Please put me together, Daddy, like you would put a puzzle together.

Yours

3

Now I took on another obligation.

Each morning I had to be at the groundfloor windows to see Sonja off to her job. I was being weak about this. Some mornings I made myself not go.

But in the afternoons I'd show despite myself.

She always stood to watch me, grinning much love, and I had time to write on my fingers,

Be cool.

I could see her twice: once at the mainfloor windows and once again when she went down the basement corridor that led to the workroom right under UT.

I started thinking about this.

UT is Tshaped too. 2stairways at the elbows of each arm. Right across from my office is a door leading down to the women's workroom. I'd seen Pepper open it up a couple of times for the con electrician to go down, but he always supervised any cons who went down.

At lunchtime on Wednesday

I didn't go. I hung around the bare unit, me and a substitutehack aide because Pepper had to go see about 1 of his legs that he said he had bursitis in; he wouldn't be back till after lunch.

The women always came back to work just a little before the conguys and Winders got out of the messhalls. All the grills were locked off when this happened, 1st of all the 1 at UT.

When I went to the windows, I could see Sonja going. I could hear their chickenchatters singing below under my feet as I went back to my office opening, where I stood for a moment looking at the utility door that led down to where they were.

I went in and sat down and typed an Underground to Sonja:

Lay that thing out for me down there, the whole joint.

Then I rolled the little thing uptight and went out to the entrance,

where the substitutehack was just opening it up with his bigkey. 'You still got time to eat.' He grinned at me; there was a sparkle about it.

'I know it.'

I went out and down the corridor to the Barndoors

where I hung the kite under the wallhung ashtray bucket with a piece of Scotchtape. Then I stuffed off down near the Cokemachine, buying 1, then I came back down to UT and around the hackoffice, where the newguy looked up and said,

'Didn't go, huh?'

'Somebody told me we were eating kosher today, but it's really southern Iowa.'

I went into my office and sat down. The hackchair had lumps in the pillow I'd put down to ease my ass.

I think I waited a long time before I heard the guys' voices coming back from lunch;

then Joe Antman came in from his meal over front in the main building, and Pepper returned intact.

That afternoon

I came down to the Cokemachine on another errand and found that the kite was gone. She'd copped.

This line of thought carried me over to the next day:

I went to breakfast,

where they had bananas for a pleasant change. So I checked my drop. The quick note said:

Daddy, this is to the best of my ability. Please don't be angry. You know I'm willing to do anything you want me to.

It had a diagram inside.

I lured Pepper into my office just before it was time for them to leave at 4o'clock.

He flinched when I closed the door behind him.

'What was it you said you wanted to talk to me about?'

'Nothin but that talk we were supposed to have.'

'Oh,' he said, blinking. '*That* talk.' He had a RobertHall black trenchcoat on his arm. 'Ohyeah. Well, I guess you know how I feel about that.'

'Yeah, that's why we're gonna talk it out right now.'

'Talk about what?'

'You know what. I don't have to tell you. It's about that bottle of haircoloring and the note.'

He had a spasm. 'Listen, I hope you don't take that serious.'

'Naw, I ain't. But Joe Antman would, and so would Captain Koyle, and so would Dr. Mossler.'

He got hungup fumbling around. 'Suppose I give you some money?'

'Get yourself together, fool. What could I do with money?'

Then he began to get desperate. 'Listen, you'd just better give me what you have before somebody gets in trouble.'

'What kind of trouble?'

'Well, real bad trouble, for 1 thing. You might even get hurt.'

'Are you threatening me with violence?'

'Naw, I was just tryin to tell you how serious a thing like this is.'

'You're God Damn Right it's serious. And don't you ever pucker up that hole in your face to threaten me again. I'd beat the shit out of you, you God Damn Ignorant hillbilly. I could beat your ass right now and then just turn over the haircoloring and your doofus note, and they'd excuse me for it. You shut up from now on and do just as I tell you.'

He began to collapse, I could see, and I got my strength back.

'From now on, I'm the policeman. From now on, it's me who can bust you. Do you understand that?'

After a longtime he said Yeah in a small voice.

'So these are the things you're going to do. From now on, if I have anything coming from my woman in the Barn, like cigarets or anything else I might need to support me over here, you're going to pick it up. Do you understand that?'

He said Yes he understood that.

'But that's just for openers, you hack, you screw, you policeman. I might tell you to give me the key to the front door.'

I was beginning to terrify him.

I exulted.

I tasted my lips and found them like love.

Wednesday morning

I got the moves from Koyle's clerk for guys who were supposed to go out into population, and Bob Trent was on the list. I was surprised. I went into my office and destroyed his move card and substituted the name of another dopie. It'd be weeks or so before they found out about it, and even then it might be overlooked.

I didn't want him out of my reach just yet.

That afternoon, I checked him out when he went down to the Chapel for singing. I followed his limping figure carefully. His routine never changed: between the hours of 1 and 2. The Chapel doors were always open for anybody who wanted to get in.

He met his little ratfriend

and they sang those God Damn Spirituals together.

It was just a matter of finding the right moment.

4

Wednesday night I got a pass from Cambridge. It meant me and Sonja would be meeting him together the next day.

This was the first time I'd done a bit where I'd paid so much attention to personal grooming. My moustache had grown out of that Ralph Cooper bag into something thick and Stalinistic. My eyes were clear. What I saw in the bathroom mirror didn't offend me the way it used to.

I was even a little nervous, getting ready. Like 1 time I can remember I had a girlfriend when I was around 12. The oldfolks called it Courtin. I was the same way then, doofusly giddy. I came way over from Brooklyn to shine shoes on 42nd Street, some of them shitty, to buy ones for myself to show off in. I wore those shoes for 3years after. And it seemed like the memory of her seeped right in through my feet each time I put them on.

But I made myself shape up. I didn't want to tilt Sonja's image of me. Of all the women I've ever met,

I find I'm most vulnerable to whores.

A lot of things went through my mind when I thought about that. And Damn It, it was raining again; I could see from the bathroom windows to the courtyard below. The rain has always been my enemy. It seems to melt my will. I remember trying to cop in the rain: nothing has ever made me more miserable than copping in the rain.

Now the pall that overcomes this place when the weather is foul overcame it. I could barely see myself in the mirror. Then I had a chill, and thought,

I shouldn't have been thinking like this.

The clock in the Dayroom said it was only 10minnits from the time I was supposed to be there,

so I hustled it up, smearing my armpits with Mum and

my justwashed body with the cheesy Commissarygrease some guys used to screw sissies with around here; then I got into the government jockeyshorts and Tshirt and newpressed congrays with a white Banlon. My wallmirror said it all kind of matched. I wore the plainblack Stetsons I'd gotten busted in 3years before.

And I thought about the shoes I bought from 42nd Street.

I was sitting across from Mr. Wallers' desk when she came in escorted by 1 matron. Naturally, she had to sit on the other side of the room, but I got up to move around and fake looking at some of the goodbad paintings from the ArtGroup that hung on the walls,

and I had a chance to look her over well, with her knees all exposed and bare up to the place where her cunt must've started under the shortbrown skirt, and I had a chance to say under my breath,

'Hello, love.'

Mr. Wallers took out a handkerchief like a kite and blew his nose.

'Daddy . . .' she began as I moved back where I was supposed to be.

There was no 1 else on the floor but we3.

I sat down. She was wearing glasses today that gave her a kind of secretariallook, and it was amusing that a whore could look like a secretary just by putting glasses on.

10minnits after 2, by the wallclock,

Dr. Cambridge came out grinning at us.

'I'm so sorry to keep you waiting. Won't you follow me, please?'

So that brought us together, walking sidebyside in the hallways, Dr. Cambridge a little in front, talking about something we weren't paying any attention to because we were feening on each other so hard, and when we made the bend to the psychoffices

I got her ass in my hand and nursed the twitching softness of it while I looked both ways. Dr. Cambridge didn't see anything.

This joint was giving me a feelhabit. I did it again just as we entered his office. She stank of something sweet and carnal. Her lips were red as crayon, and she trembled eachtime my hand touched her.

'Sitdown, won't you?'

We took seats facing his deskchair, where he sat suddenly and relaxed. Sonja's skirt pulled up over her smoothlonglegs when she crossed them, and she boldly reached over and took my hand between the space of our chairs. Dr. Cambridge acted as if he hadn't noticed.

'How's it been going for you?' he asked me.

'The days pass. Nobody can stop them.'

'And you, Sonja?'

Her teeth were so perfect when she smiled, I wondered if they were false. 'Nothing much. I've got a new job since the lasttime I saw you; I'm down in the garmentshop now.'

'You like it there?'

'Naw. It's all kind of a bitchy situation. There's a dyke problem. I've been wondering whether I should put in a Form 10 to change my job, but I've got to ask my man 1st.'

'Well. He's sitting right next to you.'

She batted her eyes. 'He might not want me to ask right now. Do you, Daddy?'

'No.'

She squeezed my fingers. 'I'll do whatever he advises me.' She recrossed her legs, and I knew Cambridge must be getting some disturbing gappers.

He leaned back and put his fingers behind his head and batted his elbows. 'The garmentshop seems to be a good place for you, Sonja. At least you'll be earning 2days a month goodtime, where you weren't earning anything before on your other job.'

'Well,' she said, 'I think my man is the most qualified to tell me what I ought to be doing, so I'll take his advice whenever he tells me.'

Dr. Cambridge watched us silently for a long while. Then he looked directly at me. 'I'm sure you'll advise her well.'

'She might not need any.'

'Well, if she does I'm sure you'll tell her exactly what to do.'

'To the best of my wisdom, that's right.'

'Sonja. The last time you were here, you told me something about Love and a New Dedication. We didn't have enough time then. You can finish now, if you want to.'

She put wary bigeyes on me, but couldn't tell anything. 'Oh, it wasn't anything much, you know, Doctor, that I haven't said before in the past when I talked with you. I just always said that I looked for that 1 time to really be in love with a man, without considerations, and I feel like I am now.'

'Do you feel like you're *loved*? That was an important part of what you meant.'

'Yes, I do, I feel like I'm loved. I know my man loves me.'

'How can you know about love when you haven't had sex with him?'

'Oh, you can know about love without sex,' she said. 'I've loved men without sex a fewtimes before, but not in this way. I've always kept a piece of myself *for* myself, but with this man I can't keep anything.' She looked to make sure I wasn't drugged. 'He *gives* me myself,' she tried to explain. 'You wouldn't know what I mean unless you were a woman.'

'I know what you mean; I don't have to be a woman.'

'Oh, sure then, you understand. I listen to his voice everyday, and it's right, like a bell, so you've just *got* to know when a thing *sounds* right. This man sounds completely right for me. I'm going to have him.'

Dr. Cambridge pulled his arms down and grabbed both knees. 'Maybe I ought to tell you what my experience has been in these kinds of relationships between addicts, and I've been here a few years: They never work out.'

Sonja was disturbed. 'How can you say that about us?'

'Because I'm speaking from a statistical viewpoint. It's hard enough for 1 person to readjust from narcoticsaddiction, but when 2 are paired it invariably leads to recidivism. 1 is strong enough to recover alone; 2 aren't.'

'But that doesn't have to go down with us,' she said, a little distressed. 'If 2people love each other enough, I think they can do whatever they want to do.'

'And so do I,' said Dr. Cambridge. 'But this applies only to 2people who've never been strung out on drugs before. If 1 of you regressed, what's to happen to the other? If 1 of you loves the other enough, chances are it'll be easier to become addicted than try to fight the other's illness.'

Sonja shook her head in a convinced way. 'That's not always true, I know a couple in Manhattan who met downhere, and they're getting along all right right now. They've even got a little restaurant and're making a little money. I know this broad well, because she used to work with me out on the Coast, and she sends me cards all the time telling me how she's doing. She's got to be doing like she says, because junkies don't have time to send cards out to anybody.'

'I'm not saying there aren't exceptions to the rule, Sonja, but by and large affairs begun here in the hospital and carried on to the Freeworld involve some sort of tragedy. I mean drugtragedy. I just wondered if you 2 had thought about anything like that.'

'What's to think about?' she said, her ignorance beginning to show.

'And what do you think about it?' he said, looking at me.

'What can I say against a statistical viewpoint?'

'I wouldn't be surprised if you had a lot to say,' he said.

'What difference would it make what I said? Everything is already predicted, you say, so it's foolish for me to say anything. You've got all dopies in a neat littlebag; what's good for 1 is the same for the other.'

'That's not what I meant.'

'But it's what you said. And it really doesn't make me any difference anyway what the United States Government thinks I am.'

'Or what it thinks Sonja is?'

'Nor what it thinks Sonja is.'

She squeezed my hand again.

Dr. Cambridge took up another tack. I began to feel his pressure, and resent it.

'I'm hoping that both of you *do* have love,' he said thoughtfully. 'It's the best possible substitute for junk. A lot of addicts are cured, but they substitute things like liquor, or maybe they become gluttons – it all depends on the attitude. But some of them fall in love, and they never use again.'

'I thought you said it couldn't happen that way,' Sonja leaped on him.

'I said I thought if 2people loved each other, they could do anything they wanted to do.'

'That's just 1 family of thought.'

'Oh,' he said, as though I'd stepped on his toe, 'you think there're others?'

'Of course. I could just make up my mind never to use stuff anymore, and I wouldn't need anything to drink or smoke or eat or fuck. It'd be a simple matter of making up my mind.'

'Then why haven't you stopped using drugs up till now?'

'That's too simple a question to answer.'

'Then let me make it more profound. Why is drugs like a person to you?'

'Because it hurts my life': I didn't hesitate to tell it.

'Oh,' he said.

'Yes, that's the reason. People and drugs are the only things that hurt your life. How can you even dare question 2 absolutes like that? You won't find anything pat in my life, if that's what you're looking for.'

'But what about Joyce?' he said.

'Okay, what about Joyce? You had to get around to it sooner or later.'

'Joyce was a prostitute.'

'And I turned her out.'

'Isn't there something typical about that?'

'No, only in your world, your great whiteworld. Joyce was a prostitute because she *had* to be.'

'But I didn't ask what she *had* to be,' he said. 'I was asking something else. I was trying to point out that there *are* pat things in your life.'

'What's so pat about Joyce and me?'

'Because you both followed a pattern.'

'Don't be stupid. Followed a pattern by whose Law?'

'Survival's. I've heard what you and Joyce were at least a hundred times.'

'But not out of my mouth or Joyce's mouth. You're depending too much on what you've read.'

'Well, then,' he said, leaning back and waggling his elbows, 'maybe you can tell me how it was different.'

'How it was different? Yeah, I can tell you how it was different. It was different because that was the way I wanted it to be.'

'But that doesn't say anything.'

'Then you're not listening. It was different because I didn't want what we had to be any different than what it was.'

'And the child too?'

'Yes, and the child too.'

Sonja wasn't understanding, an archhigh doofuslook on her face, but I tuned her out because these questions somehow had to be answered.

I'd lost my context, or allowed the doctor to make me feel that way. It's very rare that I allow myself to get turned on like that.

I think we stared at each other, but Sonja was completely out of it. She squeezed my hand a little tighter now, and licked her lips to make them shine. Suddenly I'd forgotten about her flesh. It was more important then, I think, to see that Dr. Cambridge saw me as I really was.

I don't know why, but I couldn't have been startled any less if suddenly a star had fallen at my feet

and I had seen its outside break to show the world the face within was me.

'And what about the child?' he said.

'What about it?'

'You seem to be so definite about your beliefs. I want to know what you think about your child.'

But I hadn't thought about Joye for months, except the time my aunt sent money.

Sonja's womanscent was a great deal more than she could've ever known. I knew the doctor was an enemy:

He watched me for reaction time.

But I decided, What the hell,

and then began to tell it all the way I really felt.

'What we're talking about is another thing altogether, and it has nothin to do with Sonja or how she feels about me or how you feel about us. Because I don't really giveashit what you think.'

'But maybe you really do.'

'Ohyeah, that's what you'd *like* to think, and that's something I don't care about, either.'

'You said,' he said, 'something about the way Sonja feels about you, but how do you feel about Sonja?'

'That knowledge doesn't belong to you – it doesn't even belong to Sonja. What I feel about anything is my right, and I'm not obligated to disclose it to anybody or anything.'

'You seem angry.'

'What do you care? All you care about is hearin about the kid, or so you say. You think maybe bringing this thing up will rupture our relationship; then you'd have Sonja all to yourself again.'

She looked wideeyed, redlipped and bewildered.

'Don't you know Dr. Cambridge is in love with you?'

'That's not true,' he said, sitting up straight. 'You've managed to shift to the offensive. That's very good, but you've used a lie to do it.'

'I've never been known for my veracity about anything.'

'No, but this is a lazy kind of evasion, and not characteristic at all of the kind of person you really are. It's the 1st time I've seen you afraid about anything.'

'You can just stop that shit right now: I'm not afraid of you or anything like you.'

'I'm sure you're not, and that's not what I implied. You became defensive the moment the subject of Joye came up.'

I told her, for her ears: 'Joye is a cripple. She got crippled because her mother used stuff when she carried her. She'll never be anything but a cripple.'

When I looked at him,

he seemed surprised:

'Ah,' he said in a long smilingbreath.

'Well, that's what you wanted to hear, wasn't it? That's what you wanted Sonja to hear.'

'What I want isn't important. It's what you want, and what Sonja wants. What *I* want more than anything is for you both *not* to want drugs anymore.'

'But I *don't* want drugs anymore,' Sonja said. 'All I want is this man.'

'Yes' – he nodded – 'you've told me about that.'

'You said something about being in love as an antidote.'

'I couldn't have meant it precisely like that. Addicts tend to magnify their excesses, whether it's drugs or love, Sonja, and we can't forget that the addict is a fantasist, as well. Right now, in this environment, which is anything but normal, it really might seem true that you're in love.'

'I'm old enough to know when I'm in love with a man,' she said, squeezing my hand again in a fierce way.

'Perhaps you are and do,' he said. 'But this is a unique situation, and what you're saying you feel is not very different from what others said before you 2 came along.'

He was working at a disadvantage, but I actually admitted to myself that I wanted him to be successful, and I didn't see why he couldn't see

that the schematics of our 2lives allowed us to hear him objectively but reject him at the same time. The balance was a strange 1:

Cambridge was death on me, for the sake of Sonja, and I knew it. But now it was less easy for me to be angry with him even though Love, the way I knew it and the way he spoke about it, was like a lizard and a snake in the same cage. He couldn't know what she was, or even myself, the way I'd lived with these personalities. I'd lived with Joyce: just paint Sonja with a yellowskin:

and saw her earn our bread with her crotch and mouth, those 2 whorecomputers, and when Joye came I didn't know until I saw her face that she was mine.

Even though I felt a tiny sense of hate for him, I couldn't blame him. He knew nothing but the gist of me, but this is all you need to know of anyone.

'You're making this like a war,' she said tragically. 'What're you tryin to do?'

'Just *show* you, if I can . . .'

'You're not God,' she said. 'You can't *show* anybody anything. You're only a psychiatrist!'

'Don't misunderstand me, Sonja.'

'No, but it's you who misunderstand us. Because if we're unhappy and we find out we love each other, why shouldn't we have that happiness?'

'I'm not saying that you shouldn't,' he said brutally; 'I'm only saying you should open your eyes and *see.* You've been an addict for 25years. You're almost 40years old. What do you intend being for the next 25years?'

She hadn't wanted him to say that, and she looked at me in a childish littlegirlway for what to tell him next. But I let her squeeze it out on her own.

'My man will tell me what to be.'

'What is it,' he asked, 'that he'll tell you to be?'

'Whatever it is he wants,' she said defiantly, 'and whatever it is he wants is mosttimes right for me, I know now.'

'But this is complete submission,' the doctor showed her.

'I know that; don't you think I know that already?'

'But you've already completely submitted to drugs, and what happened then? Can you trust that this man will totally satisfy your need to submit?'

'I never have totally needed to submit. But I *need* to sub*mit* right now, can you understand that?'

'Yes, I can understand that. But who will you need to submit to next month, when you leave here?'

'It'll still be him—'

'But can you be sure?'

'With the kind of lugs you're droppin on her, it'll be hard for her even to submit to a douche': That broke the spell, and he shifted his attention.

'I'm very glad you came up here today,' he said. He looked at his watch.

'I'm glad you're glad about it.'

'You don't mind returning next week?'

'Not right now, but I might have afterthoughts.'

'I hope not.' He stood and smiled and stretched. 'I have a book you might like to read: it's by Dr. Ellis.'

'I couldn't fit it into my schedule – I'm reading about *Sex and the Office* right now.'

He picked that up right away, and laughed.

'This is the end of our period.'

I stood. Sonja stood, pulling the tightskirt down over her widehips. She looked hurt and a little worried.

We were all awkwardly silent,

then Dr. Cambridge came to life and escorted us out to the hallway, freer in unobservance of us than he'd been before, so Sonja took the opportunity to breathe this hot message in my ear:

'You *do* love me, don't you, Daddy? Say Yes.'

But thankfully the doctor turned and I had the chance to nut up completely.

More and more,

I could see,

she was beginning to sound too much like Joyce once had.

43½

Joe Antman came in drunk the nextday.

It was shocking, but I knew Joe was 1 helluva cunthound, or so he said, and was having a lot of trouble with his wife.

He wobbled with drunken dignity into my office and sat down. His eyes were cloudy and harsh.

'You don't know how they are,' he told me definitively.

'Ohyeah, I know how they are.'

He fixed me with a steady gaze. 'No, you just *think* you know how they are. You never had a wife like mine.'

'And you never had a wife like mine, so we're even about that.'

He lit a Marvel cigaret with a staggering flame.

'Damn, Joe, why don't you take the rest of the day off? You could get busted in your condition.'

'Naw, naw, they don't dare bust me, not with what I know about this joint; they wouldn't dare try to do anything about my condition.'

'Well, ain't it kinda stupid to give them any hint about what your condition is? Why don't you take your ass on home? Sam'll pay you for the day anyway.'

'Home?' he said with greatbig eyes. 'Do you know what you just said? You said Home.'

'Yeah, I know what I said.'

'You don't know what it is *not* to have a home,' he said sadly.

'I know what it is not to have a home. . . .'

'Now you think you bein halfassed brilliant,' he said, puffing smoke at me. 'Ain't that what you think?'

'Naw, Joe, that ain't what I think.'

'You think *I* don't know what it is being deprived?'

'I never said that.'

'You think *I* don't know what it is not havin nobody?'

'That's not what I said.'

'Just because you black.'

'Now you're really fuckin the subject up.'

He puffed and blew smoke and leered at me. 'You're lucky, did you know that?'

'And you're drunk.'

'Hell'—he grinned—'I know that better than you do. I know you're lucky better than you do, did you know that?'

'Awshit, Joe, get the fuck out of here; I got work to do.'

'Naw, I'm serious. Do you know *why* you're lucky?'

'All right, go ahead and tell me.'

He put his finger under my nose and said the words slowly, 'Because you're dead.'

'Awshit': I typed incohorently on the typewriter just to get away from him.

'And you know that's true,' he insisted. 'You're a deadman. Something killed you, so you don't have to worry about anything anymore.'

'I hate drunks.'

'I'm not so drunk I don't know what I'm talkin about; I'll remember what I'm talkin about tomorrow.'

'I hope not.'

'Do you know what's wrong with you?'

'The only thing wrong with me right now is a guy named Joe Antman.'

'I'll tell you what's wrong with you. You wanna make everybody else dead the way you are.'

'Now, that's a God Damn Stupid Thing to say': I turned to look at him.

'But it's real, and you know it is,' he said seriously.

'I wonder how I got to be your project today.'

'You're dead, just like your wife, and you want everybody else to be dead too.'

'Joe, you're buggin me.'

'How can I bug you? How can you bug a deadman? You're a ghost, did you know that? I know all about you.'

'Yeah, just like everybody else, you read the records.'

'Ahyeah, I read um,' he said with a wink. 'And I know all about that Trent bastard, and I know how his move out to population got lost somekinda way, and I know you had somethin to do with it.'

'I never saw any move for him.'

'That's shit. You held him over, and I know *why* you held him over. You let me tell you' – he chopped these words up – 'You'll be a damn fool if you don't let loose the past, and you'll just keep right on bein the dumb fucker you always been.'

'I don't know what you're talkin about, Joe.'

'Ahyeah, you know what I'm talkin about. I know what you plannin to do, and I'm here to tell you you can be bigger than any shit like that.'

'Boy, the stuff you dream up.'

'I'm not dreamin,' he said. 'I quit dreamin a long time ago, just like you.'

That made me angry: 'Why are you givin me such a hardtime, Joe?'

He stomped his Marvel cigaret out on my floor. 'Because I'm not afraid of you. Because I'm the only 1 can talk to you. Because a ghost like you just don't intimidate me. Because I learned a longtime ago that a ghost is just a ghost, and I like the hell out of you, boy, and I don't like likin ghosts.'

'You don't have to like me.'

'Nobody has anything to say about what they like. I like you, and it's a God Damn Hardship for me. My workduties don't call for anything like that.'

'What are you tryin to tell me, Joe?'

'What am I tryin to tell you?' he said, in a reflective bag. 'What Am I Tryin To Tell You? I'm tryin to tell you the samething I told you when you said that stuff about a Home: that you just gotta wake up, Lazarus.'

'Joe. Get outta my office.'

He stood and grinned and waggled from side to side

just a little bit, and he combed his blond hair with his fingers.

'You know why I understand you so good?' he said, and turned to go, then stopped and looked at me:

'Because maybe I'm a little dead myself.'

5

Little Joe had been away on the Experimental Level for over 2weeks,

and I happened to meet him coming back with the little satchel he used for his boxingstuff, with his eyes all bleary and a trim bit of smile on his mouth.

'Awman,' he said.

'What's happenin?'

'Awman, I just come offa the reefertests and I'm still cool. They give us reefer chocolatebars to eat.'

'Chocolatebars? You mean they put reefer in candybars up there?'

'*Si*, man, that ain't nothin. They even give it to you to drink, but it's all gushy and funnylike.'

'Don't you ever get any to smoke?'

'Ohyeah, they give you that too; they even let you roll your own joint.' He grinned in a happyfoolish reefer way. 'But I'd rather have it in candybars any day.'

'Seems kinda impersonal to me.'

We started back to UT together, since you couldn't loiter around in the hallway when the broads were running.

'Next week I'm goin on the morphine experiment,' Joe said, then got a little smug when he said, '*Tu sabe* morphine, man?'

'*Si, chico.*'

He started to giggle. 'Hey, you speak Puerto Rican pretty good.' He kept giggling and laughing at me. The whites of his eyes were as red as fire. But then he got sober for a moment. 'The only thing I don't like about the morphinetest, you gotta kick coldturkey.'

'Then why go through the hassle?'

'Cuz it *feel* good, man, you crazy? And they give me 2days' goodtime for every test, and you see how this cut the 10year bit down? Already I earned 288days outsida my statutory goodtime, just from goin on experiments. That's a year.'

'Naw, there's 365days in a year.'

'You dig me, man; when you doin a dime 288days is just lika year for me.'

'Yeah, but you're leavin out almost 3months.'

He shrugged and grinned. 'I can pick those up anytime later.'

'Tell me some more about the Experimental Level.'

'Why'ont you senda copout into Dr. Brice, and why'ont you go up for yourself, man? I can't tell you nothin,' he giggled; 'I'm too high right now.'

'Don't gimme that shit, and stop rubbin it in. You gotta have at least a year and a ½left on your sentence before you can go up, and I ain't got that much time left. I'd go up if I could, because I wanted to get in on the LSDtests.'

He looked at me in a queer way. 'Why'd you wanna get on LSD?'

'Because I never been on LSD.'

'Yeah. Well, I guess that's 1 good reason, huh? I knowa guy on the level holds the record for LSDexperiments. You know Bobby Tolliver?'

'Yeah, the guy plays bass in the band, little dark-skinned guy.'

'*Eso es.* This guy Bobby has took off 300times.'

'Oshit, man, don't tell lies like that.'

'I'm no kiddin you, man,' Joe said indignantly. 'You can ask anyone here; Bobby Tolliver hold the record for LSD all over the world, and he did it right here doin his 10years. With the goodtime he make, he only do 5years, and you know you do 6–9 for the dime.'

'300jags seems kinda fantastic.'

Joe licked his finger and crossed his heart. 'But it's true; I don't bullshit you. But for me, I don't like that stuff, because they asked me if I would and I said No. Guys who take it see a lotta funny things. I see too many funny things when I don't take nothin. Don't *you* see a lotta funny things when you don't take nothin?'

'Yeah.'

'So. That just proves what I say. Give me a little morphine or stuff any day; I'll let them other guys take LSD. Some guys upstairs say they even took it with morphine.'

'Ohnow, Joe . . .'

He stopped to look at me with a bulldog face. 'For why you don't believe what I'm tellin you, man?'

'Because you're a liar.'

'Yeah,' he agreed, 'I'ma liar, but I ain't lyin now, and you should see some of the things the docs mix up up there, like morphine and coke together.'

'Well, that ain't nothin but a speedball.'

He winked knowingly at me. 'What about when you gotta drink a reefer malted behind it?'

'I don't know why I let myself get hung up with you. What would be the sense in a combination like that? Even if a guy got the M and coke together in the Freeworld, where the fuck would he get the malted reefer?'

Joe shrugged and giggled, redeyed. 'That's *his* problem, man.'

Just as we came abreast of the garmentshop steps,

a matron came up with 5broads. 1 of them was Sonja, looking tired and very drugged and dressed in something that looked like a blue sackcloth.

Me and Joe did a hesitationwalk, feening criminally.

'*Como tu chocho*, Sylvia?' Joe hollered at a sleekhipped little Spanishgirl with bumps on her face, but this was prohibited,

talking to the broads,

and I thought for a moment the matron would bust him. But she didn't seem to care, and only glared.

And the littlebroad replied, flushingly pleased:

'*Tiene mucho hambre, Joseito, mucho hambre.*'

And I felt my flesh tingle as I passed Sonja and looked without speaking into her big deep eyes,

because I knew hers was hungry in the very sameway.

MY DADDY LOVER,

This torture is too much. I can hardly stand it; I almost reached out and grabbed you today in the hall. Oh, Daddy, you looked so good to me and you were just what I needed to see after going thru that hassle down there with that bitch who runs the spot who got caught with the con broad going down on her. I don't know how to tell you, Daddy. I need you, Daddy.

Daddy, you said you were arranging something. Please, please go ahead and arrange it so we can at least have each other before its too late and I have to go home. I know already it will be good and you will be good for me; if only I could just suck your tongue for a few moments and feel you against me, not to mention inside of me. That would mean so much wouldn't it, Daddy?

Remember, Daddy, the first time I saw you? But I didn't even see you first, I felt you, because I felt you behind me and when I looked around I thought you were going to kill me. I don't know why but I did. If you could only see your face sometimes. There's murder in you, and I wish there wasn't. When I look at you I feel like something angry is massaging me all over. Who are you, Daddy? I keep asking myself over and over again who you are, but nothing ever tells me the answer.

Yours

5ɛ1/2

Pepper had got to the place where he was so scared of me

I thought I'd better use him before he completely blew his cool and jammed up wires all over the joint.

So

when Joe Antman had to leave 1 day, a hot Tuesdaynoon, and left Pepper in charge with another substitutehack,

I pulled him into my office very quietly and squeezed the door shut and stood with my back against it without saying anything.

He tried to make himself look like he was all together. 'Ah. Did you happen to have somethin on your mind? I'm kind of busy right now.'

'You think I only visit here? I *live* here; I know how busy you are.'

He bobbed his head. 'Yeah? Well, it kind of depends on what it is you wanna talk about; then maybe I'd be too busy about somethin or nuther.'

'Ah. I see defiance in your eyes.'

'Well, I don't know what you might be seein, but 1 thing you might be seein is how I don't see where it makes sense for me and you to talk about nothin.'

'Oh, yeah?'

'Yeah.' Then he folded his arms and clicked 1 heel.

'Oh, yeah? Well, then maybe you better check it all out on paper again, because you're beginning to prove what a God Damn Fool you are.'

'I don't see where we gotta check anything out on paper.'

'Naw? Well, what about that stupidnote to that broad Rose From Seattle that told about what you was gonna do for her the minute she pulled up. What about that? And it's all in your handwritin, stupid.'

He fumbled around for a longtime, then uncrossed his arms. 'That don't prove nothin.'

I could only stare at him.

'I could just say I was foolin around in my spare time. Practicin handwritin. How could anybody prove different? And what could *you say*? *you*, a convict? They'd *have* to go on my word.'

'All right. Now, you listen to me, you God Damn Fool. If you don't do exactly as I tell you to do, here's what's gonna happen to you:

'You will immediately be called to your immediate superior officer, Joe Antman, who is going to lay all the goods on the table and call you all sorts of unfortunate assholes.

'Then Joe Antman will shake his head and get up to take what he knows down to the Headman Police, because Joe Antman ain't fool enough to let some ignorant emptyheaded hotballs blow a good thing for him.

'Then they'll come back and Gestapo you down to the Headman Police, who might spit on you if you get between him and that bucket he uses.

'Then they'll take you over to Mossler, who'll look at you like you were a piece of green shit from outerspace. And he'll ask you only 1 question: 'How soon can you manage to leave the hospital?'

'And here you are, comin home way ahead of the usual time you get in, and your old lady's gonna know rightaway somethin new went down, and she gonna be on your ass to tell her what it was about, and what are *you* gonna tell her, you God Damn Fool, about that doofus note and the bottle of haircoloring? And how you gonna tell her about the Temporary Suspension Till Investigation Is Over? And what're you gonna tell the neighbors, sucker? And pretty soon, even your own *kids* get squeezed in a pressure like that. What's your old lady's name?'

'Marge . . .'

'Marge will soon cease giving It up the way she used to and start complainin about her Tubes. And prettysoon you'll find yourself jackin off in the toilet in the middle of the night when everybody else is sleeping.'

He couldn't think of anything else to say but,

'What do you think you can call yourself?'

'A hero': But I thought then I might've tried too hard. 'I'm robbin the rich to take from the poor. I didn't get you into all this shit; you got in it all by yourself; remember that when you get up on the stand. What's your little kids gonna think about they daddy?'

He was shocked. 'They wouldn't do *that*, would they?'

'Oh, no? You don't think they *would*, huh? You just watch how they leap into your ass. They'll disown you, Writing Lovenotes To A Damn Dope Fiend. You know how small this town is. They're gonna crack your ass for you, buddy, and everybody connected with you, and that goes for your kids. You might even have to move away from this area. Ohman. You'd be in a world of trouble if this shit ever blew out.'

'I don't see where there's any need for it ever to come out,' he said quietly. 'Seems like it might be able for you and me to solve this problem all by ourselves.'

'That's the way I see it.'

He didn't say anything for a longtime, then, finally, asked me tiredly,

'Okay, Watchu want?'

'I wanna fuck my woman. I want you to open the door across from this 1 leading down to the garmentshop where all the broads are, and I want you to let me inside and stand guard till we get off; then I'd want you to let me out immediately, or immediately after I gave you a signal. That's what.'

I could lose my job for that.'

'That's not all you could lose your job for.'

'How do I know you won't rat out on me anyway?'

'Cause I might wanna use you to do it again.'

'But you're supposed to give the note and haircoloring back to me!'

'I didn't say that; I didn't make any statement about that. But I'll say right now I'll return those things when you convince me that you're playin all the way down the middle on me; that's when I give it back, and not before.'

'Listen. How can I trust you'll do what you say?'

'Just by openin your eyes and seeing that I'd have a lot more to lose than you. Fool.'

The business with him happened on a Friday,

Which meant I had to sweat it out over the weekend wondering whether or not he'd commit suicide.

Then

Monday came, and it was earlymorning, about 7:40, when I saw him coming down the hallway ahead of other hacks in the unit, the 1st on duty,

and I knew it had to be this day or the next, because Pepper was primed on hysteria and very likely to wipe me away if he happened to have a backlash.

I followed him into the hacks' office as be opened up. 3 or 4 young Winders were waiting out in front, 2 of them white with asslong hair. The blackguys looked like they'd been carpeted up the backbone.

'How you doin this mornin, Mr. Smith?': I went over to the bigboard and started snatching out Removals and Moves.

'Oh, ah, I'm okay,' he said.

'You sure?'

'Yeah, I'm sure.'

'I just wanna be sure I know everything on your mind.'

'You can trust me.'

'That's what Judas said.'

'That's a helluva thing to think about anybody.'

'Well, I think it about you; let's not make any mistake about it. I don't trust you as far as I could hurl the Headman Police. So I'll just come back from time to time to run this little plot to you in stages.'

'Don't you think you oughta tell me *every*thing about it?'

'I hope you didn't do any drinkin before you left home.'

'No, I meant in case of an emergency or somethin, so I'll be able to help you out of a tightspot.'

'The 1st emergency comes up, I'm busted. I don't need you to give me that kinda information. I just wonder how much doublereverse you'd do if something *did* go down, so you be careful of tightening the screws in case something like that goes off. Just do what I tellya; that's all you need to know.'

We exchanged Undergroundnotes at noon:

> DADDY,
> *now at 1:45 we have our coffeebreak at which time there is nobody in the office, and the stairs are at the left of the desk. But I would have to get one of these other broads to pull for me, and I don't know one broad down here I'd trust that much. But what you say is urgent, and I will get somebody even if I have to pay them. Anyway, I will be there at that time somehow, please believe me, Daddy.*
>
> LUV

> LUV:
> *Don't you touch anything I've already told you to do. From the layouts you gave me I can see it as being nothing but extremely easy. Don't you dare complicate a hair of this plot.*

> DADDY,
> *Did you know today was the 27th of May and its three days to Memorial Day?*
>
> LUV

> LUV:
> *Please do not send me anymore kites.*

At 1 o'clock I came in and told Pepper what to do next.

'But what if somebody sees me? Joe's back now.'

'Don't start trembling on me, you bastard. You just be standin by that door at 1:30, at which time you will stick your key in the lock and open it.'

'I didn't say I wouldn't do that.'

'No, you wouldn't dare say you wouldn't do that.'

'But how do I know exactly when, since I ain't wearin a watch?'

'Ohshit, don't worry; I'll let you know when.'

Then I went into my office and did a little private trembling. I was working with unpredictables: Sonja and Pepper. The next hour could very well find me going to the hole.

Tamerlane came into the office and asked me if I knew anything about the moon.

'Why, man?'

'I just wondered, thass all,' he said, 'since just about everybody is interested in the moon these days.'

'I ain't.'

'Let's see what you know about it.' He opened the place where he had his thumb in a book.

'Waittaminnit, Tam—'

'Now lissen, this ain't gonna take long; I just want you to hear what this guy's got to say about the moon.'

'What time is it?'

He looked at his ham of a wrist, and watch. '1:20.'

'I got to be pullin up in a few minnits.'

'Well, lissen, you got a few minnits to lissen to this. It's somethin might interest you.'

'I'm interested enough, Tam.'

'Not till you hear this. Now I'm quotin him.'

'Go ahead.'

'He says: 'We know nothing about the rays of the moon; they may be anything, electron or neutron particles dispersed directly at us. That is why we must protect our feet as well as possible, for these rays, when bouncing off the sidewalk, enter the bottoms of everybody's feet, sometimes causing damage to the soles of the feet. A patient may sometimes even limp' . . .'

'Yeah, yeah, okay, Tam—'

'Waittaminnit, waittaminnit, man; this is the most interestin part, 'cause he says here: "Moon rays have been referred to as Spoon rays, but this is far and away from being the whole truth. Granted, a June moon will offer many opportunities to a spooner, but are the moon rays always healthful to us? Scientific evidence says No. If you are interested in my program, Dr. Earle

Spencer's Campaign for Common Sense About the Moon, send $2.98 for a postpaid copy of my booklet, *The Right to Talk About the Moon.*"'

'Where did you get that shit at, Tamerlane?'

'Some old Texasdopie gave it to me over on the other side, said he been subscribin to this guy for years.'

'Well, he's dealin with a hot subject.'

Tam nodded over the book for a couple of minnits, then suddenly looked up.

'Doesn't somethin seem wrong about this to you?' he asked me.

Then
at 1:26

Joe Antman wanted me to take a dopie's jacket around to the Dispensary, and I had to do a lot of faking out before he turned the bag over to Tamerlane. I told Joe I was sick and was going upstairs to lie down for a while,

but I slipped on over to my office and closed the door and waited for Pepper's knock. It seemed like 20minnits before it came,

then I got up and went quickly out and across to the door Pepper held open, inside blackly accepting me. Then the door was shut, and darkness. I was on the top landing. To my right the stairway curved down, then curved right again. I could hear sewing machines going, and women's voices.

It was hot. I had on a pair of scuffs, so I kicked them off and took off my shortsleeved shirt. The sweat began to roll down my chest and make slick little patterns. I spread the shirt on the floor for her to lie on.

Below, the women kept babbling. A grimy window let in a little light, because it was barred and 3feet over my head.

Then I heard a broad's voice say very authoritatively,

'Coffeebreak, girls.'

The machines whirred down. Some broad said her ass was tired, in Spanish. Then the chatter became undercurrent and bugged me, but I knew the reason why. It was almost 5minnits already.

Then I sat on the landing next to the shirt, and hugged my knees. I couldn't tell anything down there that sounded like her.

Then a fewminnits later I heard a bustling on the steps below, like a cluster of birds being frightened,

and I saw her turn the lowerlanding, head down, not having seen me yet. She was in my arms before we knew it.

I sucked her tongue, a warm brinish thing, and pulled her into me where I could feel her flesh and the length of her against me, where I could rest My Man on her thigh, and for 1 terrifically wonderful moment we were stayed, and the mixture of sex and fear and frustration glued us together like wax figurines.

I don't know what to say about myself.

Because it was something like those exhilarating moments when you have a strange key, and you go to a strange door to put it in,

and suddenly all of you knows the key *is* going to work, and that combination, that mechanism of release factors, is the only way it could possibly be.

We eventually settled on the floor in the dirtydust, and I saw she wasn't wearing panties, in expectation. I grew a flag.

I pried at her.

Her pussy smelled wonderful.

I joked around with it for a minnit.

Then I came over her and squatted over her and felt her breasts and sucked each of their large brown nipples for a longtime, and manipulated her bigass into position under me,

and then I rose and unbuttoned my conpants and dragged them down over my ass, and at that very moment something smelled like roses. I became a spirit; I was lost. If there was a time to bust me, it was right now.

I entered her cunt like a proud prince; it was tight and afraid. And I made a few motions in heaven before my mind let go, but right at the beginning we were frightened, this remembrance. I didn't feel the velvet of her until she felt my own, when all her lids fell and made their mouths into shapes to suck me in.

We were socketed into each other.

I couldn't remember being so deep and warm before, and her insides scrubbed the black muscle of me with slick angrystrokes; then suddenly I couldn't hold it any longer, and came,

and settled down in the morass it made, like I was coming in for drydock.

'Come, baby?' she said in my ear.

'Whaddayou think?'

'I figured you might have. Wanna go for seconds?'

'Soon as I have my tanks refueled, which need not necessarily be today.'

'Ohbaby, Daddy, I can make you, like now, like there, like feel the way you feel in my mouth?'

A twitch developed in my eye.

'See, Daddy?'

'Yeah.'

'Is it . . . ready?'

'It's gettin ready.'

'Oh . . . Daddy. There. It's ready.'

She hopped on top of it, and we wrung it out till we both got off, pasted in sweat and short of breath near the end. It was very good.

Pepper gave me the Emergency Knock.

We had to get up, all out of shape, and I took her to the landing and stood there kissing her and sucking her for 20foolish seconds more; then she went tipping down to the second landing, and disappeared.

When I came out, Pepper had holes for eyes, like Daddy Warbucks.

'He's in there talkin to Joe Antman right now.'

'Who is?'

'Captain Koyle.'

It was just terror: Captain Koyle had come over for a social visit with Joe Antman,

but no 1 had missed me.

The Four Part

1

We had fried eggs on Mondaymorning after having fried eggs on Sundaymorning,

so I could tell something was getting set to jump off.

Lunchtime convinced me. We had a beefpattie with french-fries and a french salad and thickrich cups of piercingcold milk.

'Somebody from the Bureau visiting us today,' Matthew told me in the hallway after lunch, 'and a broad from 1 of the big New York papers is coming around to do a story about the joint.'

'I hope they stick around past suppertime. I haven't greased this good since I've been here.'

'Oh, the menu'll keep improving over the next couple days. We'll probably get steak tonight.'

And we did.

When I got back to the unit

they'd sent down about 5young faggots from the Shooting-gallery. They were ghostboys, eyes sunken and black around the rims, hair matted in curls to the shoulders, mouths looking as though someone had cruelly scrubbed lipstick off.

'Take um down to the barbershop,' Joe Antman told me grimly, 'and have that shit cut off.'

Little Joe was doing handstands.

It's hard trying to walk from UT down the long hallway, then down to the basement and the long corridor there and make the bend right to the barbershop door,

with 5 faggots.

It's a lotta work, because you've got to try and make sure none of the littlebroads gets kidnapped on the way over and on the way back. Guys loved faggots here in the hospital. They loved them harder than they do in Lewisburg or Atlanta, where there are no women.

I never could understand it.

3faggots by the names of Queenie, Bubbles, and Kasavubu are famous for being perpetual Winders, and they're old faggots, all of them,

but the dopies treat them like royal cunts,

3depraved old men.

However, these were young faggots, lean little lambchops, and 1 almost did get lost in the dressout room behind the tall rows of shelving for everybody's clothes; but the guy who pulled him blew his own cool by talking too loud, and the dressout hack told him to Get The Hell From Behind There.

They got outfitted for 2weeks with congray, and I remembered it was MemorialDay only after we came back past the CCdesk,

where 4hacks sat leering at the boybabies worse than the cons,

and I saw the big calendar there saying it was. Maybe that's why they laid out in the messhall, but Matthew usually knew what he was talking about.

I nosed around, nudging a few guys on the way back, loitering with the 5birdfaced gays in front of the Cokemachine, drinking a lonely cup in the crowd,

and I got a chance to listen to a few people who'd heard about visitors from the Free, and a couple who had seen them.

Then I ran into George Prospectus on the way back.

'Hi.'

'Damn. Ain't they moved you outta UT yet? They're keepin you longer than anybody else.'

'I guess you could say I've got connections.'

'Looks like it.'

'No, but really,' he said, 'it's because of Dr. Uxeküll. I told him I didn't want to get into any rhubarbs over there on the Eastside about anything.'

'Any what?'

'Rhubarbs. You know.'

'Awyeah.'

'They tell me guys even steal your shoes from you over there.'

'They tell you correctly. And they beat up Winders.'

'Well, I wouldn't be too overly worried about defending myself. I may look frail, but I know a few things.'

'They've been known to rape guys over there on the Eastside.'

'Ohwell now, really, it isn't that bad, is it?'

'You'll never know till you go.'

'If that's meant to be a challenge—'

'It's not meant to be anything but a statement. Don't go to Harlem in ermine nor pearls.'

'I never *have*,' he said seriously.

'Then that explains why you're such a God Damn Tramp. Tramps ingratiate themselves always.'

He was getting red. 'I don't know why it is I get so God Damn Mad everytime I talk to you.'

'I thought it was just the opposite.'

Tamerlane had a Scotchtaped Undergroundkite for me when I came in.

'Um.' He looked the boys over. 'You don't have to worry about these. I'll give um rooms.'

Then I went into my office and locked the door and slit the tape off the kite with a razorblade.

DADDY,

I don't know how to tell you what I've been thinking, and it all came after our set. You must have known I thought it was beautiful, and you filled me. I didn't take a shower, just to keep you in me. You radiate in me.

But I've been feeling other things, and I remember you silent all the time. And that was when I lost you. When I couldn't find you again until it was all over. Daddy, do you know what I'm trying to say? I didn't feel you, not your real *self, because you wouldn't give me that much all at once. I understand, and please don't get mad because I'm thinking like this. I just felt like I might not have meant anything to you.*

But she didn't understand.

I *did* feel something. She ought to have felt it. It was in all my moments with her, when we filled each other, even when we opposed each other at the instant of come. It wasn't like Joyce, or any other woman I'd ever known, and I still wasn't done with the ache of having her:

To have a woman after so long, in this impossible place, almost killed me with pleasure, and it made me feel like a man for the 1st time in years.

I found myself typing an Underground, trying to explain. Then I snatched the God Damn Paper out and asked myself what the hell I thought I was doing.

She didn't think I thought about her? I thought about her, I thought about her, I confess it, and I cared about her.

Somenights, I remember, I'd reread her lightheaded kites of the day 8 or 10 times, and tuned out on myself everytime, being too drugged with myself to even recognize the words I read.

She thinks I didn't. It's stupid.

I turned around and looked at Robert Shelton for comfort. But after a while he got sick of looking at me, and kept turning his eyes away.

2

I didn't see her till the dance following MemorialDay.

They decked out the basketball court in the gym, hanging streamers and setting up tables on the righthand side under the women's upstairs seats. And 1 part, in the middle at the far wall, was reserved for the joint band. There were about 10kneeslats with the legend *Narcoleers*, and Whim was to play at the black baby spinet. I stood around and watched them setting it up.

And Doug crept up on me. 'What's happenin, Killer?'

'Ohman, do you have to creep up on me like that?'

'I didn't know your life was in danger.'

'No, man, it's just the way you always manage to pop up when I don't expect you. *Some*thin must be givin you a cue.'

'Now you're acting suspicious.'

'*Me* acting suspicious, whaddaya mean *me?* You're gettin to look more and more like Charlie Chan. Gimme a little air, Doug.'

'Well. God Damn.' He laughed quietly. 'I wonder how I stepped on your toes.'

'You never stepped on my toes.'

'But you've got an attitude.'

'It's easy to have 1 in a joint like this.'

'I still say I stepped on your toes.'

'You can say what you wanna.'

'Just stop for a minnit and look at yourself,' he said. 'You're really *drugged*. You look like a marriedman.'

'Now lissen, Doug . . .'

'Yeah, that's what you look like, a marriedman. I told you to be careful when you got on the pink.'

'Ahman, please don't whip me with this shit.'

'How can I help hearin about your big romance? It's all over the joint. She's been talking to other broads about you, and they've been writing it in the kites they send over here.'

'What do they say about me?'

'They call you SweetDick; how come you didn't guess? I didn't ask what they said about you; guys just tell me, that's all.'

'Well. It don't mean nothin.'

'Yer old lady gonna be at the dance tonight?'

'Yeah, she's supposed to come.'

'I saw her with some more broads waiting for the elevator up to 5. Not a badlookin old broad.'

'I dig her lines. She mighta had a little class at 1 time, when she was a young ho'.'

'There's still a glimmer.'

'She's got a good body.'

'I could see that.'

'But it's probably the biggest thing in her favor.'

'All that's nice. But have you really gotten into somethin with her?'

'Whaddaya mean, 'Somethin'?'

'I mean somethin emotional,' he said, 'like you and Joyce had when I knew you in the World.'

I pulled up on him, but he followed me through the weightroom up the thin staircase to the main basement level. The sublevel descent branched out in long dark storage areas.

We came up in the basement corridor right in front of the recreation office and walked slowly around to the staircase at CC.

'You know I'm hip to the thing you had with Joyce.'

'Lissen': I stopped. 'Don't start that soapopera buddybuddy shit with me, Doug. Joyce is dead, and that's the end of that. She was just another filthy dopefiend bitch.'

His face froze. 'I thought she was a sorta good woman.'

'Maybe she woulda been for you, but for me she was a heckle. That's all a whore is, a heckle.'

'Are you tellin me what you feel about that other broad? Sonja?'

'I'm not tellin you how I feel about anything, but you just

keep pressin my button. You been itchin to bring this subject up for months. And I'll tell you what I suspect, Douglas; I suspect your intentions.'

'What are you talkin about?' he said in a harsh voice. 'Joyce is dead, like you said.'

'Maybe not for you. Maybe you had somethin goin with her in the Free, and I didn't know about it.'

'You had a good woman, man,' he told me solemnly. 'I never saw Joyce do anything that wasn't cool. She was all your woman.'

'That's the funniest shit I've heard all year. How could a whore be all *my* woman? A whore belongs to everybody.'

'You know better than that. Joyce was enough in herself to show you better than that. I knew her when she was a little kid, long before she copped you and got strung out, and she was a goodsweet kid. She was still the same after she got to be a woman.'

'You don't say.'

'Yeah, I say, and that's not all I'm gonna say. Because the reason Joyce got strung out was you, and the reason she was a whore was you, and the reason she's dead today was because of you. Oh, you can flex up if you wanna, Killer, and knock me out, but it's all been said now.'

I got to the dance late,

and I thought for a minnit the hack on the door wasn't going to let me in. But something happened that distracted his attention, so I walked right in. He didn't follow to check me out.

The band was going. The court was loaded up with dancing couples, and there were about 5 or 6hacks standing around the walls, and 2matrons. The Headman Police was there too.

The lights were low. There were jagged little clusters of people sitting at the tables in the rear, and the whole thing smelled of atmosphere. I had to remind myself that I was doing a bit in a penitentiary, but I couldn't really get over the fantasia, or the bittertaste in my mouth from the impacts.

I became delirious from the collective odor of women, stewed in a rectangle of bodyheat; it chewed away at all my senses.

Everybody seemed to be dancing in release, some guys with their hands around broads' buns, and the girls were sized up against them, hot bellies hunting for the knot, the pipe, denied.

Whim had the band grooved, and the music was like hot meltedbutter. Lomo did something erratically beautiful for 32bars.

I twisted through the dancecouples over toward the rear-tables. I popped out and stood there looking around until I heard her calling me.

'Over here, near the back.'

The light was quite dim where she was, and I couldn't see her face until I wiggled halfway through the tight clutch of tables.

'I'm having coffee,' she showed me when I sat. 'But they got Coke, too, over at the refreshment table. Want me to get you 1?'

'Not right now.'

'Don't you want anything?'

'No, baby, I just want to look at you for a while.'

'You like this dress? I like the seams at the waist, and it's 3inches over the knees. I got it today in a package from my father. My Going Home clothes.'

'It's a Wow dress. When exactly do you leave?'

'The 24th.'

'I didn't know it was that soon.'

'I've been telling you all the time how soon it was, and what I'm going through because of it.'

'It just comes as a surprise.'

'Daddy, you know I don't want to leave you here.'

'You can't do me any good in here.'

'I know that, Daddy, but that still doesn't keep my mind from bending everytime I think about leaving you here in this God Damn Place.'

'You're the 1 who needs worryin about. Just think about what you're goin into. Are you ready?'

'Yes, Daddy, I'm ready.'

'I mean, maybe you thought you were ready the other times too. You were tellin me about Synanon.'

'OhDaddy, that was a mistake from beginning to end. It was a relief to get back to stuff, what with the hassle I had there.'

'You don't suppose you'd be just as relieved to get out of here?'

'Really, Daddy, stuff hasn't even crossed my mind.'

'Lissen, Sonja, you ain't a chicken no more. Your attitude had better be different. I want you to have yourself together when you leave out of here.'

'I'm together, Daddy, I'm sure I am. I don't need stuff anymore. All I need is you; that's the kind of attitude I'm leaving with, and I intend to do everything I can to straighten you up when you come to the Coast.'

'That's 10months away.'

'Really, baby, it isn't that far off, and I'll be laying, like you tell me, and I'll really be straightened up by the time you show.'

I wingspreaded my hand on her thigh under the table.

'There's only 1 thing I need from you, Daddy. . . .'

'Why should you need anything?'

'I just need this 1 thing, that's all I'm asking.'

'What thing? Do you want an Obligation?'

'Ohno, Daddy, please. I just want you to reassure me.'

'Do you want me to say Yes, I'm coming? Yes, I'm Coming. But will you be ready when it's that Time?'

She put her forehead in the palm of my hand. 'Please don't doubt me, baby. Not this 1 time. Don't do it now; do it later, after time shows you how much I care. Then you won't be able to. I'll show you I need you; I'll just live all my life for you.'

'Tell it to me in a different way.'

'I love you, Daddy; I love you, Daddy; how can I tell you anything else?' Then she reached like a snake with her mouth and touched mine. 'You are Right for me, I know it; I've felt it before but not this way. I'll do anything to have you.'

'You can't have me with stuff.'

'OhDaddy, I've told you I don't need stuff anymore; you're my crutch—'

'Now I'm a crutch.'

'OhBaby, I didn't mean that, whatever it sounded like.'

'You selected the word.'

'But I didn't mean that. I meant something else. You are my support, my spirit; you make me strong, Daddy, in places I've never been strong before.'

'Have you ever asked yourself Why?'

'There's no answer in me. Why should there be? Just so long as we both know what's real. You're my Chance, Daddy.'

'Chance for what, to be what?'

'To be a woman. To be full and round with you. I feel like swallowing you sometimes, putting you all the way down in the bottom of me.'

We shifted, so I could see the sharp black edges of her wide white eyes, and the quick, beautiful way her thick toplip curved, and our hips and thighs and calves met and glued themselves.

'OhDaddy, I had so many things I was going to say to you, and now that we're together I can't think of a God Damn 1. Oh, let's dance. Do you wanna dance, Daddy?'

'No.'

'Ohplease, I want to feel you against me, Daddy.'

So we went out on the floor. It was crowded. Lomo was doing something. She filled my arms, and her full sharp scent filled me; I seeped with it. We made music, like cream is poured from a big cold pail.

That was when I began to need her. I consciously did not want her to go, and there wasn't much I could do to read the feeling off.

Full woman, living woman in my arms, and it doesn't matter it's only Sonja: I didn't even bother to imagine it was somebody else. Allwomen. It's hard to explain, because you come so close, basically, to what everything is about.

And

holding her, cooked with her warmth and smell, I strained against her throat in the overcoat of shadows, kissing it and tasting it good in my mouth, she melting into me. I said it and meant it,

and said it again.

'I love you, love you.'

3

Joe Antman pounced on me as soon as he came in Monday-morning. Over the weekend some of Sonja's Undergroundkites to me got cracked by Pepper and he foolishly turned the whole bundle over to Joe, not thinking for 1 moment that he might be incriminating himself.

Joe came into my office. 'You can't say that I ain't tried to be fair with you.'

'Naw, Joe, I can't say that.'

'You goin with a broad named Sonja over in the Barn?'

'You see my mail when it comes in; you know who's writing me.'

He didn't have a mad look on his face. 'How'd you go about screwin this gal?'

'Who says I screwed her, Joe?'

'These Undergroundkites she sent you say so, tellin about how it felt.'

'She was just imagining things.'

He waved the little bundle in my face. 'This ain't no imagination. This is enough to convict you.'

'I don't see why we have to go to court about it, Joe.'

'I wanna know how you did it.'

'Oh, you want me to bust myself?'

'Naw, nothin like that. This is just between me and you. How'd you do it?'

'Do you really believe I'd tell you?'

'Well, you don't have to tell me,' Joe said; 'these letters tell me; they tell me just how it was done.'

'Stop playin police on me, Joe.'

'The least you can do is tell me,' he said impatiently. 'You know I'm not gonna turn this stuff over.'

'Yeah, Joe, I know that, but I wouldn't tell you even if you busted me.'

'1 thing I know is,' Joe said cannily, 'you had to have an accomplice. Now, who could you use for an accomplice? Who would be sucker enough to let you hook them up some sort of way and have to payoff? Who is the biggest fool in this county? Who is the Fool?' His eyes lit up.

'Aw, quit pushin, Joe.'

'I know.'

'Boy, what an imagination you got.'

'I know. Don't tell me I don't know. I know.'

'Nobody can blame you for what you think.'

'I know who the droolin fool is.'

'Why don't you let it rest for a coupla days, Joe?'

'I know,' Joe said, winking at me wildly. 'I *know*.'

And left.

After that, Pepper gave me a demerit for an untidy bed for almost every day of the next 2weeks.

3E3/4

DADDY

We have one more session together with Dr. Cambridge before I leave. I saw him today in the unit and asked if we could. I'm so very happy about it. I've asked for correspondence privileges, but that will be pending his approval.

I get sadder and sadder as the days pass, and I seem to get more depressed about leaving you here. This is such an evil place, Daddy. Even the bugs around here are evil; now they're starting to come in. Do you have those horrible hardshelled beetles over there on your side too? If you try to kill them, they make sounds like real people and squish out juice and entrails when you hit them, like something human. I can't stand them. I'll be so glad to leave here but so hurt to leave you. Yes, I know you love me, Daddy; I know it now. It was just so hard for me to understand at first. I've never been loved your way before. You are a special kind of man for me.

I feel myself ebbing away, like a spirit.

Yours

4

I ate lunch with Matthew in the Number2 messhall. It was a little quieter here, mostly whities and Puerto Ricans.

'I put your name down on our slate to run against the Patients' Council when they have elections next month,' he said.

'Why?'

'Well, I just thought you'd dig it.'

'That's what you're always thinkin. I'm just askin you Why?'

'Why what?'

'Why *should* I, man? What good is it going to do me to run for the Patients' Council?'

'You really don't haveta if you don't wanna.'

'I'm not sayin I don't wanna. I just wanna know Why should I? Can you answer me that?'

'You don't even know whether you'd dig it or not,' he said.

'I used to be on 1 of these concouncils. They're all rubberstamps; they all go along with Policy. Even if we did get elected, what do you think they'd allow us to do? No more and no less than the last councilbody, that's what. I don't know why you get in such a God Damn Sweat about this.'

His face got black and intense. 'It's just a matter of seeing something done right for the 1st time, that's what drives me.'

'You crusader.'

'And what are *you?*' he asked me, angry now. 'With your hip semantics, and isolationism?'

'You're confused.'

'Not as easily as you are. But I could ask you what you're crusading for, and you couldn't tell me in so many words.'

'I'm not crusading for anything.'

'That even *sounds* funny, doesn't it? Say it again.'

'I'm not crusading for anything.'

'See the way it sounds? You didn't tune up today.'

'I'm a conscientious objector against crusades.'

'Yeah, that sounds a little bit better, but you know and I know it's all bullshit.'

'Why don't we tune each other out?'

'That's all right with me,' he said, returning to his tray. But after a while, he said,

'Think about it anyway.'

I got a feeling out of this last meeting I didn't want to have.

Monday she would be gone,

but we still had the long weekend together, and the imminence of her going would grow. I didn't want that.

George Prospectus came out of the Branch-5 doors and stuck his hand out at me. 'Well, wish me luck.'

'For what?'

'Dr. Uxeküll is releasing me and my wife tomorrow; he thinks our treatment is completed.'

'Well, that's nice news for you and your wife.'

We shook hands.

'I thought you'd be glad to know.'

'Yes, I am. It's good to see somebody get the cure around here.'

'I'm sure Dr. Uxeküll has the answers.'

'Yeah, he's fulla answers. You think you're ready?'

'I've never been so ready before.' George grinned.

'Maybe you won't think so when you hit the street.'

'What's out there that can make me feel any differently than I do right now?'

'Stuff.'

Dr. Cambridge came out and picked me up early, before Sonja came.

He motioned me to the chair I sat in the last time we had a visit, then sat himself.

'How've you been doing?' he asked.

'Fine.'

'I'm sorry you couldn't come back for the other meetings.'

'I told you I didn't know whether I would for sure.'

'Sonja was disturbed about it.'

'I've discussed it with her.'

'Monday is her releaseday,' he said, putting his hands behind his head, 'but I suppose you know that.'

'Yes.'

'Has she talked her plans over with you?'

'Some of them.'

'Do you approve of them?'

'I'll wait and see what happens.'

He watched me for a long time. 'You seem more relaxed now.'

'That's because I feel more relaxed.'

'Good. I see you're getting into things around here. I noticed you at the meeting with the Council.'

'And I noticed you. I got a very distinct impression from you.'

'Oh? What was that?'

'That you were like 1 of those people who watch executions.'

'I don't understand.'

'You know what I mean. The way you sat by and let Dr. Uxeküll run that garbage, and you didn't say anything. You knew what he was doing.'

His face showed I got to him. 'I'll admit that Dr. Uxeküll wasn't completely accurate about some things.'

'Then why did you let it happen?'

'It wasn't a case of my letting it happen or not.'

'But you did, and you knew it was a lie. I'm just asking you these things; I don't expect an answer. Just to see you compromise yourself is enough for me. There was something obscene about it.'

'I hope you're being as objective as possible about this situation,' he said.

'I'm trying to be.'

'Don't let it be a case of trying to find chinks in my armor. There's plenty of them, let me tell you. You saw me act in a way you felt to be dishonorable, but certainly you know there are deep motives behind every dishonorable act.'

'That doesn't excuse them.'

'And it doesn't excuse me by any measure,' he said. 'Yes, I let Dr. Uxeküll say what he did—'

'For reasons of politics.'

'For reasons of politics,' he confessed. 'For 1 thing, he's my colleague, much as I might disapprove of his methods.'

'But you're bound. Another guy told me the same thing once.'

'Yes, I'm bound. And for another thing, if I want to continue what I'm doing I've got to be careful not to shake the boat of Policy. Third, I am loyal to the image of the hospital, however much I know it to be a contradiction. I wish it could die in that 1 image. It's an anachronism, but not the thing it stands for.'

'And what's that?'

'Relief . . .'

'Relief for the Tormented.'

'That's right. You know what it's supposed to mean.'

'Then why doesn't it mean that?'

'Because you're dealing with the mind of Policy. We're still using 20year-old treatments for addiction. The whole thing's got to be updated. If I had my way, do you know what I'd do? I'd turn this place into a warehouse and establish centers in the 3major areas of narcotics addiction—New York, Chicago, and Los Angeles. I could do it with the same money we get here. This would allow us to follow up cases closely. I'd fire everybody that has a damn thing to do here, and I'd start with new people who had some sort of clue to the problem. I sincerely feel this is the only way.'

'We came the long way round, sidestepping your dishonor.'

'I'm not trying to be evasive about it. I want you to understand why I kept my mouth shut when I shouldn't have.'

'I understand.'

He almost smiled. 'Of course you do. You understand. In your way.'

'In whose way should I understand? Yours?'

'If that's possible.'

'That's not possible.'

'Then you'd better teach yourself how to understand other men,' he said, 'or you may find yourself acting as dishonorably as I did.'

The Five Part

1

Down in the deepdark,

in the middle of Saturdaynight, I had the dreams. 2 of them. 1 was about Joyce, but I could never see her face, and we were both running around this big deteriorating old house, looking for 6bags we'd hidden there. My skin crawled.

Joyce stuck her tongue in my ear. 'I'm dead, Daddy, but that's no reason for you to be afraid. Come on, let's find it, me and you till the bitter, you always say.'

Then the dream exploded in patchwork light, and this time I saw the bloody woman on the road, but the face wasn't hers; it was the face of some other woman I couldn't identify but knew. The snow sprayed like moths over her tortured face. And then it faded into the grinning face of my mother, and her false teeth opened to say quite plainly she was pleased with me, and she added a word she so seldom used,

and I heard it plainer than I've ever heard it before:

and I rose in tears, crying, the moment I heard her gentle voice say,

'John.'

DADDY,

do you have everything you need to know? The address of my father's house in Frisco? And the phone number? Remember when you get out of here to call me directly, collect. I'll be waiting for you at the airport, and don't worry about money while I'm gone. I'll be sending it along regularly.

I'll be getting your wardrobe together, so please send me all your sizes. I know a tailor who fits the stars who used to handle a little business for me. He'll do me a couple I know for a bill apiece. So don't worry about that.

Daddy, I have to cut this letter short because I've got to pack all my stuff up and get cleared out. The new girl who's going to take this room just came in and is trying to give me a hand. I'm in the process of destroying your pink kites, such lovely things. But I won't be allowed to keep them. Each one I destroy tears me up inside.

Love, love, and more love. I will write again two times before I leave, and I'll drop a pink in the box Monday so you'll get it Tuesday.

Yours

2

I went to eat with Tamerlane Sundayevening.

'What's the matter?' he said.

'Nothin.'

'You don't look as though you feel too good.'

'No, I feel fine.'

We stood a longtime in line. It finally came out baked beans and yesterday's fried rice. Tam loaded up.

'I can't understand you, man.'

He chewed on a piece of bread as we went down to the diningarea. 'What's that?'

'How you can do this dime so easy.'

'I don't know. But it don't seem to be so easy at night, when I lie down and think everything over good. I just keep asking myself what I can do about it. And I keep comin up with the same old answer. Do it.'

DADDY,

I'm all squared away and ready. My heart is so heavy. I'm torn between two extremes, you and the Free. Oh, Daddy, if only you were leaving with me now everything would be just so right. Our house is so big, and my father even has a library. We live on the hump of Frisco, and at night it all lights up below like a bed of diamonds. I know that will thrill you. It will be just us three. All he wants is for me to be home with him, and he will love you too.

I kept one of your letters because I couldn't destroy it. Its one of my most favorite. You say in it 'Nobody likes being measured in terms of death, and that's basically what everything boils down to: How long will it last? That goes for everything conceivable, and it goes for the feeling that exists between us. Stuff is a bad hiccup – you hiccup it until you get sick. I've asked myself that same basic question. Really, then, that's the only instruction I can send you home with. Just keep asking yourself, How long will it last?'

Oh, Daddy, what I have with you will always *last, you know that.*

I know the way to go, the way you've led me, though I know faster ways. But, Daddy, I believe in you and know you're thinking of nothing but my welfare. I'll be cool like you say for a couple of months and, Daddy, don't worry about me getting hung up with stuff again. You've given me all the defense I'll ever need against that.

Yours

I began to see she didn't understand a God Damn Thing.

3

Joe Antman has an uncanny way of feeling things. All day I'd been depressed, and at noon, when I didn't go down with the rest of the unit to eat,

he came in to rap and fart around in general. But I nutted him out and continued my filing and staffingwork.

When I came out of my office I saw Bob Trent standing in front of the hackoffice Jeffing around with Pepper. The sight of him made my flesh go prickly all over. He gave me a sick little grin when I went past them into the office, and Joe must have seen a look on my face I couldn't hide.

'Why don't you go on upstairs and rest yourself?' he said.

'I ain't tired.'

'You look tired to me.' He was watching me hard. 'Take the rest of the day off.'

I told him maybe I would, then finished my filing and went back into my office. Trent was still laughing and giggling around with Pepper. I felt like I had a fever.

Joe came in before I could clear out. 'Where you goin?'

'I thought you said I should rest myself.'

'Yeah, I know what I said, but what are you gonna do?'

'Maybe drop off at the corner for a beer with the rest of the fellas.'

Joe blocked the doorway. 'Don't start that shit. I can see somethin workin on you.'

'Yeah, Joe Antman, as usual.'

Then his face got so soft and gentle when he spoke, it frightened me. 'Maybe you don't know it, but I got an investment in you. I *own* some of you, boy, because you been planted in *my* garden. The way you grow is the way *I* grow.'

'Now, lissen—'

'No, *you* lissen. Maybe I ain't sayin this right, or maybe

you're too much of a God Damn Fool to understand what I'm tryin to say. But even the world changes, the seas and the mountains and everything else. If somethin as great as that can change, why can't a man?'

I tried to think of something sharp to say,
but for once couldn't.

I'd written my aunt a letter, and she was so surprised to hear from me she sent 5dollars airmail.

I was waiting at the Commissarydoor that afternoon when Matthew ran down on me.

'What's happenin?'

'I got 5dollars. You need anything?'

'A tube of Colgate and 2El Productos.'

'All right.'

The line moved ahead a little.

'Wasn't that your old lady I saw leaving this morning?'

'Yeah, she went back to the Coast.'

'Then you must be in mourning.'

'Don't say stupid things.'

'Do you have correspondence privileges?'

'Yeah, we can write each other. Dr. Cambridge approved it.'

'How do you feel about it?'

'It's too soon for me to feel anything. I gave her some assignments. If she carries them out, I see no reason why we shouldn't hook up together.'

'You really feel like that about it, huh?'

'Yeah, I do.'

The line moved up.

'That broad ain't no chicken,' Matthew said.

'I told her that. She's a vet, and vet enough to know about herself.'

'I hope it works out.'

'Everything works out.'

'You don't have to sound like you're in love.'

'I wasn't trying to sound like I was in love.'

'Don't be so serious about everything. I know you've thought this whole thing out. The broad is an exwhore and exdopefiend, and all of her best years are gone. She's gotta have more to offer you than just a hothead.'

'You're right. I've thought about everything.'

'Good.'

We got to the window. I got the toothpaste and cigars 1st, and blew the balance on coffee and cigarettes. We came out.

'Have you been doing any thinking about our last conversation?'

'What? The election? Yeah, I've been thinking about it.'

'Are you gonna run with us?'

'I ain't through thinking about it yet.'

'Okay. Well, let me know when you make up your mind.'

'I will.'

'Seeya.'

'Seeya.'

After I left Matthew

I went down to the weightroom. Only a fewguys were working out, and nobody saw me when I took 1 of the short ironbars the enthusiasts used for forearm curling. It fitted with not too much bulge under my congrays next to my thigh. I was wearing a thick sweater, so you couldn't tell anything at all. I put a hand in my pocket to hold it against my leg as I walked.

Then I went back upstairs to the main basement corridor, where there were only a couple of cons hanging around and the 1 hack near the laundry. Nobody saw me when I slipped through the Chapel doors. I went back to the john at the rear of the stage, closed the door and squatted on the toilet, listening.

My hand was slippery with sweat as I hefted the bar and made my arm and muscles accustomed to its weight. I sat there for a longtime, thinking how good it was going to feel to bounce it off Bob Trent's skull. And I had no remorse, until I thought about Joe Antman, but I canceled that out by imagining I was about to perform a religious act, almost like exorcising a devil. I wasn't worried about the investigation afterward, because I wasn't the only guy in the hospital who had a motive, and nobody was going to force me to cop out on myself. It would be impossible for Bob Trent to tell anyone what happened.

I thought I heard a noise out in the Chapel, so I crept over to the door to listen. It was nothing. He was late today. I hoped he wouldn't bring his snitchfriend with him, because that meant I'd have to off both of them.

I went back and sat on the toilet. Even though my hand sweated, the bar was as cold as ice, like a thing that had been buried for ages in a glacier and then suddenly melted out. It made me think of what Joe Antman had said about mountains.

I heard the Chapel doors open and close, and the sound of it made me come up like a spring and almost leap to the door. It sounded at 1st as though he was talking to someone,

but I realized he was merely singing to himself, feeling alone with himself, and I waited for what I thought was long enough for him to go over to the organ in the corner where Sonja and I had stood that night with my hand cupping her, and lay back the cover, then click it on and wait for it to warm up in that throaty whirring sound it made. Then the 1st testing chord, then I heard him begin in a 'Wings Over Jordan' baritone:

'Oh, I'm on my way to heaven and
I'm sooo glad. . . .'

I came out under the cover of the electric thunder.

'Yass, I'm on my way to heaven and
I'm sooo glad, 'cause the world can't
Do me no harm. . . .'

He was singing so hard he didn't see me till the last moment, when I was only an arm's reach away. His fingers froze the keys in 1 long distant shriek of horror, and flecks of spit from his singing began to bubble out of the corners of his mouth when he instantly knew what I was about to do. I felt as though I was in a dreamstate, with the bar raised over my head, too many pounds of violence for me to care about, making it come down toward the spot at his temple where the hair had fallen out, glimpsing the way his redbrown eyes swelled, seeing the veins still puffed in his shortthick neck from singing. And the organ screaming like an unfucked woman.

Then, just before I could strike him, he grabbed his head with both hands and began to blubber in a series of dirty sounds that actually caused my trajectory to slip and slice inches past the target of his skull. I don't know till now what the fuck caused it. The bar crashed into the keys, and several of them leaped from the boards. He didn't even move, just sat there blubbering snot with his face hidden from me and his dumpy body twisted in a deathexpectant knot.

I moved around for a better shot, and raised the bar again.

But this time

it wasn't like it had been before. Infuriatingly enough, I didn't hate him that much anymore.

I thought of what Sonja had written me about the bugs that crawled in the windows of this joint,

and I knew that killing Robert Leroy Trent would be just like killing 1 of those foul hardshelled creatures.

When I got back, I got a delayed Underground from the Runner in the Photographic Lab.

I went into my office and closed myself away and read it.

DADDY,

I am going Daddy, I am going. That's the only thing that runs through my mind; I can't think anything else. This is the most painful thing of my life. But here I am crying about myself when its you who'll have to stay on here in this hell. Please forgive me, Daddy, for being so self-concerned.

Daddy, an old homie of mine just came in from the women's Shootinggallery whom I haven't seen for ages, and you must forgive me for taking time away from your pink but I just had to talk with her. We've been rapping for two hours.

Daddy, guess what? She brought a book in with her and she wants to lay it on me. It looks very respectable, Daddy, with very good names in Frisco. She says it's good for a grand per, and I wouldn't have to make too many stops. She just wants to give it to me, Daddy. It looks perfectly legit to me.

I'm going to take it on home with me. If its a good book, baby, I can really have everything laid out by the time you got there.

Oh, Daddy, I'm going, I'm going. It hurts so much to, but I'm going and I love you. I'm going.

Yours

I heard a key in the lock from the outside. It was Joe Antman. I couldn't tell anything from his face when he came in. He sat down and looked at me strangely for a long sadtime; then he took out a Marvel cigaret, lit up, and puffed smoke toward my silence.

'You want me to pack up?' I said finally.

He looked at his hands and the cigaret between his thick-fingers. 'Naw. I'll have Tamerlane do it later. He'll be real careful with your books and everything.'

'Okay.'

'They.' He puffed thickclouds twice. 'They wanted to come down and getcha, but I told um I'd bring you down myself.'

'Well, thanks for that, Joe.'

He examined me again, as though he were seeing me for the 1st time. 'Why didn'tcha kill im?'

'I don't know. Maybe you brainwashed me too well.'

'There *was* a time you woulda killed him.'

'Yeah, I guess there was.'

He puffed and puffed. 'That's the 1 thing I'm happy about

– you didn't hurt Trent any, so they can't really get you for anything but Attempt. They'll maybe take 30 days or so from you in goodtime, but they're gonna move you outta the hospital to a penitentiary as soon as they can. It won't put you too much behind schedule.'

We sat there in silence, till he said, offering me 1, 'Wanna smoke? You ain't gonna be able to in the hole.'

'I don't see how you can stand um. I'd rather smoke okra.' I saw him smile, and that made me feel good. 'Well, it looks like you lost out on your investment, Joe. There ain't many gardens I fit into, anyway.'

'That's okay,' he said. 'You started growin in my garden. You'll be able to grow anywhere after this.'

It was beginning to hurt to stretch it out any longer, so I stood and read Sonja's kite 1 more time, then tore it into tiny pink pieces and threw it in the wastebasket.

'You ready to go?'

'We don't have to be in a hurry,' Joe said.

'When do they plan to ship me out?'

'Tomorrow. To Terre Haute.'

'Then I'd better get some rest. Those God Damn Car rides break my ass.'

He threw his cigaret down on my floor and stomped it out in an angry way. Then he stood and touched my shoulder gently. 'Now, you remember what I told you about that damn mouth of yours.'

'Ohshit, Joe, how can you forget a thing you've been told 3million times?'

Tamerlane called me as we came out; I could see by his big softdog face he'd heard what had happened. He walked me and Joe out to the UTentrance; then he said:

'Take it easy, man. Seeya when I get this dime done.'

'Yeah, Tam. Look . . . if you happen to see Doug, tell him for me: tell him I apologize about that shit.'

'What shit?'

'He'll know what shit I'm talkin about.'

Then we went on down the long hallway slowly.

At CenterControl, sitting in the godchair, I could see the Headman Police waiting for me.

It happens that my cell in the hole is right across from the floor on which I used to see her all the time, silhouetted by the light of her room, and I have an insane pang of loss when I think I'll never see her again.

And I watch from my holewindow through the entire night, hoping she might come 1 last time.

But she never did. There was no girl in the window,
and I wonder now if there had ever been.

Night
June 2, 1966
New York City

PAYBACK PRESS is an independent, in your face imprint focussed on black culture and black writing. Below are details of the books we have published so far. For a further listing or for further information, please either ring or write to us at Payback Press, 14 High Street, Edinburgh EH1 1TE tel: 0131 557 5111 fax: 0131 557 5211 email: canon.gate@almac.co.uk. We will send you a free catalogue and place you on our mailing list if you wish.

THE FARM, Clarence Cooper Jr ISBN 0 86241 600 0 £5.99

This highly provocative final novel from a man who lived and died by the needle stands out as one of the greatest pieces of prison-writing ever. Awesome.

"A Richard Wright of the revolutionary era" – Negro Digest

CORNER BOY, Herbert Simmons ISBN 0 86241 601 9 £5.99

"The characters in this book are as disturbing a bunch of young punks as exists in serious literature. Simmons writes of them and their mores with diamond hard brilliance."
- The San Francisco Chronicle

PORTRAIT OF A YOUNG MAN DROWNING, Charles Perry ISBN 0 86241 602 7 £6.99

A hard-boiled and highly disturbing bombshell of a book that is a page-turner from start to finish.

"a fluent, graphic tale of tragic quality"
- The Times Literary Supplement

THE HARLEM CYCLE Volume 1, Chester Himes ISBN 0 86241 596 9 £6.99
- Introduced by Melvin van Peebles

This omnibus edition of the first three novels from Himes's legendary Harlem cycle makes for essential reading

"On every level they are simply - or rather not so simply - terrific"
- The Sunday Times

PIMP and TRICK BABY, Iceberg Slim ISBN 0 86241 593 4 £5.99
- Introduced by Ice T ISBN 0 86241 594 2 £5.99

Raw like sushi, Iceberg Slim's first two novels are cult classics, never before published in Britain until now.

"Too often, this major cultural icon for our times has been criminally ignored...Slim always told it as it was, without compromise"
- Irvine Welsh

BENEATH THE UNDERDOG, Charles Mingus ISBN 0 86241 545 4 **£8.99**

At long last reissued, this is one of the great jazz autobiographies. Seminal.

"A shocking and brilliant read" - Q Magazine *****

THE NEW BEATS, Exploring the Music, Culture and Attitudes of Hip-Hop, Skiz Fernando ISBN 0 86241 524 1 **£9.99**

"Accords rap the sort of detailed analysis surely overdue for a genre well beyond its infancy....superb" - The Face

BORN FI' DEAD, A Journey through the Jamaican Posse Underworld, Laurie Gunst ISBN 0 86241 547 0 **£9.99**

"brilliant" - Linton Kwesi Johnson *"excellent"* - Independent on Sunday

PANTHER, Melvin Van Peebles ISBN 0 86241 574 8 **£7.99**

The original novel that was stripped down and simplified to make the film. Go to the source and see what was missed and what you missed.

BLACK FIRE, The Making of an American Revolutionary, Nelson Perry

ISBN 0 86241 546 2 **£9.99**

"Evocative, powerful, sad and sweet and angry, all at the same time" - Washington Post

BLUES PEOPLE, LeRoi Jones ISBN 0 86241 529 2 **£7.99**

"Blues People's clear-sighted analysis of music as culture set a standard which every significant book about black music has followed since" - The Observer

BLACK TALK, Ben Sidran ISBN 0 86241 537 3 **£8.99**

"Read this book and make it part of your permanent library"

- Archie Shepp

All orders placed direct are postage and packing free
All forms of payment accepted